LADY GRACELESS

A Series of Senseless Complications
Book Two

Kate Archer

ARE YOU SIGNED UP FOR DRAGONBLADE'S BLOG?

You'll get the latest news and information on exclusive giveaways, exclusive excerpts, coming releases, sales, free books, cover reveals and more.

Check out our complete list of authors, too!

No spam, no junk. That's a promise!

Sign Up Here

www.dragonbladepublishing.com

Dearest Reader;

Thank you for your support of a small press. At Dragonblade Publishing, we strive to bring you the highest quality Historical Romance from some of the best authors in the business. Without your support, there is no 'us', so we sincerely hope you adore these stories and find some new favorite authors along the way.

Happy Reading!

CEO, Dragonblade Publishing

Additional Dragonblade books by Author Kate Archer

A Series of Senseless Complications
Lady Ferocity (Book 1)
Lady Graceless (Book 2)

A Very Fine Muddle
Romance Me, Viscount (Book 1)
Be Daring, Duke (Book 2)
Stand With Me, Earl (Book 3)
Sweep Me Up, Baron (Book 4)
Write for Me, Marquess (Book 5)
Convince Me, Viscount (Book 6)

A Series of Worthy Young Ladies
The Meddler (Book 1)
The Sprinter (Book 2)
The Undaunted (Book 3)
The Champion (Book 4)
The Jilter (Book 5)
The Regal (Book 6)

The Dukes' Pact Series
The Viscount's Sinful Bargain (Book 1)
The Marquess' Daring Wager (Book 2)
The Lord's Desperate Pledge (Book 3)
The Baron's Dangerous Contract (Book 4)
The Peer's Roguish Word (Book 5)
The Earl's Iron Warrant (Book 6)

PROLOGUE

R OLAND NICOLET, THE Duke of Pelham, father to seven daughters and zero sons, had spent his time at home after last season's adventures congratulating himself that he'd managed to unload one of his offspring onto an unsuspecting gentleman by way of marriage. He looked forward to escorting the other six out of the house as soon as might be possible, though the youngest had just turned eight years old. He would take them all to Town, one by one, and heave them toward the nearest fellow passing by until his house was gloriously empty.

As he liked to say—his dream was within reach.

Anyone who was at all familiar with the duke, and in particular his seven daughters, named it all nonsense. The duke was a notorious liar, his fabrications generally serving no other purpose than providing him entertainment. His children found that quality highly diverting, though the *ton* did not laugh quite as long and hard.

The duke's sister, Lady Marchfield, a well-respected countess, perhaps found the duke even less congenial than most. Her brother was determined to enrage her at every turn, which he inexplicably found hilariously funny. She, though, was intent on bringing a modicum of rationality to his house in Town and ensuring that her nieces were settled sensibly and with a minimum of gossip.

The duke's first foray into the world of London's marriage

mart had been a series of twists and turns, and going forwards and backwards, and had even found a Bengal tiger on the loose. He'd been delighted with the whole thing, as it had been far more interesting than he'd ever hoped for.

Now, his Felicity was happily settled with Mr. Percy Stratton while Grace was the next in line. The duke anticipated a fascinating time of it, as his second eldest daughter had the unique ability to trip over her own two feet. If there was an ottoman in the same county, Grace would make it her business to find it and fling herself over it. Dogs and cats rushed to get under her feet. She had a small and fading scar on her right hand from misjudging how many stairs must be gone down to go to breakfast. On that particular occasion, she'd only been off by one step, but that had been sufficient.

She would require a rather stalwart fellow who did not mind finding his bride splayed on the floor on occasion.

The duke was confident on the point that any future son-in-law of his must be stalwart. All of them, whoever they might turn out to be, had better at least be stalwart. The duke had the unique ability to take the measure of a person and then send them through a mangle like any washerwoman squeezing water from wet sheets. Mr. Percy Stratton had been put through his own mangle and come out the other side relatively intact. The duke would be interested in seeing who Grace's candidate turned out to be.

He could not predict exactly how the thing would play out, but he would shortly find it out—bags were being packed and arrangements made. In two days' time they would depart their isolated estate on the Yorkshire moors, open the house on Grosvenor Square, and assault London society with the company of the Nicolet family once more.

CHAPTER ONE

A Remote Estate in the Yorkshire Dales, 1802

GRACE NICOLET, SECOND eldest daughter of the Duke of Pelham, threw a roll across the dining table toward her father's head. The duke had just joked, as he often liked to do, that he'd be rid of them all at his earliest convenience and would not even allow them home for Christmas.

As always when this threat was floated, Patience remarked that he'd have no choice but to let them in because she would break down the doors with a hatchet. Grace, for her part, was in the habit of hurling a roll in his direction.

She could not work out why she never hit him with it, though. Her rolls always seemed to go astray and they often hit a footman instead. It was not as if the footmen minded it, she knew they laid bets on who would be hit, but she would like to know why her aim was so terrible, even when she threw it right at him.

Or at least, where she thought he'd been. People and things had a habit of moving this way or that.

This time it had been Charlie struck with her floury missile, and he snorted over it.

"Wide of the mark as always, Gracie," the duke said with a laugh. "I do not even bother to flinch or duck when you take aim."

"Maybe you should practice throwing rolls, Grace?" her

youngest sister suggested. "I have been practicing my sewing and it has got ever so much better. I sewed for an entire ten minutes today and only stabbed myself three times."

"I will keep that in mind, Valor," Grace said. What she did not say was that she *had* practiced. She could not understand how other people were so skilled at such things. How did other people manage it when that odd feeling came over them and everything moved this way and that, and their eyes could not keep up with where everything was? She sometimes ended on the floor at those moments. Most of the time though, she just went through the world a little tipped over and unbalanced.

It was a fault made worse by her name. Why had she been named Grace? It was the worst possible name she could have been given. She lived in a dread that she would be noticed as clumsy in Town, and then people would laugh because of her name. Mrs. Wenchel had once remarked that it was ironic.

Grace had no wish to be ironic!

The dessert course had come out and with it her father's bottle of port. Lady Marchfield would be shocked to her shoes that they stayed at table with her father as he drank. Their aunt had told them in no uncertain terms that it was not done. Ladies were meant to retire while gentlemen might take a reasonably sized glass of port for a reasonable amount of time before rejoining the ladies in the drawing room.

There were several problems with that theory, as Lady Marchfield had seen for herself. One, the duke never stuck to anything reasonable, two, he did not like to get drunk alone, and three, he got far more drunk whenever he *was* left alone.

He sipped his port contentedly and gazed down the table at his daughters. "I received two letters today," he said, "one was from our Felicity."

"Oh, what does she say, Papa?" Patience asked.

"She says she is wildly happy, I am sure," Verity said.

Winsome turned to her. "How would you know? You are not there. She might be wildly unhappy for all we know of it."

"Do not say so, Winsome," Serenity said. "I could just cry to think of it."

"She's perfectly happy," the duke said. "She says Stratton is a brick and she's got his temperamental viscount in hand. Hah! I knew she'd take Sir Pineapple by the throat and shake some rationality into him."

"Papa, Felicity told you backward and forwards that you are not to call her father-in-law Sir Pineapple anymore," Patience said.

"And I don't, to his face," the duke said jovially. "In any case, she and Stratton come to Town to assist Grace. Or assist me, more like it, in getting her out of the house. Then I'll be down to just five feminine setbacks—my dream is within reach!"

The duke was roundly jeered at over the notion and everybody found it very amusing.

"Who was the second letter from, Papa?" Grace asked.

"The second letter," the duke said, taking a long draught of port. "That's where things take a rather grim turn. As much as I tell my diabolical sister I do not want to hear from her, it does not put her off. That polecat has been sticking her nose into henhouses that are not her own again."

Valor laughed hysterically over the idea and whispered to her constant companion, a stuffed rabbit named Mrs. Wendover, to inform her that Lady Marchfield was a polecat.

"What has she done?" Winsome asked. "Can we stop her?"

"Lady Misery continues her quest to get a butler into my house," the duke said.

This struck everyone rather hard. Grace noticed the footmen had both gone rather wide-eyed. Mrs. Right, their housekeeper, ruled the roost. The staff looked to her as their leader and they were all very comfortable. Nobody wished to have a butler, least of all Mrs. Right.

And then when they thought of the butler Lady Marchfield had installed last season! Nobody would soon forget Mr. Sykes-Wycliff, running from the house, hysterically shouting at the duke. Why would Lady Marchfield even try it again?

"Mrs. Right shall be very put out," Grace said.

"I trust Mrs. Right will eject the newest specimen with all haste," the duke said, "just like the last one."

"Perhaps she could even stop him from getting in at all," Winsome said. "Our Mrs. Right is ever so clever at running rings round our aunt."

"He's already in," the duke said, downing his port. "Apparently, my sister has had the nerve to open *my* house and install a butler in it before I have even arrived. Who let her in? That is what I'd like to know."

This, Grace thought, was a check in the endless game of chess between the duke and Lady Marchfield. Her aunt had decided the easiest way to gain her point was to get it before the duke had a chance to make his own move.

"His name, according to Lady Misery, is Harold Button," the duke said. "Mr. Button, if you can believe anybody goes round publicly advertising such a name, has been until now the butler for some dowager or other in Somerset. Mr. Button spent years in a deadly quiet house, that dowager has since kicked off, and now he looks forward to the vivacity of working for a family with so many young people."

"*Vivacity?*" Winsome asked as if that were the most bizarre quality a person could look for.

"Yes, so she says. God only knows what she's told this poor fellow about us." The duke snorted. "If I know my sister, Mr. Button will be expecting a parade of staid and purse-lipped individuals. The jest is on him!"

"I bet she hasn't told him anything about Mrs. Right," Valor said, collapsing in giggles.

Grace agreed. Mr. Button would never have taken the position if he'd known that Mrs. Right would shortly drive him out of it. Mr. Sykes-Wycliff had found that out.

That fellow had been led to understand that the duke liked to softly knock on a person's door in the middle of the night and then clobber them when they opened it.

He'd also believed the story of the duke's annual servants' hunt where the staff ran round the moors and he chased them on foot and shot at them. Supposedly, the year before, a young footman had been hit, still walked with a limp, and currently lived with his mother. Mr. Sykes-Wycliff had believed all of it, though it was nonsense.

Anybody who knew the duke was aware that he was a very sound sleeper but for his snoring and shouts, and he did no creeping round the house in the night whatsoever. As for the servants' hunt, if such a thing were ever tried out, the duke would be on horseback, as he was not a very great walker.

Mr. Sykes-Wycliff did not know the duke well enough to perceive these facts. He'd believed everything Mrs. Right told him and had experienced a complete breakdown of the mind, just like Mr. Herring had, all those years ago.

Grace could not imagine what the new butler would be told, but she was certain Mrs. Right would think of something. They were all very comfortable living without a butler, especially the duke, as he trusted Mrs. Right implicitly. She understood his ways and was not forever fanning herself over them.

Further, they'd all agreed that it was a kindness to any incoming butler to be driven mad and driven out, so he might land himself in a house where he was truly needed.

"Now my girls," the duke said, "this time we make the trip to Town without the uncomfortable company of your miserable aunt. I suspect things will go a deal more smoothly than they did last time."

All of the duke's daughters nodded in agreement, though they all secretly wondered if that could be true. The nearest town of moderate size from their estate was only an hour away, and yet none of their trips *there* had ever gone smoothly.

"Valor," the duke said to his youngest daughter, "this time round, no more hiding away in linen closets at the inns. It was very inconvenient last time to notice you were missing and have to backtrack an hour. Several times, if I recall rightly."

Valor shrugged. "It was Mrs. Wendover's idea. I *said*, Mrs. Wendover, we shouldn't do it. *She* said, we have to do it because traveling is scary."

Grace pressed her lips together to stop from laughing. Valor's stuffed rabbit served a whole host of purposes, one of which was to be blamed for any crimes Valor might have committed. And why not? Mrs. Wendover did not mind if anybody was cross with her or if she were to be punished with no dessert.

"You can tell Mrs. Wendover that idea is firmly off the table," the duke said.

"I'll try, Papa," Valor said. "But we all know Mrs. Wendover is guilty of stubbornness. Even the vicar says so."

"He said *you* were guilty of stubbornness, Valor," Winsome pointed out. "On account of claiming one of the ten commandments is too strict."

Valor lifted her chin in defiance. "There are times when something must be stolen. It cannot be helped."

Grace well knew Valor meant that biscuits must be stolen at every opportunity. The poor vicar did not know *what* the girl intended to steal. He was a nervous sort of person and his imagination had seemed to run wild on the subject. Grace had more than once seen the vicar surreptitiously scanning the altar to assure himself that the accoutrements of his calling were still there whenever Valor Nicolet was nearby.

"Will we stop at the same places we did last time, Papa?" Serenity asked. "Everyone knows how sensitive I am to other people's moods, and I did feel very deeply in my heart that some of the innkeepers were rather distressed by our visit."

"Oh yes," Winsome said. "Remember the fellow who shouted at us as we pulled out of the yard?"

Verity snorted. "Never again! He shouted never again."

"It was on account of Papa asking for things that did not exist," Patience said. "Remember, Papa? You would ask for brocabbage pie and say it was a Yorkshire staple, and then they'd all run round trying to figure out what it was, and then you'd tell them you just made the whole thing up."

They all laughed heartily at those fond memories.

"I can't say I won't trot out the brocabbage pie gambit on occasion, as it is amusing," the duke said. "People will really believe anything. But this time, we take a different route. I am determined that you shall see a thing you never saw in your lives. It is something your sainted mother was very fond of and something that not every person ever gets to see."

This stirred up a vast amount of speculation, but the duke would not give up his secret.

Grace was delighted. She had thought the real excitement would be in London. Now the adventure was to start as they made their journey there, whatever it might be. Her father was really a dear to think of it.

MILES DELATORE, VISCOUNT Dashlend, eldest and only son to the Earl of Gravesend, very quietly breathed a sigh of relief. They'd been adrift for two days and, finally, land had been spotted. A strong current was funneling them into a bay.

He was very quiet about the sigh, as he did not wish his only crewman, known in the wider world as his valet, Moreau, to perceive that he'd ever been less than confident of their survival. He *had* been less than confident, though.

They'd set off on Tuesday for some deep-sea fishing on his twenty-two-foot sloop, *The Marquessa*. He'd designed and helped build the boat with his own two hands and he'd taken her far out of sight of land dozens of times. This time, though, his luck had run out. A sudden squall had come up and hit them hard.

It had been a terrific effort to simply hold on and avoid being thrown from the boat. That would have been the end, as nobody who'd been thrown off a boat in a squall had much hope of getting back on it again. Waves and currents were a devilish thing, and they were not things even a strong swimmer could overpower. Boat and swimmer would drift ever farther apart until the swimmer was forced to realize they were doomed.

His earl would have cursed him to hell and back if he left the world in such a stupid manner without leaving an heir behind him. It would not be so much for missing his son's company as it would be knowing the earldom would pass to Miles' cousin.

Rupert Burdock, Baron Montclave, was all sorts of things at once—dull, snide, untrustworthy, a schemer, a climber, and not someone who would be sorry to hear Miles was dead.

Miles had thought he might sail out of the squall or at least keep the sloop from going broadside, but the wind had shredded his sail like a razor through paper. They had been buffeted about in all directions, waves crashing over their heads, and Miles bailing the water out as fast as he could. His valet, on the other hand, had wrapped himself around the mast and shouted that God must let him live as it was not his fault that Lord Dashlend was "un idiot extraordinaire."

How *The Marquessa* did not go over he still did not know, though he supposed it must have been a divine intervention. He was kept alive for something, though he could not think what. He led a sporting life, going from one thing to the next—sailing, boxing, fencing, hunting, jockeying his own horse at the races— he was usually in motion. It was endlessly entertaining, but he did not suppose he was a very important player in God's grand plan.

Perhaps God had been intent on keeping his high-strung valet alive, though that seemed even less likely. Moreau's contributions to the world were keeping Miles' clothes immaculate and complaining about the awfulness of the English. When he complained too much about the English, Miles suggested he ought to go back to France. Then, quite suddenly, the French were awful too. Moreau's sport of choice was complaining, and he always played at the top of his game.

Perhaps the likeliest reason God had seen fit to save them was the Lord could not countenance Baron Montclave becoming the next earl.

When the squall moved on and the water becalmed, the real recriminations from his valet had begun. Miles had spent the past two days bobbing on a windless sea and ignoring the ever-present question of why he'd not built a boat that could carry a spare sail. That question was looked at backward and forward, usually ending with a disgusted sigh. Then Moreau's eyes would inevitably drift to the ale cask and note that Miles had brought very little food and not enough drink.

As the excursion was just meant to be a casual afternoon at sea, the only drink on board was ale, and his valet had been verging on drunk most of the time.

Just now, Moreau stood at the bow, looking longingly at the stony beach they drifted toward. There were breakers to be got through, but they had made it.

"What is it will happen when we go into those waves?" Moreau asked.

"I cannot be sure," Miles said.

"Mon Dieu, why did Moreau think the captain of the ship would be sure? I drink the last of the ale, as it may be the last I ever drink! What an ending for Moreau! Drinking terrible English ale instead of superior French wine! Une injustice!"

Miles did not answer but found those ideas rather rich. He was slowly dying for lack of anything to drink as his valet had drunk most of the ale already. If Moreau thought it was so terrible he might have left more of it in the cask.

They approached ever closer to the waves. They were large rollers that did not break early, which worked in his favor. With any luck, the sloop would coast into shore until the keel scraped the bottom.

Moreau finished the last of the ale and staggered to the port side of the boat. "Moreau abandons this cursed vessel and swims to shore! He does not go down with the ship!"

With that, his valet went over the side and disappeared into the waves.

Miles had no time to look behind him to see what his drunken valet was doing. He kept the tiller steady and steered *The Marquessa* up and down the rollers. On the last trough, he felt the familiar scraping under his keel that slowed the boat. As the sloop ran aground, he abandoned ship himself as the boat would soon go over.

He jumped off the starboard side and swam under the mast just as it slapped down on the water. The waves pushed him clear of it. He crawled his way out of the water, the surf mercilessly hammering him on the head, and stood up on the rocky shore.

Moreau came tumbling in and lay like a banked fish gasping for air. *The Marquessa* was on its side and being pushed back and forth by the waves as they came in and then receded.

The sun was out though. He was alive, his drunken valet was also mysteriously alive. All in all, things could have been worse.

The boat had come in very close to shore and Miles waded out for the bowline. There was no pier to secure it to, but he would make do by looping it round a boulder on the beach.

Once that operation was completed, with no help from his valet whatsoever, Miles began to think about which direction they ought to walk to find civilization.

MRS. RIGHT HAD been the duke's housekeeper for these past twenty years, ever since her husband had breathed his last and she was forced to sell their little shop and find a way to sustain herself. She had been determined to tuck away the money from the sale of the shop to fund her retirement. She was young and she was a strong specimen of a woman—she would work while she was able.

As a matron who was well used to running a household, she was hired on in the duke's house. She was meant to be what the duke had named a second in charge, deferring to the current housekeeper at that time, Mrs. Kendall.

That lady suffered from some sort of nervous condition and was often not able to attend to her duties.

Mrs. Kendall was too much affected by the duke's original way of going on, combined with the lonely remoteness of the house. She was forever taking to her bed on account of it. One day, a cousin came and collected her, as he had become concerned over the letters she wrote hinting about wandering out to the moors to be lost forever. Mrs. Right was speedily promoted and had run the house ever since.

Acting as housekeeper was a pleasant way to maintain oneself. She quickly fell to adoring the duke's children as they came on the scene and she had respected the duchess, who let her get on with her work. She even developed a soft spot for the duke, despite his eccentricities. When the duchess died, Mrs. Right had become the children's de facto mother, the person they ran to with any and all difficulties. Her loyalty to her girls and the duke ran deep, and heaven help the mistaken person who inconvenienced any one of them.

The only thing not so comfortable in the whole situation was being bossed about by a butler.

She'd managed that problem though. Mr. Herring had been driven out years ago and there had never been a replacement hired.

Then last season, Lady Marchfield had been determined that a duke must have a butler in his London house and had installed Mr. Sykes-Wycliff. She'd driven him out too, and in the process nearly driven Lady Marchfield mad.

Mrs. Right had been certain Lady Marchfield would have learned her lesson.

She had miscalculated, though. She had been informed that a certain Mr. Harold Button was already installed in the house in Grosvenor Square.

Well, Mr. Button was on the verge of learning a thing or two about tangling with Mrs. Agnes Right. Like those before him, he would rue the day he thought to boss her about. In fact, like one of those before him, she might enact what she'd privately named the "Herring Gambit." It had worked marvelously on that very first butler and it would work again.

As the carriage jostled along a lonely road on its way to London, Valor said, "Mrs. Right, you will convince Mr. Button that he ought not be our butler? The last butler was scary—he was mad all the time."

"Do not you worry, you dear little mite. Mr. Button is about to be convinced right down to his shoes."

CHAPTER TWO

GRACE HAD SO far enjoyed their travels as they headed toward London. They were a regular caravan of carriages, two of their own and the rest rented. Her own carriage carried herself, Serenity, Valor, and Mrs. Right. Another carriage held Winsome, Patience, and Verity, and she supposed the arguments in that coach went on all day. Verity would pose some new fact that was likely not a fact, Winsome would challenge it, and Patience would toe-tap over the tediousness. Her papa was ensconced in his own carriage with the two footmen and his valet, Reynolds.

Lady Marchfield had last year pointed out that a duke should not be riding with his footmen and his valet, but the duke had inquired who he was to talk to if they were shunted off elsewhere. Lady Marchfield had suggested herself so that they might discuss plans for the season. The duke had marched her to another carriage and shouted, "Not on your life!"

Just now they traveled down a rather narrow bit of road and Grace felt as if they were taking a very roundabout way to Town. However, the duke had told them he had a reason for it, he was to show them something special. She wondered if they were getting close to it as she could not see why else they had left the wider and better maintained roads.

She did feel they had traveled into a county they had never been through. The air smelled somehow different. It was not unpleasant, but it was less grass and hay and more... she could not even come up with a word for it. It was very fresh and invigorating.

The lead carriage carrying the duke slowed and stopped. Grace peeked out the window and saw her father hop out and stride over, standing between the two carriages carrying his daughters.

Patience hung out the window. "Are we almost there, Papa? What I mean is, are we almost somewhere?"

The duke nodded. "In another quarter of a mile, you shall see the secret I've held close. Keep your eyes wide open and prepare to be amazed!"

The duke hopped back in his carriage and the caravan set off again.

"Mrs. Right," Grace said, "I feel certain you know where we are going. You will know what it is that our mama was so fond of."

"If I did, I would not spoil the duke's surprise for the world," Mrs. Right said.

Valor slipped her hand into Mrs. Right's and clutched Mrs. Wendover with the other. "Is it a scary surprise?"

"My girl, I have told you ten ways to Sunday that when you are by my side, naught can hurt you."

"Oh that's right, you do tell me that a lot."

The discussion then fell to all the times Valor had been certain disaster was poised to strike but didn't.

There was the time she became sure that the bull who ruled their farthest field had figured out how to unlatch the gate and would bide his time. When nobody was looking, he would free himself and trample them all. That bull had grown old and his only interest in life was grazing—he would not be inclined to gin up the energy to trample Valor or anybody else.

Then there were the endless amounts of times that she could not be convinced that the woman's screams she heard in the middle of the night were just a fox's cries. She had even consulted the vicar on the matter, who explained that a fox's cries *could* sound very like a woman frightened or suffering. Valor hinted to the vicar that she very much feared that it must be him torturing all those screaming women if he wanted to cover it up instead of rescue them. The duke had to step into the ensuing set-to and remind the vicar that he owed the duke his living.

Just three days ago, Valor had woken Grace with the sad news that they had a terrible ghost. That unearthly creature had kidnapped Mrs. Wendover and she was now likely lost forever. Valor had been very against going back to the scene of the kidnapping, but Grace had marched her back to her room. The stuffed rabbit had been in her usual lost location, which was under the bed. Valor claimed she had not been able to check there before imagining a kidnapping because everybody knows that under the bed at night is scary.

Faced with all these false alarms, Valor shrugged. "You will be sorry, though, when I'm right. I still don't believe it's foxes."

Grace giggled and peered out the window. They had just gone down a lane hemmed in with tall trees. Very suddenly, the vista opened.

"Is that… is that the sea?" Grace asked, nearly breathless from the sight.

This caused Serenity and Valor to fling themselves to her side and look out the window.

"It's so big!" Valor cried.

A tear rolled down Serenity's cheek. "Who ever could have imagined such wonder and majesty?"

Both of her sisters were right. Though they had all known of the mighty ocean, though they'd all seen drawings and maps galore, though a painting of it tossing a mighty ship sat over their drawing room mantel, this… it was almost too much to take in!

A deep blue endlessness in either direction leading off into a horizon. The Netherlands, Belgium, and France were out there somewhere and they could not even see them, the sea was so vast.

The duke had hopped out of his carriage and called to Grace.

"The carriages can go no further else they will not be able to turn round—we go on foot!"

They piled out of the carriage and hurried down the lane to the duke. Patience, Winsome and Verity were out of their carriage. The footmen had wasted no time either. Only Reynolds took his time and attempted to look dignified—the duke's valet was a rather grim specimen in every situation.

Everyone followed the duke through a twisty tangle of a path that ended in stone steps leading down to a narrow beach.

Along with the majesty of the sea, they were now cognizant of a thing they had not seen from their prior location above the shore.

There was a boat on its side with waves crashing over it and two men staggering up the beach. Both men had their jackets off and were soaked through, so they had clearly been the crew of that boat. Despite being jacketless and wet, they both seemed to be dressed rather fine.

Particularly the gentleman on the left. He was tall and athletic looking. Even with his dark hair plastered to his head, he looked very dashing. The one on the right seemed to be having a breakdown of some sort—he was jumping up and down and shouting something. Grace began to wonder if he were the gentleman's butler, as in her experience butlers were always so prone to hysterics.

They had all hurried down the steps and though Grace paid close attention to her footing she missed the last as it was covered in sand and she went down with a thud. This caused Charlie to trip over her and then Thomas to fall over Charlie.

"Causing another pile up, eh Gracie?" the duke said, helping her to her feet.

Grace did not answer, because of course she had. The two gentlemen were staring in their direction and she hoped they'd not seen how it happened that three people had fallen down.

The duke turned to the two gentlemen and shouted, "What-ho! Shipwrecked, are you?"

The dashing man shouted back. "I suppose we are, though we've at least managed to land on the right island."

The duke turned round and said, "Well, it seems we encounter more excitement than I'd planned. Let us go see what has gone on with these two fellows."

Very naturally, they were all in eager agreement with this plan and set forward to meet the two shipwrecked gentlemen.

Grace's shoes filled with sand and small stones. While she did not know what footwear would be suitable for walking on a beach, these rather flimsy slippers could not be it. Charlie gave her his arm while Thomas assisted Mrs. Right. The duke picked up and carried Valor, else she would have fallen behind. Reynolds would no doubt have assisted either Patience, Serenity, Winsome, or Verity, but they had run on ahead.

By the time Grace reached the party, Winsome was interrogating the gentlemen regarding how they were shipwrecked and Verity was interrupting her with the idea that shipwrecks were a very common thing. Patience had gone down to examine the boat, while Serenity wept at the shoreline over the majesty of the view.

"The Duke of Pelham," the duke said heartily. "And you are?"

Both gentlemen bowed. The dashing gentleman said, "Viscount Dashlend, son of the Earl of Gravesend, Your Grace. This is my valet, Moreau."

The duke laughed. "Dragged your valet out to sea, did you? What say you, Reynolds? Would you ever put up with such shenanigans?"

Reynolds shook his head gravely, as the last thing he would ever be involved in was shenanigans.

"This man understands Moreau!" the valet cried, pointing at the duke. "Merci, Your Highest and Most Holy Grace."

This caused the duke to laugh even harder. "Well, Dashlend, you've got yourself a hysterical man there—maybe the sea is not the place for him. And you," he said, pointing to Mr. Moreau, "I am just Your Grace, do not add holy to it and hint I'm the pope, thank you very much."

Mr. Moreau seemed nonplussed with the duke, though Viscount Dashlend looked rather amused.

"Now," the duke said, "you might as well meet all these setbacks by way of progeny—there is Patience, staring at your boat and wondering how you managed to tip it over. Serenity stands next to her, weeping as usual, probably to do with the majesty of nature. Here is Valor, the youngest, do not worry about her, she'll be terrified of you. You already met Verity and Winsome—one names a fact and the other sets out to prove it wrong. Here is our good Mrs. Right, my housekeeper—she runs the whole circus. And finally, the eldest still left at home, Lady Grace. I am taking her to Town in the hopes of getting her off my hands at the earliest possible moment."

Though this was quite a usual speech for her Papa, Grace could not help but hear it as a stranger might hear it. Felicity had told her of that odd feeling, as she had experienced the same herself. It was one thing to know what the duke meant, and another to take what he said on its face.

The viscount looked as if he were working hard not to laugh. His valet was looking with alarm back and forth between the duke's daughters.

Viscount Dashlend bowed and said, "Charmed."

Was he, though?

"I suppose we'd best get you out of your current predicament," the duke said. "We are going to an inn not a mile off—I'll put you up while you make whatever sort of arrangements one makes when involved in a fiasco such as this."

"That is exceedingly kind, Your Grace," the viscount said.

"Patience! Serenity!" the duke called to the shoreline. "Come now, we have two wet people to transport."

Patience, never one to linger as a habit, came running back. Serenity was a bit slower, as her weeping over the majesty of the sea had no doubt clouded her vision.

"Reynolds," the duke said, "I leave it to you to rearrange the carriages in some suitable fashion."

Reynolds nodded gravely and set off to do the duke's bidding. Grace did not know what arrangements the valet would make, but Reynolds was one for quiet efficiency. She did not suppose he would come up with any whimsical ideas like putting the viscount in her own carriage.

"Let's get this caravan going," the duke said.

"Lady Grace," the viscount said, "may I escort you to steadier ground?"

Grace nodded and had every hope that her pink cheeks could be attributed to the brisk sea air.

Her sisters were all very wide-eyed at the idea, especially Valor. "Be careful of rogues, Grace," she whispered as Grace went by.

Grace pretended that she had not heard that. The idea had come from Mrs. Right. Before Felicity's season, she had told them all what they could expect in Town. The men were feckless rogues, and the women were fan-waving furies.

Their opinions on the matter had veered wildly over the course of that season—one moment they were convinced it was not true, then it was true, then it was not true again. Mr. Stratton had turned out all right for Felicity, but who really knew?

"Lady Grace," the viscount said, "I presume from your father's speech that this is your first foray into Town?"

"The first where I will be out," Grace said. "I was there last year when my sister, Felicity, had her season."

This seemed to register something in the viscount's mind. "I was not there, I was on the continent on business for my father...but, Lady Felicity? I seem to have heard about a tiger and then she wed Stratton?"

"Yes, that is right," Grace said.

They had come to the steps and Grace was determined not to fall over. She leaned heavily on the viscount's arm.

He seemed to perceive her trepidation over them and said, "There now, well-worn steps like these only require one to go slowly and not get ahead of oneself."

Grace nodded, really very gratified at his consideration. How extraordinary that she would have met with her first single gentleman in such a situation. At least, she supposed he was single, but then perhaps he was not—how to find it out?

They had reached the top of the steps with no tippings over, which was just as she hoped for. Viscount Dashlend escorted her through the twisting track and it was really very narrow in some places. Grace was not certain she'd ever been so close to a gentleman outside of her papa. In truth, she was sure she had not. There was one moment where really they should have gone in a single file. Their shoulders touched. It was rather exhilarating.

Reynolds had made arrangements with the carriages. One of the luggage coaches had been rearranged to permit just enough room for two people. Horse blankets had been laid down on the seats to accommodate the wet passengers.

"Jump in, sailors," the duke said to the viscount and his valet. "We're off to The Dolphin and the Dove—what a name for an inn, eh? What does a dolphin want with a dove? Nobody knows, least of all the innkeeper!"

With that genial assessment, Grace went to her own carriage and very slowly and elegantly got in.

THE CARRIAGE DOOR was shut by the duke's valet, who gave both Miles and Moreau a very stern look before making his dignified way to the duke's carriage.

They stared at one another.

"Well, how propitious that we are rescued so easily," Miles said. "I had thought we'd be roaming up and down the coast looking for help from the local people. I imagined we'd end up spending the night in somebody's hayloft."

"What is this family?" Moreau asked.

"Were you not listening? The Duke of Pelham and his daughters."

"You know what I ask."

Of course, Miles was pretty certain he did know. What an extraordinary introduction. He'd been introduced to ladies by their fathers hundreds of times. In all of those times, he'd never heard a father refer to a daughter as a setback and then describe them in further unflattering terms. He'd wondered if the duke was drunk, but then he'd decided that was not the case.

"Was he drunk?" Moreau asked.

"I do not believe so," Miles said thoughtfully. "I believe he may only be eccentric. Highly eccentric."

Moreau narrowed his eyes. "Moreau is eccentric. This is something else."

Naturally, Moreau *was* eccentric. One had to be eccentric to talk about themselves by name, as if one were Louis XIV using the royal we. The duke's was a different sort of eccentricity, though.

"This is English ducal eccentricity," Miles said. "Something you will not be familiar with."

As Miles expected, this brought an end to that particular line of inquiry. Though Moreau claimed he knew quite a lot on nearly every subject, he freely admitted that the habits of the English were beyond his understanding.

They fell into silence as Moreau became distracted by examining his wet clothing and quietly sighing over it.

Miles did not give too much thought to his clothing, as that was Moreau's problem. His thoughts were much more taken up with Lady Grace.

She was very pretty, really. Her hair was a lovely shade of blond and not at all short of ringlets, as the sea breeze had helpfully revealed. Her cheeks were dimpled, which was charming. And then her eyes—so many blond ladies were blue eyed, but she was not. Her eyes were such that they might be taken for brown, but when one was closer one saw they were actually more olive with hints of gold. He really thought those eyes and her refined bone structure lent some sophistication to what might have been only a confection of blond curls and dimples.

Lady Grace also seemed a good-natured sort of lady. After all, she had not looked at all perturbed to hear herself described as a setback, nor the duke noting he was looking to get her out of the house as fast as possible.

Miles paused. Because, of course, that was why a lady came to London to begin. No father outright ever said it, but he supposed they all secretly harbored the duke's ambitions. And then, the duke had quite a number of young ladies to settle. Miles had lost track of exactly how many of them had been on the beach as they'd seemed to be a regular swarm.

Thoughts of settling all those young ladies inevitably brought on ideas of his own situation. He really ought to get on with it. The squall they'd been through, how close they'd come to disaster, impressed upon him how each day could be his last.

Should that day come earlier than later, it would mean that a certain Rupert Burdock, known to the wider world as Baron Montclave, would step in as his father's heir. That alone would send his father following Miles to the great beyond with all haste.

Miles' father and his father's brother, Cyril, had been oil and water since childhood. The earl had been the direct line in the earldom. Montclave's father Cyril might have gone on as a mister all his life, but he had been gifted the barony for services rendered to the crown. Most unfortunately, their estates bordered one another. The barony was far smaller and that seemed to be a constant needle in that family's side.

As neighbors, they could not avoid knowing one another. The earl had gone to great lengths to instill honor in his brother, to no avail. There had even been instances when the earl had wondered if an accident had been an accident, or some plan of Cyril's to get him out of the way so he might move up a spot in life. If the earl had died without issue, Cyril would be next in line.

Cyril went on to wed a viscount's daughter who seemed equally dissatisfied with their lot. Then Montclave had been born to Cyril and his lady.

It was said that when a son arrived, there had been much celebration in that household, as Miles was not yet on the ground and they had high hopes a son would never arrive to the earl's household. As the years passed, it looked more and more likely. It almost began to look assured. The only circumstance they really feared was that the countess would die and the earl would remarry to a younger and more fertile lady, thereby producing a son at the last possible moment.

Miles' mother was nearing thirty when she became with child, much to everybody's surprise.

Still, Cyril and his wife held out hope that the earl's offspring would be a girl. It was not though.

Since then, Cyril had died and Montclave had taken on the mantle of Baron.

Montclave went out of his way to be some sort of obsequious friend, but Miles was not particularly fooled. There was always an undercurrent of something there—anger, resentment, scheming...something untrustworthy.

How delighted Montclave would have been to get a letter that Miles was lost at sea.

"I'd really better do something," he said quietly.

"Oh I see," Moreau said. "We go out to the deadly depths of the ocean with no spare sail only to crash land in barbaric English wilderness and be taken away by an eccentric duke. But *now*, you would like to do something."

"That is about the size of it."

"Mon Dieu."

"Mon Dieu all you like," Miles said. "In the meantime, fix my clothes as soon as we get to the inn. I am all but certain the duke will ask me to dine with him. I must be presentable."

"Fix your clothes?" Moreau asked, as if he'd just been directed to fly to the moon. "I see. So what do you imagine? Moreau will blow on them to dry them out?"

"I've not imagined anything," Miles said genially. "You are the valet—it's your problem to imagine."

"Oh yes," Moreau muttered, "it is always my problem. The world sits heavy on Moreau's shoulders."

Miles stopped himself from laughing. Moreau had one duty in life—to see to Miles' clothes. If that was the weight of the world, he'd like to know about it.

Moreau peered out the window. "And here we are at the Dolphin and Dove, another eccentric English inn. What will they serve, I wonder? Oh I know, not dolphin and not dove, it will be beef. It is always beef."

"Let us hope you are correct," Miles said.

They had pulled into the yard and it was apparent the duke had written ahead that he would be arriving with a caravan of people and carriages. Staff swarmed the duke's carriage as if he were the prince.

"We'd best take ourselves out and manage on our own, I think," Miles said.

"Yes, why not," Moreau said. "We are nobodies now."

Miles was often fascinated by the workings of his valet's mind. The highs and lows of it were dramatic, to say the least. He wondered how the fellow slept at night, with all these tragic musings running circles round his mind.

"Wallow in self-pity all day long if it suits you," Miles said, jumping down from the carriage. "Just do something about my clothes."

CHAPTER THREE

G RACE FELT SHE did very well in the innyard. She wished to take a few surreptitious glances at the viscount they'd found shipwrecked on the beach while not being observed.

She'd also very much wished for the duke to invite the viscount to dine, which she'd been looking for an opportunity to suggest before Valor beat her to it.

"Papa," Valor said, "are we to have a stranger at our dinner? I'm worried about it."

"Hah, nothing to worry about. Good thought, though." The duke had turned to the viscount and his valet, who were just emerging from the luggage carriage. "Dashlend, do dine with us—I'll send over some clothes, at least they'll be dry. My valet will set you up. And your hysterical man there, too. Two hours to get settled."

The viscount had expressed his appreciation for the courtesy, though his valet seemed somehow affronted.

It was well that the duke had allotted two hours to get settled, as it had really taken that long. It seemed the duke had written explicitly on how he wished the rooms to be arranged. However, it could not be done exactly as he'd ordered without tearing down some of the inn's walls and the innkeeper was firm in his opposition to such a move.

Finally, it was sorted out to everyone's satisfaction, including what to do with the two extra people they'd brought along. At least, Grace thought most of the party was satisfied with the arrangements. She could not say how satisfied Reynolds was to be sharing a room with the viscount's valet, the footmen having wriggled out of it by noting that they were both very loud snorers and could only be tolerated by one another.

Grace was in a large room with four single beds shared with Serenity, Verity, and Patience. Mrs. Right was housed with Valor and Winsome. There was very conveniently a connecting door between the rooms and that was what had really held things up for the innkeeper until he'd had the idea of moving extra beds in. Though the room was large, the four beds only allowed for the narrowest of spaces to move around them. It was found to be satisfactory, though, as all the sisters were well used to being nearly on top of each other as a matter of course.

Serenity was working on Grace's hair, catching one ringlet and pinning it down just as another set itself free.

"I really wish to look well this evening," Grace said. "It is my first evening out in company with a strange gentleman."

"Do you think him strange?" Patience asked. "I did wonder."

"I mean strange in that he is unknown to us," Grace said. "We have only been introduced and we do not know a thing about him. For instance, is he married? He does not wear a ring, but then he might choose not to as a matter of preference or he might have been leery of wearing it while at sea."

"He cannot be married," Verity said. "It is a well-known fact that if a gentleman were married, and then he almost dies at sea, certainly the first thing he will say is that his wife must be sick with worry. He must get word to his wife right away. Lord Dashlend said no such thing."

Grace pondered that. It could be true. Of course, Verity made up quite a lot of what she said, but this one made a deal of sense. If a gentleman were married, he would wish to get word to his wife that he had survived his ordeal at sea at the earliest possible moment.

Mrs. Right came through the connecting door and said,

"How do we get on in here? I've just managed to convince Valor that Mrs. Wendover does not in fact know that there are murderers in the area, as Mrs. Wendover has never been here and does not read the newspapers."

"I suppose Mrs. Wendover will not be left behind when we go down for dinner, then," Patience said.

"She will not. That was the compromise, in the end. Goodness, Serenity—how many pins have you put in Grace's hair?"

Serenity shrugged. "I lost count. You pin down one curl and another makes its escape. Also, I was thinking of the sea."

Mrs. Right, ever efficient, took over for Serenity and pulled out a dozen pins and started over.

"Will you dine with us, Mrs. Right?" Verity asked. "It is one thing at home, where you like to have your cozy dinner with Cook and Thomas and Charlie, but here you are always with us."

"Why should this night be any different than the past nights?" Mrs. Right asked.

"Patience says a viscount won't like it, but I say our papa will not care," Verity said.

"Since when is the duke meant to care what's got a viscount's back up?" Mrs. Right said. "I will dine with you and I have every hope that word of it gets back to Lady Marchfield. It will drive her mad."

"We ought to tell Mr. Button about it as soon as we arrive," Patience said. "I bet our aunt has told him to report on the doings of the house. We could shock her before we've even unpacked."

"Very good thought. Now, as to this Mr. Button," Mrs. Right said, "do not be at all alarmed if I pretend at being frightened of him. I am not, and I will not be, but I have a plan in mind for that hapless fellow."

All the sisters nodded, as they placed a great amount of faith in Mrs. Right's plans.

"Mrs. Right," Verity said, "I've told Grace I am sure the viscount is not married."

Mrs. Right nodded sagely. "He is as unattached as the day is long. There was naught said about a worried wife upon his rescue. She would either be a terrible harpy he cannot stand the sight of and would not mind faking his own death to escape her, or she does not exist. Lord Dashlend seems too sensible to wed a terrible harpy, therefore there is no wife."

Grace was vastly relieved. It seemed the question had been satisfactorily settled.

"There we go," Mrs. Right said. "I have undone Serenity's fanciful stylings and your hair is looking very well. As are your cheeks, you are blooming, my dear."

Grace supposed she might have bloomed a bit more with that compliment. But she really did wish to look well this evening.

MILES HAD BORROWED stationery from the innkeeper and fired off a letter to his butler in Town. Wainwright was ordered to bring a carriage, clothes, and money. Once he had money, he could arrange for someone to tow his boat to a port and have it repaired. He'd already arranged with the innkeeper to employ a watch at the beach so that some enterprising young sailor did not put a sail on *The Marquessa* and make off with her.

As for the evening, Miles had been the slightest bit concerned that the duke was planning on sending over some of his own clothes for him to wear. It was a kind gesture, and not one he could refuse without insult, but the duke's middle section had seen a few more bottles of port than Miles' ever had. Or even if Miles had consumed just as much port as the duke, his younger years and habit of pursuing sports had seemed to keep its more rounding effects at bay.

Fortunately, a combination of clothes had been delivered by the duke's valet. It would be the duke's valet's best coat and pants, paired with one of the duke's shirts that had been hastily pinned to take it in, along with one of the duke's neckcloths.

All in all, it was far better than expected.

As for Moreau, he'd also been left with some of the valet's things. Mr. Reynolds had made clear he handed over what was "his oldest set." Though it was "his oldest set," Reynolds cautioned that he expected it to be returned to him in good order.

The effrontery of it had left Moreau surprisingly speechless.

Moreau had gone from swimming in the sea to swimming in the duke's valet's oldest set of clothes. He looked faintly ridiculous as he hung Miles' clothes across the window to dry out. "Now you go down and have beef with the mad duke and his battalion of strange daughters while Moreau struggles on alone."

"That sounds right," Miles said, and left his valet to complain to himself. He jogged down the steps and made his way into the private dining room reserved for the duke.

The duke and his family, and surprisingly his housekeeper too, were already gathered. If Miles had harbored any doubts about the eccentricity of the duke, having his housekeeper at the table washed those doubts away.

"Ho there," the duke said jovially, "here is our hapless sailor. You look a deal better now that you are dry—do not you think so, Gracie?"

Lady Grace had the sense to blush at this rather forward comment. Miles said, "I will not ask anyone to comment on my appearance, either earlier today or this moment. I pray Lady Grace has the generosity to forestall judgment until I am back in Town and appear more usually."

"I am not certain I would judge at any time," Lady Grace said.

Miles smiled at her. "Perhaps not aloud."

"Sit here, Dashlend," the duke said, motioning to an empty seat beside him. "I'll need you on this end of the table, far away from my youngest. I've promised her I'd keep you away, you see—you are a stranger, so you may well be a murderer."

"Mrs. Wendover said he might be a murderer, Papa," Lady Valor said. In a voice so quiet she could almost not be heard, she whispered, "I was only thinking it."

Miles sat down. He presumed Mrs. Wendover was the housekeeper just now at table, though he thought he remembered another name for that lady when she was introduced. But whatever her name was, why should she suspect him of being a murderer?

"I do not suppose many murderers arrive by capsized boat, washed up on the beach," he said.

"Hah! That's right, Valor!" the duke said, motioning the waiter to fill their wine glasses. "Not much of an entrance for a murderer!"

Lady Valor seemed to consider this point and took to whispering to a stuffed rabbit on her lap.

The duke said, "Well now, I suppose this could-be-a-murderer at our table cannot be expected to remember all the names of this ghastly horde. That's Patience, Verity, Winsome, and Serenity. Valor would have already made herself memorable. There is my esteemed housekeeper, Mrs. Right—she runs the place. And then, my second eldest—Grace."

Miles nodded to all of them and tried to keep their names straight. Who was this Mrs. Wendover who thought he might be a murderer though? A governess? Perhaps she'd declined to walk down to the beach and had stayed inside a carriage?

He did think it was rather hopeful of the duke to name his daughters as temperaments that they might or might not possess. He had always thought, whenever he met with a Lady Charity, or Faith, or Constance, that it was a rather risky proposition.

"Rest assured, Lord Dashlend," Lady Winsome said, "I explained to Valor that you cannot be a murderer because a murderer is more sly. They like to sneak up on a person. Why? Because the murderer knows that people do not just stand around waiting to be murdered."

This very predictably sent a shiver through Lady Valor and she clutched the raggedy stuffed rabbit in her arms. It rather sent a shiver through Miles too. It sounded as if Lady Winsome had given some careful and extensive consideration to the habits and strategies of murderers.

He thought to turn the conversation to more usual subjects, as this was the first time murderers had been the topic at any dinner he'd ever attended and he was hoping it was the last. "Lady Grace," he said, "may I ask what are you looking forward to in Town? I suppose attending balls must be high on the list?"

For some reason, the mention of dancing gave the lady a rather stricken look. Miles began to wonder if the duke had failed to hire a dancing master for his daughters.

But no, it would be too absurd. In truth, it would be barbaric. One could not send a lady to Town without the necessary skills to attend a ball. Certainly not a duke's daughter.

"Oh yes, dancing, certainly," Lady Grace said.

It was not said very convincingly.

"What she means to say, Dashlend, is our Gracie has two left feet," the duke said. "Best to know it now—surprises like that never do anybody any good."

Lady Grace blushed furiously. Lady Verity said, "Grace is really a very good dancer. Except sometimes she's not. A very common condition."

Was it a common condition? What did it even mean, except when she's not? What condition?

"I suppose you attend Almack's?" Lady Grace asked.

Miles nodded. "I will miss the season's opening ball due to my current circumstances, but will likely attend the second Wednesday. I will admit, it is not my favorite place. However, one does not like to offend the matrons of society, so I do my duty."

"It's the supper, isn't it?" the duke asked. "I would like to know what those blasted women are thinking about. Do not give me lemonade at midnight, thank you!"

Miles attempted to suppress his laughter over the duke's outrage but was only partially successful. "It is rather dreadful."

"Our sister, Felicity," Lady Patience said, "found Almack's supper very terrible."

"Very, very terrible," Lady Serenity confirmed.

"Our aunt thinks it's marvelous," Lady Winsome said.

"Lady Misery thinks everything dull is marvelous," the duke said.

"Her real name is Lady Marchfield," Lady Valor said, clutching her rabbit. "In case you're wondering."

"She's very…proper," Lady Grace said.

"Ah yes," Miles said. "Lady Marchfield. A very formidable matron."

"Formidable? Well, that's one word for her," the duke said. "Not one I would use, but most of the words I *would* use are not for young ears."

"Papa is very put out, on account of our aunt installing a butler in his house on Grosvenor Square," Lady Grace said.

"His name is Mr. Button," Lady Patience said with a certain hint of disgust.

"We do not require Mr. Button," the housekeeper said in a dark tone that sent another chill down Miles' spine.

"Maybe I'll leave Lady Misery at another cyprian's party," the duke said, laughing and taking a rather large gulp of wine.

Lady Valor collapsed in giggles. "That was so funny. Even though we don't know what a cyprian is."

"Not all of us know, in any case," Lady Grace said.

Three waiters streamed in with a variety of dishes. Miles supposed Moreau would feel very vindicated to hear there was a beef platter. However, since they were so close to the sea, there were two different fish dishes too. No dolphin or dove, though.

"Where are we on the brocabbage pie?" the duke asked the waiters.

Both of those fellows looked abashed. Miles could not imagine what brocabbage pie was, but it did not sound very appealing.

The innkeeper himself hurried in and the waiters looked at him with some relief. One of the waiters said, "His Grace inquires into the brocabbage pie."

"Ah yes, as to that, Your Grace, our cook does not have that recipe."

The duke wrinkled his brow. "A *cook* does not know how to make brocabbage pie? A *cook* cannot make what is an esteemed and beloved Yorkshire staple?"

The innkeeper shook his head sadly.

"Tell him, Papa!" Lady Valor said, before burying her head in her stuffed rabbit and giggling hysterically.

The duke nodded at his youngest daughter. "You may tell your cook I would consider him mad as a spring hare if he made a run at making that particular pie. You see? It does not exist! I made it up!"

Miles stared at the duke. The duke's daughters all laughed heartily at the ruse. Lady Patience said, "Well done, Papa."

"Oh yes, I see," the poor innkeeper said. "A very fine joke, Your Grace." The fellow bowed and hurried from the room. Miles would not be surprised if he were hurrying toward a glass of brandy to calm himself after that particular joke.

The dinner commenced and Miles learned quite a lot about the Nicolet family. He had, of course, heard of Lady Albright's tiger getting loose and Stratton stepping forward as the hero of the hour to rescue Lady Felicity.

There were other things he'd not heard though.

He was given more detail about the cyprian party that had been mentioned. Apparently, the housekeeper had accepted the invitation on behalf of the duke and Lady Marchfield. When the duke realized what sort of party it was, he left his sister there to fend for herself.

This story struck all of the family as particularly hilarious, especially the part where Lady Marchfield arrived to the duke's house to yell about it.

Miles was at a loss as to how a housekeeper could send a duke and a countess to a party put on by low women and still keep her position.

The dessert course was passed uniquely, as he heard about the various tortures thrust upon Stratton when it was felt he might have tricked Lady Felicity regarding his feelings. There was a pile of chains left on his doorstep, his grocery order was changed to only cabbages, his wine order was canceled, and his clothes were donated to charity.

All of this was said to have worked out well, as Lady Felicity and Stratton had wed. Since then, Lady Felicity had taken Sir Pineapple in hand, whoever that person was, and Blueberry was turning out to be not much of a mouser.

After dinner, he was pressed to take some port, though the ladies remained at table. He initially thought this odd arrangement was on account of being at an inn. That was cleared up when it was explained that the duke got too drunk when he was left alone with the bottle.

Well past midnight, he staggered up the stairs to his room. He found Moreau sitting morosely by the window, fanning Miles' clothes in the night air.

"Moreau was forced to dine with the duke's staff," Moreau said. "That valet is grim-faced and kept staring at his 'oldest set' of clothes, even though they were on my person. He leaned forward anytime food or drink came near Moreau's lips as if Moreau is in the habit of missing his mouth."

Miles settled himself in a chair. He knew perfectly well from experience that Moreau was on the verge of recounting his entire evening.

"The duke's footmen were very drunk and kept winking at a kitchen maid until she winked back," his Valet said, looking mournfully at the clothes hanging by the window. Then, naturally, they were terrified of the girl. Three of the coachmen came in and demanded bottles of wine on the duke's charge. The valet attempted to refuse them, but they said they would rip him limb from limb and he acquiesced. Then those brutes went off with the kitchen maid and the footmen nearly wept over it. For all I know, maybe they did weep. They had to go out to the yard to vomit out all the wine they drank so who knows what else they did out there. As you might suspect, they came back in and drank more wine. Then they sang terrible English songs."

"You think all English songs are terrible, no matter who sings them."

Moreau ignored that comment. "The valet attempted to send them to bed, but of course they had prior viewed the coachmen's success, so they told him they'd rip him limb from limb. He took them both out by their ears. At that moment, Moreau thought to himself, this has been a delight indeed, and now I retire. One might have thought Moreau might find peace in his bed and he had closed his eyes, but no—that valet comes into the room and claims he must always have the bed by the window for his nose problems. Moreau was forced to relocate himself here to sleep on the floor, lest he cover the valet's face with a pillow in the middle of the night. But never mind Moreau's charming evening. I suppose you had a very pleasant dinner with your new friends?"

Miles smiled. "They are completely mad, and so are you."

CHAPTER FOUR

GRACE HAD BEEN up very late, as the moment they retired to their beds at The Dolphin and the Dove a minute examination of Viscount Dashlend had commenced.

Verity approved of him, as he'd admitted to disliking Almack's, which she thought was a very brave stance.

Serenity approved of him, as she sensed in him a sensitive soul. She pointed out how stricken he looked upon hearing of all that had been done to Mr. Percy Stratton before that gentleman wed Felicity.

Patience said she could not decide, which was very aggravating. She did not, as a habit, like to dilly-dally on deciding. It seemed the sticking point was that he did not put up a vigorous defense against the charge that he might be a murderer. She did not think he was, but she would have expected a more robust explanation than murderers did not arrive by shipwreck.

All through these discussions, Grace made herself out to be merely curious over her sister's opinions while holding no firm opinion of her own.

She did have an opinion, though. She thought Lord Dashlend was rather marvelous. He was such a strapping specimen of a man. He had very dark hair and eyes, and a nose with just a touch of the Roman in it, and a squarish chin. She'd never seen such a man.

He was so genial too. Grace understood from Felicity that a

person encountering all of the Nicolets at once might feel a bit overwhelmed. Aside from his flinching when Winsome explained why he could not be a murderer, he'd not seemed overwhelmed at all.

What was a question, though, was that she really could not gauge if he thought anything particular of her. She could not measure what sort of effect it had on the gentleman that she possessed two left feet. She did, everybody knew it, but perhaps so early in the acquaintance was not the moment for her father to mention it.

There would be no end of ladies in Town who did not have two left feet. Why should Lord Dashlend be interested in a lady not so blessed?

Grace knew very well that her father would have mentioned it thinking it would be helpful. After all, he'd been ever so helpful to Felicity with Mr. Percy Stratton.

But then, she could look on the side of hope—there was every chance she could become more graceful than she currently was. Perhaps she was already improving. It was true that she had missed that last step down to the beach, but it had been covered in sand. Anybody could have missed it. Other than that, she'd acquitted herself very well.

In truth, it seemed to her that these long carriage rides somehow did her good. She'd noticed it last year when they'd gone to Town. It was a very odd thing, but the jostling of it caused her to feel steadier on her feet for days. She'd even tried it out at home by hopping up and down and it did seem to help.

She'd fallen asleep keeping hope in her heart. Grace did not know what other gentlemen she would meet in London, but she had met Lord Dashlend.

He was exceedingly interesting.

THE FOLLOWING MORNING had been the usual Nicolet confusion of somehow getting everybody going in the same direction. Grace had been sure to go down early for breakfast. She was rather thrilled to find Viscount Dashlend already there, sitting across from Mrs. Right.

The Viscount rose as she made her way to the chair by Mrs. Right. The housekeeper poured her a cup of tea and said, "I've just told Lord Dashlend all about our last butler, as he inquired about the one that awaits us."

"Poor Mr. Sykes-Wycliff," Grace said. "We all do hope he's settled himself in a house that really needs a butler."

"Might I ask," Viscount Dashlend said, "is there a particular reason why the duke's household does *not* require a butler?"

Mrs. Right's teacup came down on her saucer with a quiet clatter. "I'm the reason, Lord Dashlend. I, Mrs. Agnes Right, am the reason the duke does not require a butler."

"I see, yes of course," the lord said hurriedly.

Just then, a boy who worked for the inn ran in and said, "Lord Dashlend, this was just delivered by fast messenger." He handed over a sealed letter.

Lord Dashlend opened it and scanned it. He seemed very pleased with his contents. "My butler is on his way with money and clothes and my carriage. He has already written to a local shipwright. He is pleased that I am alive, as he sent out various search parties looking for me, though it seems they looked in the wrong place—I was much further south than they imagined."

"That is very good news," Grace said, though really she had been hoping that there might be a chance the lord would continue relying on the duke's hospitality.

Lord Dashlend suddenly laughed. "He writes that I did not mention the fate of my valet, but he presumes Moreau is alive as things never do go his way."

Mrs. Right laughed heartily at the joke. "A clever butler. Now that might be somebody I could tolerate, as opposed to these ridiculous fellows Lady Marchfield sends my way."

"Really?" Lord Dashlend said.

"No," Mrs. Right answered.

Valor hurried into the room, dragging her stuffed rabbit

behind her. "I made it through the night," she said, settling on the other side of Mrs. Right.

Lord Dashlend looked at Valor enquiringly.

Valor stared back and said, "From murderers, Lord Dashlend. As you can see with your own eyes, I am not murdered."

Grace noted a small smile playing at the edge of his lips. "Yes, as anyone can see, you are looking very vital and alive."

Valor nodded. "Mrs. Wendover woke me twice in the night because of scary noises, but nobody got in."

"And you woke me up both times to tell me what Mrs. Wendover said, you naughty little mite," Mrs. Right said.

"She made me wake you up, she said you should be informed," Valor said, once more throwing Mrs. Wendover to the proverbial wolves.

"Is Mrs. Wendover the governess?" Lord Dashlend asked.

This sent them all into the giggles. Valor held up her ragged stuffed rabbit. "This is Mrs. Wendover."

Lord Dashlend seemed very surprised to find it out. Grace realized that all along he'd thought Mrs. Wendover was some mysterious lady hidden behind a door somewhere.

The duke strode into the room and said, "Well, here is part of my unfortunate brood, though heaven knows where the rest of them have got off to."

Grace had reached for a roll to throw at her father's head, but then put it on her plate. That habit had begun to seem rather childish. At least, while Viscount Dashlend was in view.

The duke noticed and gave her a wink. "Well then, Dashlend, I suppose you've sorted yourself out?"

"Yes, Your Grace," the viscount said. "Your help through this mishap has been very much appreciated."

"No bother, no bother at all," the duke said. "Now I suppose you'll like to come to dinner when you get yourself back to Town."

Grace noticed the viscount's eyes widen just a bit before she put her eyes on her toast.

"Delighted," the viscount said.

She wondered if he really was delighted. He might be, or he might have only been polite.

"Tuesday next," the duke said. "You'll be back by then I am sure."

Before the viscount could say whether or not he would be in London by that time, the door to the dining room crashed open.

"Papa," Serenity said, a single tear meandering down her cheek.

"Let me guess," the duke said. "You've found another dead bee in a garden. I've told you time and again—bees do die on occasion. If they didn't, we'd be overrun with them and you would not like it."

Grace naturally noticed the confusion on the viscount's countenance, as he could not know that Serenity wept over any and all dead things she came upon.

"No, Papa," Serenity said. "It's just that I am afraid you will not like what I am to tell you and I should just cry and cry over it. But there is room in the carriages—there really is. It will be fine, I promise."

"We do not need room in the carriages—Dashlend here has got himself sorted on his own."

"Not *him*," Serenity said. Grace blushed at her tone, as it seemed to say that the viscount was of the least importance.

Patience, Winsome, and Verity appeared behind Serenity.

"Have you told him?" Patience asked.

"Have you mentioned how usual a case this is?" Verity asked.

"She has not mentioned how usual it is, because it is not," Winsome said, challenging Verity's supposition.

The duke sighed. "I am afraid this is not a circumstance of a dead bee."

"No, Papa," Serenity said. "It is about a dog who has tragically lost one of his legs."

The duke sat up a little straighter. "I see. Now, you girls sit in here and close the door behind me. I'll have a word with the innkeeper and we'll put the poor thing out of its misery. Patience, cover Serenity's ears, and Verity, cover Valor's so they do not hear the shot."

The viscount had jumped from his seat. "I will come with you, Your Grace."

"You cannot shoot him!" Serenity cried.

"Why would you shoot him?" Patience asked.

"It is the kindest thing," the duke said. "It would not be kind to prolong its suffering, even though the necessary outcome upsets you."

"He is not suffering, though, Papa," Serenity said. "He is ever so cheerful."

This news seemed to take everyone aback, as nobody could imagine a dog who'd just lost a leg being at all cheerful.

"Verity," Serenity said, "do go and get him while I make sure nobody goes looking for a gun to shoot him with."

Verity hurried off and everyone stared at one another, very afraid they were to be presented with a dying dog.

"You will fall instantly in love with him," Serenity said. "I feel that deeply in my heart."

"I do not often agree with Serenity's brand of heartfelt codswallop," Winsome said, "but in this particular case I daresay she is right."

Grace did not know what to think. They were to fall in love with a dying dog, and then perhaps even more strange—Winsome agreed with Serenity.

The door opened and everyone at table braced themselves for what they would be forced to witness. Valor went so far as to go under the table, taking Mrs. Wendover with her.

Verity came through with a very small dog with a rough-looking tan coat, bulging brown eyes, and three legs.

There was no blood though.

"You see, Papa?" Serenity said. "He is perfect, but for the missing leg."

"He really is so perfect," Patience said. "Look, when he wags his tail, his tongue hangs out."

"He gets around just fine," Winsome said. "We don't think he even knows he's one leg short of a set."

"We had a confidential conversation with the innkeeper," Serenity said, "and it seems this poor little mite has no home. He just hangs round the inn." Serenity took that moment to burst into tears. "Hoping for scraps, Papa! Scraps!" she cried.

"All right, all right, settle down, my girl," the duke said. "No need to go blubbering over a stray dog."

"But that is just it, Papa," Verity said. "That is the good news—he is our dog now!"

The duke sighed long and deep. He turned to Mrs. Right. "What is your opinion on this, Mrs. Right? I will be guided by your judgment."

Mrs. Right considered the matter. She said, "He will need a deal of looking after, but on the other hand, we had seriously considered bringing a pair of stoats into the house. I reckon he will not be as much trouble as that."

Grace had almost forgotten that Felicity had even gone so far as to read books about stoats after viewing a pair at Lady Albright's house. They'd not gone forward with the idea only because none of them knew where to locate a pair that might wish to join the household.

"I see," the duke said. "So it is out with the stoats idea, and in with the three-legged dog."

This caused a pandemonium that went on for some minutes and involved much kissing of their father's head and cheeks. The dog seemed relatively unperturbed by the ruckus and spent his time staring at the food on the table.

Serenity, so attuned to others' feelings, took the dog from Verity and fed him a rasher of bacon and a buttered roll.

"Might I inquire as to what this undersized cur's name is?" the duke asked.

"His name is Nelson, Papa," Winsome said. "You know, like poor Lord Nelson who lost his arm."

Lord Dashlend snorted over it. "Nelson will be very flattered, I'm sure."

Serenity, Verity, Patience, and Winsome stared at the viscount, as if to communicate to him that they did not find jests at Nelson's expense at all funny.

"Now you see it, Dashlend," the duke said. "You see what I have to put up with. I'm trying to get them out of the house and they're bringing creatures into it."

Valor emerged from her location under the table and looked warily at Nelson. "Is he going to get bigger? How big? Does he bite?"

Mrs. Right patted her hand. "Do not you fret over it, my dear. Even if he were to chase you, he'd never catch you."

"Oh I see," Valor said, "because he's only got the three legs."

"That's right."

"And also, Valor, he's blind in one eye," Serenity said.

"Of course he is," the duke said. "It's not enough that you have dragged in a mutt of unknown parentage who lost a leg somewhere or other, but he's blind in one eye too. I would expect nothing less."

"Mrs. Wendover does find it reassuring that he's only got three legs and one working eye," Valor said.

The duke rose. "Of course she does. Well now, we better get this circus moving. Serenity, you are in charge of that dog—if we leave him behind somewhere, that's where he stays."

This appeared to strike terror into the hearts of Serenity, Verity, Patience, and Winsome. "We will all work together," Winsome said. "We will have eyes on him at all times."

The other girls nodded their agreement.

"I will pack up some food in a napkin," Verity said. "It is a well-known fact that dogs will follow who feeds them."

"We will need a leash, I will go find something we can use," Patience said, sprinting from the room.

"I will pat his head," Serenity said, "so he knows he's loved and we hardly noticed that one of his legs is missing and he's practically blind."

The viscount rose from his chair. "Your Grace, I will take my leave of you, as it appears you have your hands full at the moment. Thank you for your assistance yesterday. I will have your clothes returned in good order when I am back to Town."

"You should bring them back yourself," Valor said. "I am pretty convinced you are not a murderer and you could see how Nelson gets on."

The viscount nodded and said, "If Lady Grace is agreeable."

Grace almost fell off her chair. She steadied herself and said, "As you wish, Lord Dashlend."

It was a rather nonsensical answer, but Grace did feel it had a certain elegant nonchalance to it.

"Perhaps I do wish, then," the viscount said.

"All right, all right, I think that's settled," the duke said jovially. "Now, time to shove off with this collection of lunatics."

Grace rose and curtsied to Lord Dashlend. What a morning!

RICHARD BURDOCK, SECOND Baron of Montclave, stood in the drawing room contemplating his mother.

"You will need to be on the scene, whichever way it goes," the dowager said.

The *it* in question was regarding whether or not Dashlend was alive.

Lord Dashlend was his cousin and also, conveniently, his neighbor. Because of the proximity, the servants of both houses often spoke. Occasionally, something of import was said and that news traveled straight back to the baron and the dowager.

Never had a more important piece of information arrived to their drawing room—Dashlend was missing at sea. Fishermen had been hired and had gone out for two days with no sight of the viscount and his valet.

"He always fancied himself the yachtsman," Montclave said with a derisive laugh. "Very fitting that he should meet his end that way."

"If he *has* met his end," the dowager said. "We must not allow hope to cloud our thinking. If he is dead, wonderful—all problems are solved and you are the new heir to the earldom. If he somehow survives, he is not yet wed and has no issue. We must arrange to keep it that way."

"I do not see how I am to stop him from a wedding," Montclave said.

"Nor do I," the dowager said, her tone tinged with impatience. "That is the sort of thing where one must size up the situation. If he lives, keep track of him. If you perceive that something is developing and heading toward a church, find a way to get in the middle of it. The past year has been very convenient as he was mostly on the continent. But now, he will be in London and encircled by hopeful ladies looking to tie him up in matrimony."

Montclave did not think it was much of a plan. "Perhaps he is not inclined to the married life. After all, he hasn't bothered with it up to now."

"If he is alive," the dowager said, "I expect his misadventure at sea will have put some starch into him. He will come back a changed man and may well decide it is time to do his manly duty."

"I suppose the earl will point that out, even if he does not see it himself," Montclave said morosely. "The servants say the old fellow is irate that Dashlend might be dead without leaving an heir behind him."

"If the earl were not abed with his gout, I suspect he'd be swimming the sea looking for his only son. Get yourself to Town. We do not know where news of his fate will land first. He keeps that ridiculous boat of his nearby Hull, so news may arrive to London before making its way here. If it is known here first, I will send word."

Montclave stopped his pacing. "I have an idea. Why do not I install myself in his house in Town, under the guise of leading the search for my dear cousin? The earl cannot travel just now even if he wished to. Ought I not step forward to lead the search from the comforts of Dashlend's house in Town?"

The dowager, a spry lady of late middle years, nodded vigorously. "Excellent, Montclave. Very clever. It is in these moments that I see your father in you."

He set off to give direction to his valet on what ought to be packed. He would move into number five, Chesterfield Street. With any luck, Dashlend was dead and he would not be required to ever move out of that house.

As the new heir, his life would be transformed. The clubs would fight for his membership. He would be invited everywhere. He would be given the utmost respect.

It would all suit very well.

CHAPTER FIVE

M ILES SAT IN the sunny garden of the inn with a pot of coffee, musing over his circumstances. He had noticed, throughout the course of his life, that when one was in the middle of a thing, one did not have the faculties to really examine it. It was only when the moment had passed and there was time for reflection that clarity arrived like an oil lamp to illuminate the darkness.

The duke and his daughters, their alarming housekeeper, and their newly-acquired three-legged dog, had departed the inn two days before. While waiting for his butler to turn up with money and clothes, Miles had plenty of time for reflection.

It really was some sort of miracle that he had not been forever lost at sea. And then, there was something to the duke being on hand at the beach at just the convenient moment that smacked of divine intervention.

Could it be so? Were the fates attempting to tell him something? If they had been all along trying to communicate, he supposed they'd finally thrown up their hands and decided to almost kill him to see if he would perceive the message that way.

Nothing in his life before that squall at sea had hinted at the precariousness of his existence so directly. He was extraordinarily lucky to have been born into a title; he'd always recognized that fact—there was not much difference between himself and a local farmer but for education and money. But even the extraordinarily lucky could be taken out of life in a moment.

He was well aware that there would be plenty of the *ton* who would vehemently disagree over luck having anything to do with their position in life. They soothed what might be a twinge of conscience for having so much and others having little by the idea that there was a nobility in their blood that made it right.

It was all nonsense, of course. If one traveled far back in time to the first titles handed out, what did one find? A bunch of men at the right place at the right time who backed the right side.

As he was so lucky to have been born on the finest bed sheets, perhaps he ought to recognize that the luck carried responsibilities. He must have an heir. To fail to do so would put the earldom into Montclave's hands. The thought was intolerable.

In any case, he was not at all opposed to wedding a lady. He'd just not spent any time thinking about it.

Now he did spend time thinking about it. He spent time thinking about what qualities he would seek. His mind kept circling back to Lady Grace—she really was rather terrific.

Her family was odd, to put it mildly, and led by the oddest of them all—the duke. He supposed that did not signify though. If anything, he was rather charmed that the duke did not put on airs, as any duke would be expected to do. He did not peer down his nose at all the world, but rather met it with good humor. He met it eccentrically, if one were to face facts. The whole idea that he did not require a butler was strange indeed. And then there was the brocabbage pie...

Miles suspected the duke did not think there was anything particularly special about his blood either. Certainly, his daughters did not put on the sort of airs one so often saw from ladies highly placed. They did not practice the reserve Miles found vaguely unpleasant. They were not persnickety, but in fact rather casual. They had not insisted on a puffball of a purebred dog, but had gone wild for a three-legged, half-blind cur.

It was too soon to come to any firm opinions, but he was invited to dinner on Tuesday next. He was also invited to personally return the duke's clothes. He would take up both of those opportunities. He would not confine himself to only that either. Miles would rein in some of his activities to make room for the sort of social events one went to when one was interested in meeting a lady. Less fencing, boxing, and racing, more dancing, routs, and whatever else the matrons of society were up to these days.

His musings were unceremoniously interrupted by his valet. Miles did not suppose it would be a pleasant interruption, as Moreau was looking very red in the face and perspiring.

"Moreau has walked miles to a laundress, as we are in the middle of nowhere and no civilized transportation is to be had. Then, Moreau waited hours for our clothes to be laundered and pressed, and then he staggered back again. This, all under the English sun which never comes out unless Moreau must exert himself.

"As you might imagine," Moreau went on, "the company of the laundress and her two unfortunate-looking daughters was a delight. It seems those genial ladies are in the habit of trading in the business of local news. How I was regaled with interesting facts! It seems a young farrier has run off with a shopkeeper's daughter! Where was this shop, I wonder, as I have not seen any shops! But that is a small matter, as I was fortunate enough to be told the entire tedious story."

Miles dearly hoped he was not to hear the story too, though he supposed his wish would not be granted.

"I am not certain I could have carried on with life if I had been forced to struggle forward without the details of that fascinating interlude. Apparently, the shopkeeper's daughter was always known as a flirt and may have flashed an ankle at the young farrier. There was even speculation that she paints her face to give herself a blush. Ah, but now my head is filled with this important information, and I can sleep peacefully at night. Also, that butler of yours has just pulled into the yard with your carriage."

Miles leapt to his feet. It was really very typical of Moreau to list out all his complaints before getting to the real point. His carriage and clothes and money, along with his far more sensible servant, Wainwright, had arrived.

For the past two days he had been stagnant and waiting, but now it was time for action. He would see to *The Marquessa*, make arrangements to get her back to Hull, and then he would set off for Town.

Somewhere in London, his future was waiting for him. His duty was waiting for him. He had been given back his life, and it was time he got on with the business of it.

THOUGH THERE WERE times when Grace found the endless hours of travel tedious, she had not been bored at all after they'd left Lord Dashlend at The Dolphin and the Dove. There had been so much to think about.

Naturally, Lord Dashlend had been much in her thoughts. Grace was a rather sensible creature at heart, at least she thought so. Therefore, she did remind herself that she had only met one gentleman, briefly. She ought not get carried away with imaginings. The season was yet to come.

And then, Nelson had provided interest along the way. They made the occasional stop so the dog might relieve himself at the roadside and it was fascinating to watch her sisters care for him.

He was leashed with a silk shawl, his collar made from a pearl necklace. Serenity, Patience, Winsome, and Verity all stood round him to make certain he did not run off and be left behind.

At the various inns where they stopped for the night, Nelson was at table for dinner. The duke did at first question it, but he was roundly scolded by his daughters. He had told them all that if they lost track of Nelson he would be left behind, therefore he must never be out of sight of someone in the family.

Serenity had even posited that Nelson might be in danger of being stolen. He was so unique that someone spotting him alone in a garden might wish him for their own.

Grace thought that rather a stretch of Serenity's emotional imagination. As fond of him as they'd grown, she could not quite envision a person becoming consumed with envy over a three-legged dog who routinely bumped into things because he only had one good eye. Even had Nelson not experienced those two setbacks in life, he was unprepossessing to begin. He was very small, but he had not the charming looks of a lapdog. His eyes were of the bulging variety, forever giving him a look of faint surprise. His coat was rough, it was not quite curly but not altogether straight. He had an unfortunate underbite and his tongue seemed somehow longer than it ought to be. Her good sense told her that the luckiest day of Nelson's life had been the day soft-hearted Serenity Nicolet had spotted him.

Of course, there was a certain charm to Nelson's oddities that could not be denied. Even Winsome was defeated by them and Grace had caught her father having a confidential conversation with Nelson at breakfast one morning. She could not say how much of the conversation Nelson had taken in, as he seemed to be wholly engrossed by the platter of bacon on the table.

Finally, though, their caravan had arrived to Grosvenor Square.

As they all piled out of the carriages, the front doors swung open and a rather small and nondescript fellow dressed in a somber black suit of clothes appeared.

Mr. Button, no doubt.

"What ho?" the duke called to him. "Who are you and what do you do in my house?"

The man looked startled to be questioned in such a manner. As he would be, Grace supposed. He would not know of the duke's penchant for a jest.

The man hurried forward and bowed. "Mr. Harold Button, Your Grace," he said. "Lady Marchfield employed me to serve as your butler."

"Did she now?" the duke said, looking Mr. Button up and down.

"Indeed, she did, Your Grace," Mr. Button said. "She told me she had informed you?"

"Did she now?"

Mr. Button seemed highly perplexed. "Indeed, she did say so. She also left a letter here for you when you arrived."

"Did she now?"

Mr. Button nodded. "Again, yes she did, Your Grace."

"Well, we'll see about that," the duke said. "Here is Mrs. Right, she runs the place."

Mr. Button stepped back and narrowed his eyes upon hearing Mrs. Right mentioned. Grace supposed Lady Marchfield had painted a very dark picture of their beloved housekeeper.

"Try not to get underfoot," the duke said. "While you're here."

"While I am…"

The duke did not elaborate. Naturally, Mr. Button could not have been further encouraged by Mrs. Right's grave nod.

Grace did not suppose she needed to stay for any more of the interaction. She bolted through the doors and up the stairs, determined to secure the room that Felicity had used the season before.

She got there first, slammed the door, and locked it for good measure. Then she spent the next half hour admiring the bedchamber and the dressing room as the battle for rooms raged outside the door. Verity had twice tried Grace's lock somehow thinking to trick her into opening it. It sounded as if Serenity and Patience had rolled round the floor for a while. Winsome found the room she liked and slammed her door, occasionally shouting insults from behind it. Valor only wept, and Grace did not know why she did not just go to the room she had the year before. It was the closest to the servants' stairs and allowed her to access Mrs. Right or to slip down to the kitchens to steal a biscuit.

Nobody would fight her for it as it was also the smallest.

Nelson seemed enlivened by the whole fracas and barked with enthusiasm. Grace could hear his three paws and unusual gait click-clacking up and down the corridor.

As all battles do, the fighting eventually wound down. Not even the most determined army could fight on forever. Peace treaties were agreed to when Mrs. Right turned up and sorted everybody as to where they ought to go.

Grace peeked out and saw that the corridor was once more quiet. Even Nelson had retreated to somebody's room. She hurried downstairs, as her second piece of business was to see what invitations had come in.

There was nothing on the side table in the great hall. She made her way to the drawing room and there she found her father with a glass of brandy and stacks of letters.

"Papa," she said, hurrying to his side, "are those invitations?"

"So they are, except for this ridiculous missive Lady Misery has sent."

"Oh dear, what does our aunt say?"

"The usual nonsense. She goes on and on about our disgraceful behavior last season and how it will not be long tolerated by those in society who matter. Who are they that matter so much, I wonder? She caps the whole thing off with dire warnings that you will never make a match unless we shape up."

"That is not true, though, is it?" Grace said. "We cannot be condemned just for being ourselves? After all, what else can we do? We cannot remake ourselves in my aunt's image."

The duke laughed and said, "If any one of my girls began to take after Lady Misery, I would throw her to the street."

Grace smiled, as it was another of her father's empty threats. None of them would ever take on Lady Marchfield's grim ways, and even if they did, her Papa would not throw them to the street.

"Now Gracie, I like to learn from mistakes, whenever I do make them. Which is not often, by the by. Last year, I allowed

Lady Misery to manage my calendar. Never again—it brings her to the house far too often. You're a sensible girl, I leave it to you to accept or decline invitations as you see fit. If there is anything in there from Lady Albright and her stupid tiger, set it alight. We will most definitely not attend her."

"Perhaps she will not venture to repeat her special evening showing off her animal collection, on account of last year's fiasco."

Grace really did think it likely that the lady would not wish to repeat the experience. Having one's tiger on the loose and responsible for gravely injuring a guest could not be comfortable.

"Who knows what that old bat will do," the duke said. "But as I did fill her front hall with two thousand pence and did throw a padlock through her window, we will probably not be welcome in any case."

"Goodness, that was amusing. As to the invitations, I am sure I will be up to the task. Though, my aunt will not like it," Grace said pensively.

"Yes, I know," the duke said, laughing. "That's the other advantage of it."

Grace supposed that while Lady Marchfield would not like it, there would not be anything she could do about it. Further, it was an honor that her father placed the trust in her to manage it.

She swept up the piles of letters and put them on a side table. "I will go through them after dinner. I am sure my sisters would like to help me. You do suppose that Mr. Button will have arranged a dinner of some sort?"

The duke shrugged. "It hardly matters—Cook arrived days ago and would have sorted it all out. Meanwhile, Mrs. Right is just now downstairs with the staff. How I would like to hide behind a doorframe to hear what she's got to say to Mr. Button!

MRS. RIGHT HAD chuckled to herself when she'd set eyes on Mr. Button. If it came to a wrestling match, she could pin him to the ground in under a minute. How on earth had Lady Marchfield thought to send such a weak specimen to do battle with her?

She thought she understood Mr. Button's type—he'd been all obsequiousness to the duke, and those types were the most insidious. They did not dare throw round any orders upstairs, but they made up for it when they were downstairs. She'd seen it in his eyes as he looked over the footmen as they descended from the duke's carriage.

She would set out to make quick work of this butler and she would begin at once. The faster he could land himself in a house that needed a bossy butler, the happier he would be. In the end, it would be a kindness that she got rid of him.

Mrs. Right paused before turning the corner into the servants' hall. Just as she had suspected, Mr. Button was busy making everything and everybody uncomfortable.

"Charlie, Thomas, as my two footmen, you will be expected to meet certain standards. When I say certain standards, I mean the highest standards. I will accept nothing less than perfection. As well, I must tell you that Lady Marchfield has painted you as lax in the extreme. I hope for your sakes that she has been led astray in that opinion. As for the kitchen staff, I will demand that everything be well-timed and to the duke's liking. The maids of the house are to know that good enough is no longer good enough! I will tour the rooms on a regular basis, searching out dust in every corner. Do not let me find it. I will apprise Mrs. Right of that fact so there is to be no confusion about expectations."

The highest standards indeed. He would apprise her of facts, would he? Time to throw the cold water of reality on this little dictator. Mrs. Right hurried into the servants' hall. She stopped short and stared at Mr. Button.

"Mrs. Right?" he said in response to her stare.

She sniffed into the air as if she was deeply offended. "Sir, I do not like to be forced to speak so plainly, but there are those moments in a lady's life where she is forced to speak plainly. You will of course know what I refer to."

Clearly Mr. Button was put on his back foot by such a pronouncement. How could he be otherwise? There was nothing to refer to.

"I am sorry, Mrs. Right," Mr. Button said. "But as you did mention speaking plainly, perhaps you would do so? I haven't any idea what you are referring to."

Mrs. Right huffed and turned to Charlie. The senior footman looked at her with arched brows, as if he could hardly believe what he was hearing. It was really very good acting as he'd been well-briefed on the game.

"You see which way the wind blows, Charlie?" she said. "He will pretend to know nothing."

Charlie nodded. "Aye. Though we all saw it with our own two eyes."

"Saw what?" Mr. Button said, the tone of alarm in his voice giving him away.

"It is really too much, Mr. Button!" Mrs. Right said. "The idea that you would attempt to confuse and bewilder a poor maiden. It is really beyond reason."

"What poor maiden?" Mr. Button asked, looking round the room for a poor maiden of any description.

Mrs. Right pulled her shawl tight around her. Charlie said, "Come now, Mr. Button, we all saw you making eyes at our Mrs. Right when she alighted from the carriage."

"What... making eyes? *You* are the poor maiden? Mrs. Right, you are much mistaken! I have never made eyes at anyone in my life!"

Mrs. Right used all her self-control to stop from laughing, as she was very sure Mr. Button never had made eyes at anybody.

"Rest assured, Mr. Button," Mrs. Right said gravely, "you will find my bedchamber door securely locked at night."

"Your... your door!" Mr. Button cried. "What do you imply?"

"I will put a chair against it too."

With that, she hurried up the stairs and left the rest of the staff to frown at the butler. She did not suppose he would last a week.

MILES HAD FINALLY arrived to Chesterfield Street, and what a journey it had been. Never again would he ride in the same carriage with Moreau and Wainwright. A hysterical valet and a snide butler were a combination that did not mix well.

Moreau would go on one of his long tirades about the various mishaps that had befallen him in the past week. Wainwright would roll his eyes into the back of his head and mutter, "And yet, you are still alive. Why are my hopes always so cruelly dashed?"

Moreau would threaten to leap across the carriage and pummel him over the insult. Wainwright would raise his fists and say, "Ready when you are."

This would set Moreau to sulking, as there was no minute in the history of all time that he would ever be ready to engage in fisticuffs.

When the carriage rolled to a stop at the house, Miles did not even wait for Wainwright to get ahead of him and open the doors. A footman had been on the lookout for them and had the doors open and that was good enough.

Though, Miles could not quite understand the look on the young fellow's face. He looked terrified.

Miles paused and said, "James, what is wrong with you?"

James was usually all cool arrogance on account of being the senior of the footmen, though he was still very young for it.

"My lord," he whispered, "Baron Montclave has installed himself in the house! He turned up and said he would lead the search for you, but I told him you were already found. He said he'd need that confirmed because it might not be true."

"The presuming rogue," Miles said. "And I don't suppose he's done much looking, has he? Did he think I was lost on the Thames?"

James shook his head. "He's just done a lot of drinking, my lord. We did not know how to stop him!"

"I'll take care of it. Where is he?"

James nodded toward the drawing room.

Miles should have known. He could already smell the cigar smoke coming from that location. He strode through the drawing room doors.

Montclave had certainly heard the carriage arriving, as he was on his feet and facing the doors. "Cousin!" he said in that false ingratiating way he had. "Thank the heavens you have survived your ordeal."

"Yes, I was very fortunate."

"Indeed, indeed. Naturally, I rushed to the scene as soon as I heard you were missing. The poor earl is laid up with the gout just now and so it fell on my shoulders to lead."

"The *scene* was never anywhere near London, and you planned to lead what?" Miles asked, fascinated to know what Montclave's answer would be.

"Well, someone had to be on hand," Montclave said. "Should the worst have happened."

Miles smiled. "I see. Fortunately, the worst did not happen and you may be on your way. Very good news all round, I'd say."

"Is that the best course of action, though?" Montclave said. "I suspect you remain weak from your misadventure and may even experience a setback. Perhaps it would be best to keep me on hand to watch over things as you proceed with your recovery."

The rogue was as transparent as glass. "Nonsense," Miles said, "I am fit as a fiddle. Now, I will not hold you up." He turned to the drawing room doors and said, "Wainwright, pack the baron's things for him. Tell the coachman to hold off putting away the horses—he will take the baron wherever in Town he wishes to go."

As he turned back toward Montclave, he saw the pleasant façade he wore slip for a moment and reveal a look of real hatred. Just as fast as it had made its appearance, it disappeared again.

"If you intend to make your way back to Norfolk, you will be in time to catch a coach from The Swan," Miles said. "Do give the dowager my regards."

"Perhaps I will stay in London for now," Montclave said. "I have a friend on Bolton Street."

"Ah, a friend, I hadn't thought. Well! Very considerate of you to take time out of your no doubt crammed calendar to attend me," Miles said. He left his cousin in the drawing room, confident his staff would see the gentleman out the doors. After he was gone, Miles would order all the windows opened to get rid of that unpleasant cigar smoke.

CHAPTER SIX

THE DUKE AND his daughters had arrived in Town on a Tuesday. The following evening would have been the night to attend Almack's, and despite the duke's outlandish behavior at that location last season, the voucher for Grace had arrived.

They decided between them that they would not go to Almack's. The duke arranged payment for the vouchers just in case they changed their minds, but for now they would not purchase tickets.

The duke could not get past the idea that lemonade and stale bread was foisted on him at midnight. Grace claimed she was swayed by Felicity's opinion of it the year before and that it sounded tiresome. In any case, Lord Dashlend would not be there for the opening ball.

As well, Grace felt an enormous relief at not going because of what it was—the top of the *ton* there to stare at the ladies newly arrived to Town. She was not so confident in her dancing that she wished her first foray into a ballroom to be *that* ballroom. She did not fall down very often, most of the time she just felt a little unbalanced, but the risk that she might fall there was too frightening to contemplate.

Grace could not help but reflect on what had happened to Felicity at Almack's. Her sister's greatest weakness had been on display. Felicity was sensitive to the smells of roses and vinegar and had the bad luck to dance near a lady who seemed to have bathed in rose water. A sneezing fit had overtaken her and it was so violent she'd needed a marquess' handkerchief to mop up the explosion. If that could happen to Felicity, why would not Grace's greatest weakness come to the fore, on display for everyone?

In any case, her Papa said that a duke's daughter did not need to go scrambling around for approval. They would be invited everywhere anyway, so no need to curtsy to those blasted patronesses.

Grace had spent a lively evening with her sisters going through all the invitations that had arrived, and there were dozens and dozens of them. She had commandeered the duke's calendar, accepted those invitations that seemed both interesting and respectable, and noted them in her Papa's book. For others that they would not attend, she sent their regrets in a fine hand.

Of course, she did not know who was who in society as well as Lady Marchfield did, but she felt confident that the title and address of the person sending the invitation, along with the nature of the entertainment, told her enough.

Wednesday night had been another cozy night in, and she and her sisters had commandeered their father into a rousing game of Fact or Fib, the duke as usual drowning in blue tickets for the fibs he told.

Mr. Button was grim-faced during the proceedings. And then a little staggered when Mrs. Right was sent for so she could join in. And then positively pale when Mrs. Right helped herself to a brandy.

Nelson, on the other hand, seemed to enjoy the game immensely. Each time someone, usually the duke, was loudly named a fibber, he cast his own vote into the mix. Nelson jumped up, chased his tail for a minute, bumped into a piece of furniture, and staggered back to his bed that had been made of one of Serenity's pillows hastily covered in cambric.

Today was Thursday and she and the duke were to make their first foray into society. A dinner would be held by the Earl of Doanellen. The duke could not remember anything specific about the gentleman, but then her father was not a great one for remembering people unless they were people he'd set out to harass. However, the earl's title and his address on Bolton Street conferred a respectability. On top of that, Grace really felt as if a dinner, and the associated sitting down, would be the most comfortable way to begin her season.

It was the late afternoon and she had settled with her sisters in the drawing room for tea. Mrs. Right had already counseled her to eat more than she might otherwise do as she would wish to appear a dainty eater at the dinner. She said it was one of those ridiculous things that only applied in London.

Grace was not altogether clear why she ought to refrain from eating her fill at the dinner, other than to suppose that a single gentleman would not wish to see her eat an enormous amount and then have visions of being eaten out of house and home.

Mr. Button had been positively gobsmacked to see that Mrs. Right often attended the family in the drawing room and he had not seemed to get used to the idea. In truth, he seemed terrified of Mrs. Right and leapt out of the way any time that lady was heading in his direction as if it would be dangerous to get too near. He had set the tea tray down and been out of the room like a shot.

Mrs. Right had risen and said, "I will just go and see what Mr. Button is up to downstairs. Fanning himself, I hope."

After a half hour, Mr. Button was back and he did look as if he might have been fanning himself. "Lady Marchfield to see you, Lady Grace."

Valor snorted. "Nobody told him not to let her in," she said.

Mr. Button looked horrified over the comment. He stepped aside as their aunt strode into the drawing room.

"Grace," she said, "I could not account for your absence at Almack's last evening. I presumed you must have fallen ill."

"They decided not to go," Patience said, "on account of it being tedious."

"And the stupid lemonade," Winsome said.

"And Papa says the patronesses are harpies," Valor said, giggling into Mrs. Wendover's raggedy shoulder.

"And, Aunt," Serenity said, "I really do feel in my heart that we ought to trust Felicity's opinion of it. Which was terrible from top to bottom."

Lady Marchfield turned to Mr. Button and said, "Mr. Button, I pray you are bringing your calm rationality as an example to this household. Do bring me a cup, I will stay for tea. I can see that much needs to be straightened out here."

Mr. Button hurried to do the lady's bidding and Lady Marchfield settled herself on a settee.

"Grace, you have done yourself a grave disservice to thumb your nose at Almack's. I can assure you it was noticed."

Grace did not answer that charge, though it did make her uncomfortable. She did not wish for anyone to imagine she thumbed her nose. She only did not want to go.

"As for the rest of you, your comments are not ladylike, and they are not even true. Your father's influence will do you no favors in the wider world and the sooner you take that in, the better. Now, I have come to begin reviewing the invitations that have arrived and set your course for the season."

All eyes turned to Grace. Valor leaned over and whispered rapidly to Mrs. Wendover. The rabbit's dead black eyes did not reveal what she thought of the information just communicated to her.

"As it happens, Aunt," Grace said, "my father put me in charge of the invitations this season."

The room was in silence as everyone in it looked to Lady Marchfield to see how that development would settle.

Mr. Button arrived back with a cup for Lady Marchfield. He seemed terrified of the silence, set it down and hurried out, closing the doors behind him.

"You are to choose the entertainments? That is absurd," Lady Marchfield said.

"It's true, though," Winsome pointed out.

"But you have not... you have not gone forward with such an idea?" Lady Marchfield asked.

"I have been very careful, Aunt," Grace said. "I have only accepted invitations from titled persons who live at a good address. This evening, we go to the Earl of Doanellen's house on Bolton Street for dinner."

"Doanellen?" Lady Marchfield asked.

Such was her tone that Grace wondered if she'd somehow made a mistake. But certainly she could not have. He was an earl at a good address.

"Is he a rogue?" Valor asked.

Ever since last season's warning about rogues, Valor had been obsessed with the idea. Though, she still was not clear what a rogue was.

Lady Marchfield sniffed. "It is my understanding that the Earl of Doanellen has very cruelly left his countess to live alone in the countryside."

Patience guffawed. "Oh, I wish Papa was here," she said. "You know what he would say? He'd say, isn't Marchfield always trying to leave *you* in the countryside? It's not true, that's why it's so funny."

Lady Marchfield glared at Patience. Then she turned to Grace and said, "I do not know who you will encounter at that dinner, but you ought to be very careful of it."

"Of course I will be careful anywhere that I go," Grace said. "And Papa will take me, nothing could be safer."

"What about Lord Dashlend?" Serenity asked. "Is he going too, Grace?"

"What about Lord Dashlend?" Lady Marchfield asked.

"We met him on the road," Valor said. "He was shipwrecked, and Papa took him to our inn. After a lot of conversations with Mrs. Wendover, I am convinced he is not a murderer."

"Why on earth would you imagine that he was?" Lady Marchfield asked.

"Because he was a stranger we met on the road," Valor said

with a shrug.

"Where else does one meet murderers?" Verity asked. "It is a very common thing to meet them on the road."

"It certainly is not and please outgrow your habit of storytelling, Verity," Lady Marchfield said. "Lord Dashlend is well respected and a Corinthian of the first order. He is the only son of the Earl of Gravesend. That particular earl has *not* left a wife in the countryside and is everything genial when he is not suffering from the gout."

This buoyed Grace quite a bit. Though she had reminded herself that Lord Dashlend was the first gentleman she'd encountered and that she did not know enough about him, it had not stopped her from thinking of him. She was sensible enough to be cognizant of the idea that she might think of him so often *because* he was the first and only gentleman she had met so far. For all that, she was gratified that he seemed to be everything she had imagined.

"Though, I must inform you that it has been widely understood that Lord Dashlend is always so taken up with his sporting that he's not looked for a wife. In fact, he accepts very few social engagements during the season."

As fast as she had been buoyed up, Grace was cast back down. The possibility had not occurred to her.

"He's coming to dinner," Winsome said. "He accepted *that* invitation."

"Really? When is this dinner? I presume my brother will have the good sense, and the good grace for that matter, to extend me an invitation."

The sisters all looked at one another. Verity said, "It is next Wednesday, Aunt."

Nobody corrected Verity. The dinner was on Tuesday next, but Grace thought Verity's habit of fibbing had finally been put to good use. She did respect Lady Marchfield, but the lady was so prone to throwing cold water on any sort of merriment.

Out of the corner of her eye, Grace saw the drawing room

doors open just a crack. Charlie peered through, and then sent Nelson inside, shutting the door behind the dog.

Nelson, in his usual enthusiastic fashion, raced forward, tripped himself up, staggered back on his three legs, and licked the hand of the nearest person to him, which was Lady Marchfield.

She snatched her hand away and rubbed it with a napkin. "What on earth is that?"

"His name is Nelson," Serenity said. "He is just the loveliest dog in the world."

"Really," Lady Marchfield said. She did not say it as a question, but more as a condemnation. "Might I ask how it is that you are in possession of an ill-bred cur who is missing a leg?"

"We found him at The Dolphin and the Dove," Winsome said.

Serenity brushed a tear away. "He was living on scraps, Aunt. *Scraps.*"

"People are so cruel," Patience said. "Can you imagine? Just because he is short of one leg and can only see out of one eye, he is meant to live on scraps?"

Nelson took that opportunity to release some noxious fumes in Lady Marchfield's direction. Grace almost felt sorry for her; she'd been nearby such an eruption herself and it was near overwhelming.

Lady Marchfield staggered to her feet. "That is a wildly inappropriate dog for the daughters of a duke. I pray you keep him to the back garden. Under no circumstances go parading with him round the square. I shudder to imagine what people would think."

Nobody volunteered the information that Nelson had been out and about in the square every day since they'd arrived. Not even Valor, who pushed her face into Mrs. Wendover's raggedy form to stop herself from admitting it.

"I will take my leave. I understand Felicity and Mr. Stratton are due to arrive to Town in a day or so—I presume they also will receive an invitation for the dinner next Wednesday. Though really, to have scheduled it for a Wednesday rather than attend Almack's is bad form in my view."

With those pronouncements, Lady Marchfield sailed out of the room, her head held high.

After the door closed, Winsome said, "You know what this means? Next Wednesday, when our aunt realizes the dinner was on Tuesday, she is going to explode."

"I wonder if she will bring our uncle," Serenity said. "We do not see him near as often and he's ever so much nicer."

"I know what we will do," Verity said, "on Wednesday, we will just say that Lord Dashlend had to cancel for some reason. Then we just have a family dinner with our aunt none the wiser."

"Excellent notion," Grace said. She did not know if Lady Marchfield would fall for the ruse or not, but it would be very pleasant to see her uncle. She felt just the littlest bit guilty that they'd given Lady Marchfield the wrong day, but then she felt more strongly that she did not wish for her aunt to throw cold water on her dinner with Lord Dashlend. She did not wish to frighten him off, and Lady Marchfield was the most frightening person she knew.

MILES THOUGHT IT had been deuced odd that Lady Grace had not attended Almack's on Wednesday. Now it was Thursday and he'd thought to visit the duke's house with the excuse to return the clothes that had been lent to him. Moreau had worked diligently on the duke's valet's oldest set, and probably used too much starch in the pressing. He was convinced he could return the oldest set better than he got them, which would be a silent slap in the face to that inferior valet.

That pleasant errand was not to be. The elderly butler of an even more elderly distant cousin had arrived to the house with a message—Lady Margaret required his attendance instantly.

He'd attempted to question the old fellow regarding the cause. Was the lady in distress or was it only Lady Margaret's usual eccentricity at work? The lady lived permanently in Town and when the season began, he usually did get an order to present himself. That order usually included the timeframe of instantly.

Marcus, that was the butler's name, hemmed and hawed and mumbled about his lady getting up in years and not being able to chew meat very well these days. In short, his question had not been answered.

Miles had realized he had no choice but to attend her. She really *was* getting up in years and there was every chance she did poorly. The season before, he'd suggested she hire a competent companion who could help her manage the household, as the house had begun to look a bit ramshackle and dusty. He doubted that advice had been taken—Lady Margaret was a stubborn old bird.

He made his way to Bedford Square on horseback, the butler returning ahead of him in a hackney. When he arrived, there was nobody to take his horse. He walked him down the mews to the stables and found nothing but empty stalls—no hay, no oats, no water buckets. He finally went across the way to the neighbor's stables and asked if he could leave his horse there. Lord Marchand's stablemaster was most accommodating, though Miles had been a little alarmed when the fellow commented that "it was about time one of the lady's relatives turned up."

He made his way back to the front of the house and used the door knocker. Marcus opened it up.

"Where is Lawrence?" Miles asked. Lady Margaret's senior footman usually answered the door.

"Dead," Marcus said. "Old age, you know."

Miles entered the great hall, wondering how Lady Margaret got on with only one footman.

"What has happened to the stables?" he asked. "Where is the stablemaster or at least a groom? Where are the horses?"

"Dead," Marcus said. "Old age, you know." Marcus paused. "That's not right. The horses aren't dead, they were sold on account of the coachman being dead. From old age."

Miles looked round the empty great hall. "The other footman who was here? Where is he?"

"Dead. Fell down the stairs from old age."

This was worse than Miles had imagined it would be. "I suppose you had better take me to Lady Margaret. I presume she is not dead?"

"Her? No, she's a tough old thing."

Marcus began a very slow shuffle toward the drawing room. "Never mind it," Miles said, fearing it might take a quarter hour to arrive at the rate they were going. "I will show myself in."

Marcus very gratefully sank down into one of the numerous chairs lined along the walls. Miles supposed they were there for when Marcus could not go further.

He opened the drawing room doors. "Lady Margaret?" he said to the tiny old lady practically swallowed by her sofa. She was like a little bird sitting in a nest.

"Is that you, Dashlend? Aren't you a dear for coming to me."

"You did send an order that I was to come instantly."

"Ah, so I did. Instant always gets people's attention. They wonder if I'm taking my last breaths, you see."

Miles looked round the room and it really was in a state. There was dust everywhere, and more incredible, a pile of dirty dishes sitting on a bookshelf. He supposed that was as far as Marcus had been able to get with them.

"Sit, sit," Lady Margaret said. "You might as well relax, it will take Marcus an age to get here with a tea tray. Don't expect anything interesting on it, all we get is burned toast these days."

Miles supposed it *would* take an age, the footman had barely made it halfway across the hall before he'd had to sit down.

"Lady Margaret, it appears you have had some reductions in staff," he said.

"Oh yes, they die, you see. One hardly knows who will be

next. The flu that went round did not do us any favors."

Miles thought he could make a good guess at who would be next—Marcus was on his last legs.

"But, who is still here? I saw Marcus, who else?"

"Let's see, the cook is dead, so there is just the kitchen maid down there. She's a good sort of girl, but nobody can burn toast like she can. And then there is my lady's maid, Gwen, though after she dresses me in the morning she needs to put her feet up all day so she can undress me again at night. Her feet swell up something terrible. Now, will you stay for dinner?"

Miles was entirely nonplussed. Dinner? What were they to have? Burned toast? Could Marcus stay on his feet long enough to serve it? This situation was intolerable.

"Lady Margaret," he said, "you cannot continue on in this house."

Lady Margaret held up a hand. "Do not even suggest that I go to live with my sister in Bath, we do not get on." She paused, then said, "And I forgot, she's dead."

Miles really, really did not want to say what he had to say next. There was no choice though. His father would be appalled at Lady Margaret's circumstances. "You must come home with me. I live on Chesterfield Street, you will find it very comfortable. We'll find a place for the kitchen maid. As for Marcus and your lady's maid, they ought to be funded a retirement for whatever time they have left."

"Well now, I do not know about that," Lady Margaret said. "I would not like to hinder your bachelor lifestyle."

Miles was not certain what the lady thought went on with bachelors and their lifestyles. He said, "I insist. In any case, I've decided it's high time to look for a wife, so perhaps I will not be a bachelor for long."

"Do you? Now that is very interesting news. In my younger days, I was known as quite the matchmaker. Well, I suppose I would not mind dipping my toe in again."

Miles had no answer to that. He'd imagined that he would

install Lady Margaret to a spare bedchamber, and she'd spend her days mostly sleeping, not thinking about matchmaking.

"You know what else would be an advantage to this scheme?" Lady Margaret asked.

Miles did not know, as he had not seen any advantage to himself at all.

"That rascally cousin of yours will be very disappointed the next time he stops by and tries to wheedle money out of me."

Miles stared at the lady as she rubbed her hands together and laughed.

"Montclave?" he asked. "Montclave comes here for money?"

"Oh yes, he was here this afternoon. That's what made me think of you, now that I am examining it. Mind you, I did not give him anything, but I think he made off with a silver salver. I don't like him, I don't know why he comes."

There was another reason to get Lady Margaret out of the house. Montclave would not dare to come begging to Chesterfield Street.

Miles said, "I will make arrangements to get everyone out of this house and into mine. I will arrange for a couple of watchmen to keep an eye on things here, so that my cousin does not return and help himself."

"He'll be as mad as a bee in a bonnet, and I am glad of it. I don't like him."

Miles nodded. He did not like Montclave either.

The next hours were consumed with relocating Lady Margaret. Though the lady had mentioned that she was not certain Marcus wished to retire as he liked the work, when he was told he was to retire, he kissed Miles' hand. The lady's maid was equally delighted. The kitchen maid was more relieved than anything else. She was hired to do the chopping and peeling, not the cooking. She explained that she was as lost as a lamb on a dark night trying to make dinners.

Finally, everybody had been relocated, fed, and settled. Moreau had taken it as some sort of personal insult, though Miles had not the energy to wonder why. He sat alone in his drawing room, brooding on the idea that Montclave would go so far as to opportune an elderly lady.

Was there no low that rogue would not stoop to?

And then of course, he did spend some little amount of time brooding that he'd just installed a very elderly lady in his house who threatened to dip her toe into matchmaking. He soothed himself with the idea that it was wishful thinking on her part. After all, she could not do much from the confines of his house and he did not suppose she'd been out and about in society in quite a few years.

CHAPTER SEVEN

THE DUKE HAD somewhat relieved Grace's mind regarding Lady Marchfield's assessment of the Earl of Doanellen. He had a vague memory of the earl's lady being the daughter of the Earl of Wreckham, and then another vague memory of Wreckham cheating him at cards, and then another vague memory of not liking the fellow even before he cheated at cards. The end result was that if Doanellen had left his bride behind in the countryside, there were probably good reasons for it. Any daughter of Wreckham's was probably a harridan.

Grace did not swallow that logic whole, as her father was prone to fanciful notions, cloudy recollections, and outright fibs. However, she did come to the conclusion that if there were not good reasons why Lady Doanellen had been left behind, then surely the earl would be condemned by society over it. As he did not seem condemned, then surely there was nothing wrong.

For all anybody knew, perhaps Lady Doanellen had a wasting disease or was with child and could not travel, but she had insisted her husband make the trip. If there was one thing Grace had learned from Felicity's experience, it was that jumping to conclusions often led to jumping to the wrong one.

They had arrived and been helped down to the pavement.

"Well, my girl, this is it—your first foray into society. Try not to fall over on anybody."

"Papa, do not even joke about it," Grace said. "It is a fear that keeps me awake at night."

"Nonsense. You are a duke's daughter. You might fall down a hundred times a day and I dare anyone to say anything about it. In any case, I would likely be nearby and you can depend upon me to blame somebody for it."

Grace patted her father's hand. He really was more sentimental than people realized.

They were shown in and the Earl of Doanellen was there to greet them. He seemed very respectable, the sort of middle-aged gentleman who might be gray at the temples but had retained his vitality. A certain Mrs. Featherby, whom Grace presumed was a sister, stood by his side smiling genially.

In the drawing room, they found a mix of people which of course Grace did not know. If the duke knew any of them, he'd probably forgotten.

It was, therefore, very appreciated that a young gentleman seemed to note it and hurried forward.

"Your Grace, Lady Grace, allow me to present myself. I am Baron Montclave."

"A baron, eh?" the duke said. "Well, it could be worse—one never knows what to do with a baronet."

The baron had the good sense to laugh at this parry, though Grace did not know if he really found it amusing or not.

Grace found the gentleman rather good looking, though not quite on par with Lord Dashlend. His hair was far lighter and he was not as well built. And then, he did not have Lord Dashlend's distinction of that subtle hint of a Roman nose.

"Lord Doanellen has informed me that I will have the honor to escort Lady Grace into dinner, if Your Grace is not opposed to it."

"Why should I be opposed?" the duke asked. "You're not some sort of rogue, are you? Because I can tell you, I do not suffer rogues. As well, I'll warn you, if you're some kind of idiot—steer clear of me."

Lord Montclave did look the littlest bit startled. "I cannot claim any roguish tendencies and possess a reasonable intelligence, Your Grace."

The duke shrugged, as if he were not convinced either way. Grace was very well aware that her father was amusing himself.

To his credit, Lord Montclave quickly recovered and escorted them round the room and introduced them to the other people attending. There were those, like Lord and Lady Grimsby, who remembered the duke, though he did not remember them. His memory was often jogged by reminding him that this or that person had attended Lady Vanderwake's rout the night he set the lady's curtains on fire all those years ago. The duke still did not remember them, but the recollection of that memorable evening always tickled him.

Grace was introduced to Lady Lavender Westcott, daughter of the Earl of Wembly, a lady also coming for her first season.

Grace was rather intimidated by Lady Lavender. She seemed to have everything going for her. Too much going for her, really. She was a lovely brunette, her dress was so well put together right down to the small gold cross round her elegant neck. And then her conversation! She was charming and the things she spoke of seemed to imply that she was an excellent dancer, an excellent horsewoman, and exceedingly well read.

Of course, Lady Lavender had not claimed any of those accolades. She was too perfect to have done anything of the sort. However, if one's passion was for horses, one must be an excellent horsewoman. If one adored balls, one must be an excellent dancer. If one mentioned a whole slew of books recently read, one must be a very great reader.

Grace supposed Lady Lavender must be what Felicity had told her was a diamond of the first water. The lady who would have men bowing at her feet all season.

She certainly hoped Lord Dashlend would not be one among them.

"Shall we go through, Lady Grace?" Baron Montclave said.

Grace nodded and was led into the dining room. The lady at

the head of the table was Mrs. Featherby. She had stood by Lord Doanellen at the door greeting guests and Grace had been introduced to her there. She had assumed, rather than been told, that Mrs. Featherby must be a sister to Lord Doanellen, but now that she was examining it, she was not entirely certain.

Wine glasses had been filled and the first course set on the table. "Baron Montclave," she said, "is Mrs. Featherby a sister, or a cousin perhaps, to Lord Doanellen?"

This question, though Grace had thought it a very usual one, had set Lord Montclave fiddling with his napkin and taking a long draught of wine.

"A very good friend, is my understanding."

That seemed odd. But then, Grace supposed that if one did not bring one's wife to Town, and one did not have any close feminine relations to step in, perhaps it was not so strange to ask a family friend to act as hostess. In any case, her father was to the right of Mrs. Featherby and would likely find out all about it.

"How was your journey to Town?" the baron asked. "I understand you come from quite a distance."

"Indeed, we do," Grace said, comfortable in a subject she could speak credibly on. "We are very remote in the Dales. Our journey this year was somewhat extended. We took a rather roundabout route as my father wished to show us the sea."

"It was your first time viewing it?"

Grace nodded. "What a sight! Of course, one knows what it looks like from pictures, but to see it with my own eyes was breathtaking. And it was ever so entertaining, too. Just as we arrived, we encountered Lord Dashlend. He'd just crashed his boat and was shipwrecked. Do you know Lord Dashlend?"

The baron nodded. "He is a cousin and our estates are neighboring in Norfolk."

"Oh I see!" Grace said. That information felt like a piece of good luck. Lord Montclave would know Lord Dashlend very well. "We found him ever so charming. My father escorted Lord Dashlend and his valet to the inn where we were staying and he dined with us. And breakfasted with us too."

"Breakfast too," the baron said in a flat tone.

"I do suppose we will see him again soon," Grace continued. "My father lent him clothes, you see. Because he was very wet. And then he comes to us for dinner on Tuesday next, though I suppose we will see him before then. To return the clothes."

"Yes, certainly, to return the clothes."

For some reason, Grace got the feeling that Lord Montclave was not as enthusiastic about Lord Dashlend as she was. How odd. It seemed a very strange thing that anybody in the world would not be enthusiastic regarding Lord Dashlend.

"We had the very good fortune, at that inn, to take possession of the most charming little dog. We named him Nelson, after Lord Nelson. I do believe Lord Dashlend was just as charmed as we were."

"Was he now?" the baron asked.

"Yes, I do believe so," Grace said.

The hostess had just turned to her other side, signaling to the diners that they ought to do the same. Grace smiled at the baron and turned to talk to Mr. Gerald Howard. He was the son of a viscount and hailed from Hertfordshire. He was a very pleasant gentleman and he further recommended himself by claiming an acquaintance with Lord Dashlend and naming him a fine fellow. According to Mr. Howard, Lord Dashlend was known in fencing circles as "the man with four arms," so fast was he with a sword.

That was rather thrilling to hear. Naturally, had she been pressed to guess at it, she would have supposed that Lord Dashlend must be a very great sporting sort of gentleman. After all, she had first encountered him while sailing his own boat. Or shipwrecking his own boat, as the case was. Nevertheless, it was thrilling to imagine him disposing of opposing fencers so expediently that it seemed as if he had four arms.

The rest of the dinner proceeded in rather an odd fashion. At least, it seemed so to Grace, though it was the first she had attended in Town. Baron Montclave questioned her regarding what sort of state she had found Lord Dashlend in when she had encountered him at the seaside. Most particularly, had it seemed as if he'd swallowed any water. Then the baron had heavily hinted that he would not be opposed to being invited to the dinner on Tuesday next, which Grace dodged by claiming only her father had the authority to expand the guest list.

As if that were not strange enough, some of the diners really did consume too much wine. The party got very merry. And then perhaps more merry than it ought. There were some who seemed to forget that polite society was at table and loudly told jokes Grace was certain she ought not hear. Mrs. Featherby, the hostess, should have set the tone, but she seemed to join in on the merriment.

Mr. Howard said a few things in a joking manner that Grace did not altogether comprehend. Why Mrs. Featherby was to be known as a bird of paradise, she was sure she did not know. Was it because her dress was a trifle gaudy?

While it was a bit confusing to decide if all of it was usual, her biggest clue was her father. He was not as jovial as he might be expected to be.

Mrs. Featherby had risen to lead the ladies to the drawing room. Her father rose too and said, "I will just have a word with my daughter in the hall. Then, gentlemen, I'll happily drink you under the table."

This was met with hearty laughter, though Grace really hoped her father did not plan on it. He could be a handful when he was drunk.

In the hall, the duke determinedly waited until both the drawing room and dining room doors were closed. Then he turned to a footman and said, "Retrieve my daughter's cloak and call my carriage."

"Papa?" Grace asked, very much fearing he was unwell.

"This is no place for us, my girl," the duke said in a low voice. "Or not you, anyway."

As the party was not large, their coachman was just down the street. He pulled up to the doors in a matter of minutes. The duke hustled Grace inside and rapped on the roof.

As the carriage pulled away, Grace said, "Goodness, you had better tell me what that was all about."

"What that was all about was a rather low party hostessed by the Earl of Doanellen's mistress."

"Oh! I see. I had thought she was a sister, but then Baron Montclave said she was a very good friend."

"I did not initially perceive what the relationship was myself. About halfway through the dinner, it finally penetrated my mind."

Grace said, "Is that why Mr. Howard named her a bird of paradise? I thought it might be her clothes, but perhaps it was… her relationship to the earl."

The duke laughed long and hard over her speculation. "She is a bird of paradise in every sense of the word, clothes included."

"I should not have accepted that invitation," Grace said.

"Nor should Wembly have accepted it and brought along Lady Lavender. I'd say if he had any sense he'd pull her out as I did you, but he's in his cups. Dashed irresponsible."

"But then, how could I know not to accept the invitation, Papa? I do not know anybody personally, you do not ever remember anybody, and Lord Doanellen is an earl. Do you suppose we ought to go to my aunt and have her review the other invitations I've accepted?"

"Not on your life. I never give up a point to Lady Misery."

"But what are we to do? I would not like to end in a similar situation, or an even worse situation."

The duke tapped his chin. "I know what we'll do. I ought to get some benefit from putting up with a son-in-law. We'll have Stratton look at it. He knows everybody and he's got a reasonable amount of sense."

"Mr. Stratton!" Grace said. "He will know what ought to be done."

Really, they should have thought of that in the first place.

Grace did not know how she was to explain the evening to her sisters. Valor was already terrified of rogues. Now Grace supposed birds of paradise were to be added to her nightmares.

MONTCLAVE SURVEYED THE drawing room. Some of the guests had gone, most notably Lady Grace and her duke, who had cut out without even taking their leave. Lady Lavender had followed soon after, practically marching her father out when he'd come into the drawing room.

In truth, he was surprised those people had come at all. He had thought it ill-advised to invite them into such company, but Doanellen was determined that Mrs. Featherby would be accepted in the sort of circles he was accustomed to travel in.

Montclave did not think there was the remotest chance of that happening. The matrons of the *ton* would not tolerate a mistress at their table or in their ballroom or anywhere else. It was not so much their sensibilities offended, as it was sending the signal that they would not tolerate being themselves left behind in the countryside while their ne'er-do-well husbands squired around a more entertaining and pliable lady.

He'd said as much to his friend, but Doanellen was bull-headed on the subject and Montclave was a guest in the house, so he could not press too far.

It was convenient to have quarters to lay one's head down at night that did not cost him any money, though the convenience did come with its own sort of price. Mrs. Featherby had moved herself into the house too and she was a chattering windbag. She had no taste, her clothes were gaudy, and her manners a touch rough. She had defeated Doanellen though, so Montclave suspected she must make up for her more obvious deficiencies in private and between the bedsheets.

The earl's delusions regarding his mistress were the least of the problems on Montclave's mind, though. While he could not yet gauge what interest, if any at all, Dashlend had in Lady Grace, he was in no doubt as to her own interest. She'd been rather dogged about bringing him up. She'd come upon Dashlend just as he was dragging himself out of the sea, which must have seemed very exciting to a young lady.

They'd dined together, and breakfast too. Dashlend had been charmed by some cur they'd picked up. Dashlend was to return the clothes he'd borrowed. Dashlend was to attend them at a dinner.

Montclave had gamely suggested he might come to the dinner too, but had been rebuffed by the excuse that only the duke could invite anybody. He'd planned to get the duke well-oiled with port after the ladies retired and then opportune him on the subject, but he never got the chance.

At one point, searching for any sort of good news, Montclave had inquired of Lady Grace if it had seemed as if Dashlend might have swallowed seawater during his adventure. He'd heard that a person who'd nearly drowned could later die unexpectedly. When he'd been in the habit of haunting some rough taverns nearby the docks, a sailor had told him the story of three men who'd been plucked from the sea after their boat sank. All three were gleeful to be alive and then two of them were dead by morning.

Though realistically, he supposed the time for that happy turn of events had passed by Dashlend. Montclave would drown him with his own two hands if he could get away with it.

He was in Town to assure himself that Dashlend did not take a bride. If his cousin had an interest in Lady Grace, how was he to stop it?

That was the problem he mulled over just now, ignoring what went on around him. The drawing room had devolved into a drunken scene at Vauxhall. Mrs. Featherby was in her cups and laughing at everything Doanellen said. A few of the men were gambling far too high. Mr. Crenellen had passed out in a corner and Mrs. Crenellen sang off-key at the pianoforte.

It was just as well that Lady Grace and Lady Lavender had departed before this particular scene unfolded. Montclave would not like either of them to view the company he was currently keeping.

Somehow, he must ascertain where things were going between Dashlend and Lady Grace. If it seemed to be going anywhere at all, he must wedge them apart. He could not lose his chance at becoming the earl's heir. If he could just keep Dashlend unmarried, who knew how the fellow might end up conveniently killing himself. For years, he'd held tight to the hope that Dashlend would get in an argument with somebody and end up dead on a green, or fall from a horse he was racing, or be accidentally run through while sparring, or sink in his stupid boat.

He'd come so close on the drowning front!

One never knew when the next opportunity would present itself. He would not be so stupid as to murder his cousin as he had no wish to swing for it, but if a situation presented itself whereby he might innocently help his cousin to the great beyond, he would take it.

MILES ARRANGED TO take his carriage to Lady Grace's house to return the clothes that had been borrowed after his shipwreck. He had at first thought to take his horse, as he would always much prefer to ride, but Moreau had some sort of mental collapse over it.

According to his valet, he had slaved over the reviled "oldest set" of clothes, making certain they were perfection. They must be carefully laid on a carriage seat so that nothing should ruin his work. According to Moreau, he would do a violence to himself if another valet found reason to lord it over him. His very soul could not continue living if he were to be shamed in such a manner.

Miles did not bother to mention that a person's soul was meant to be eternal and not likely snuffed out over a set of clothes.

Listening to his valet's threats of bodily harm was not the only inconvenience though. It seemed Lady Margaret heard that the carriage had been called for. Miles found her sitting primly in the great hall with her coat and bonnet on, cane in hand.

He'd mentioned it would be an uninteresting trip, as he was only to return some clothes, but she'd replied that at her age every trip was interesting, but for the trip to a funeral parlor. That final trip was only interesting to heirs, not to the persons themselves.

She was determined to go and so there was nothing for it.

As the carriage made its way down the crowded streets, Lady Margaret eagerly peered out the windows taking it all in. Miles began to wonder when last she'd been out of her house.

If the streets were not so congested with carriages, people walking, people on horseback, and carts of all description, the trip to Grosvenor Square might be accomplished in well under ten minutes. As it was, they'd been inching along for a quarter hour already.

Precisely why he liked to take his horse.

"That new girl you sent to me is ever so clever in getting me dressed," Lady Margaret said. "She knows what she's about."

"She is your kitchen maid," Miles said. "I thought she might do for now."

"Is she? How funny I did not notice. I am too used to her presenting burnt toast, I suppose. With no toast in her hands, how could I recognize her?"

"If you wish to keep her on as your lady's maid, I do not think she would be opposed to it."

"Ah yes, I think she would suit very well. She helps Gwen too. Hah! My lady's maid has a lady's maid. Is that not ironic? Now, tell me about these people we will see."

"I do not actually know if we will see any of them," Miles said. "They may not be at home. It is the Duke of Pelham and his daughter, Lady Grace. They were instrumental in providing me assistance when I had a recent mishap at sea."

Lady Margaret leaned forward. "Did you come close to death?"

Miles was taken aback by the question, but he supposed the elderly often had the subject in mind.

"It could have gone that way. I was very fortunate."

Lady Margaret rubbed her hands together. "That sounds very promising. To meet under such interesting circumstances often bodes well. When one so young faces death, they turn their attention to the future. Very suddenly, the far off someday has arrived."

Miles did not answer, though he thought the idea surprisingly astute. That was exactly where his mind had gone.

"Of course, at my age, one spends one's time wishing someday would *not* arrive. Though, I must say that waking up in the morning is far more exciting than it used to be. There is something about opening one's eyes and noticing that one did not die in the night that is particularly cheerful."

Miles was beginning to find Lady Margaret a rather macabre personality.

"Is she pretty?" Lady Margaret asked.

"Lady Grace? Yes, she is very pretty."

"Tell me."

"Oh, well, let's see," Miles said, feeling very put on the spot. "She's got blond hair, but not too blond. Not insipid, I would say. She has an abundance of curls."

"That will look very nice when she unpins it."

Miles certainly hoped he did not redden over that idea.

"Eyes?" Lady Margaret asked. "Blue, I suppose."

"Actually no, they are more an olive color. Which I think lends some sophistication to her coloring."

"Excellent. Good teeth?"

"Uh, yes."

"Temperament? Is she pleasant?"

"Very pleasant."

"I am satisfied with what I've heard so far."

Miles sat back. He did not quite know how it was happening, but it almost felt as if Lady Margaret had stepped in for his mother, taking on the duty of examining any ladies in his view.

The carriage slowed to a stop and a groom hopped down and opened the door. As Miles had found the only way to get Lady Margaret into a carriage was to pick her up and put her in it, he repeated the operation to get her out of it. Then he fetched her cane and the clothes that were to be returned to the duke.

"Let's see what we've got to work with," Lady Margaret said, hobbling toward the door.

CHAPTER EIGHT

"H E'S COME!" PATIENCE said, from her post at the window.

"Who has come?" Grace asked, knowing very well who. She had refused to go out anywhere during the day in case he would come. They'd all endlessly speculated on whether he would come and when he would come.

Valor patted her hand. "I think it must be Lord Dashlend, Grace. Remember? We've talked and talked about him coming."

"He's brought an older lady," Patience said.

"His mother?" Grace said, her voice an octave higher than it usually was.

"I think it must be a grandmother."

A grandmother! Her own grandmother that yet lived, her mother's mother, resided in Devon and they never saw her as she and the duke did not get on. Lady Neville always sent each girl a Christmas gift and year after year it was something not very exciting, like embroidered handkerchiefs. The gift was always accompanied by a letter outlining their Christian duties.

If anyone in the room was half as nervous over the idea of meeting Lord Dashlend's grandmother as Grace was, it must be Nelson. The dear little dog was very astute at understanding the feelings of the family and when the temperature rose, he raced to meet it. Just now, he was traveling in circles.

"Serenity, do calm poor Nelson," Grace said, attempting to keep her voice steady.

Serenity swept Nelson into her arms and his little tail beat against her muslin in wild appreciation.

Thomas opened the drawing room doors. "Lord Dashlend and Lady Margaret Hawley," he said gravely.

Valor nodded at Thomas to tell him it was very well done.

The rest of them rose and approached. Grace curtsied and said, "Lord Dashlend, Lady Margaret. Do come in."

Grace would have liked to send Thomas for tea at once, but the footman had disappeared.

"Lady Grace, I have returned the clothes to your footman that I was so generously supplied in my hour of need."

Said footman popped his head back in the door and mouthed, "Tea?"

Grace nodded. Valor clapped and said, "You remembered to ask about tea. Well done, Thomas." Then she turned to Lord Dashlend. "Our Thomas is still practicing being a footman. He is getting very good!"

"Yes, indeed, I can see that," Lord Dashlend said kindly. "Lady Grace, Lady Valor, Lady Patience, Lady Winsome, Lady Verity, may I acquaint you with Lady Margaret? She is a cousin recently relocated to my house."

It was not his grandmother, it was some sort of cousin. Still, he had brought a family member and there must be something in that. As well, Grace thought he was rather marvelous to remember all of their names. "Lady Margaret," she said, "we are very pleased to know you."

Lady Margaret nodded. "Now, I wish to make one thing clear, as Lord Dashlend has made it sound as if I arrived at his house by way of invitation. That is not the case."

Goodness, what *was* the case?

"Lady Margaret," Lord Dashlend said, "I do not see the need to go into the details."

Lady Margaret patted his hand. "I do, though. You see, Lady Grace, this wonderful gentleman came to attend me after I sent a note that I required him instantly. He is always very good about that. When he arrived, he noticed that my living situation had rather fallen to shambles, as half my staff had died."

Lady Margaret held her hand up as if to stop any speculation before it began. Especially since Valor had buried her head in Mrs. Wendover's raggedy bits upon mention of the staff dying.

"They were all very old, you see, as I am myself. Flu—not to be trifled with. Well, despite my protestations that I should not like to interfere with a bachelor's lifestyle, he would insist I relocate."

"That is very kind, Lord Dashlend," Grace said.

"That's him—kind as the day is long," Lady Margaret said.

Thomas came in with the tea tray and set it in front of Grace. Goodness, it felt a bit fraught to play the hostess, all eyes on her hands and the cups.

"Lady Margaret," she said, "how will you take your tea?"

"More milk than you would think and a dash of brandy," the lady said.

"Brandy?" Grace said, working to keep the surprise from her voice. "Yes, of course. Thomas?"

As Thomas went to fetch the brandy decanter, Grace attempted to work out how much a dash was. She'd never heard of anybody putting it in their tea.

"It's my old bones, you see," Lady Margaret said by way of explanation. "The brandy soothes them."

Valor inched her way across the sofa to Lady Margaret. "Are your bones very old?"

"Old as Methuselah, poppet."

"Gracious," Valor said. "Our vicar told us that Methuselah lived for almost a thousand years."

Lady Margaret nodded. "Sometimes it just feels like it."

"I told the vicar that Methuselah must have looked terrible after even a hundred years and I asked if he was afraid to look in mirrors and then the vicar scolded me for thinking about the wrong thing."

"Hah! Take everything your usual vicar has to say with a

hefty grain of salt. No sense of humor, those people."

Thomas returned and Grace added the smallest bit of brandy to the lady's tea and handed her the cup and saucer.

Valor put her hand in Lady Margaret's free hand. "I know that must be right," she said. "I told the vicar that sometimes stealing was necessary, you know because the commandments say you can never do it. He was so cross about it!"

"Let me hazard a guess—stealing biscuits?"

"Yes!"

As Valor and Lady Margaret chattered on together, Patience said, "Lord Dashlend, we thought you'd come on an earlier day, but now we know you were helping Lady Margaret."

Serenity brushed away a tear. "It really is very touching."

"I believe familial loyalty is very usual in cases such as this," Verity said.

"Maybe not always, though," Winsome said, challenging the idea.

"I was happy to do it," Lord Dashlend said, taking his tea.

Grace was enormously pleased that she'd not spilled one drop of it.

"How do you get on in Town so far, Lady Grace?" Lord Dashlend asked. "Have you been to any entertainments yet?"

Grace was not certain whether or not she ought to mention Lord Doanellen's dinner. Then she recalled that Lord Dashlend's own cousin had been there, so there was every likelihood that he would hear of it.

"We have attended one dinner, though had I been more experienced at managing invitations, I daresay we would have sent our regrets."

"Not a well put together table?" Lord Dashlend asked.

"Um, no, it was not exactly that. We attended the Earl of Doanellen's dinner."

Lord Dashlend frowned.

"There was a bird of paradise there," Winsome said. "We've been told that's not at all the thing, though I really do not see what is wrong with it. People keep canaries and parrots all the time."

"It is my understanding that a bird of paradise is a noxious bird, though," Verity said.

"The problem was," Patience said, "the bird was in the dining room. That's what I can get out of the whole thing."

Lord Dashlend seemed to perceive that Grace's younger sisters were rather unclear as to what, or who, a bird of paradise was. He said, "Lady Grace, I notice what I believe is a fine collection of books on that bookshelf on the far side of the room. I wonder if you would escort me there and give me your comments on them."

"Yes, of course," Grace said. She was rather nervous, as she expected she would be pressed for further information regarding the bird of paradise.

They strolled to the far end of the drawing room, leaving behind Lady Margaret and Valor having a confidential conversation about stealing biscuits. Serenity, Winsome, and Patience just stared at them as they made their way there.

Lord Dashlend picked a book from the shelf and pretended to examine it. "I presume Mrs. Featherby was the bird in question?"

Grace nodded. "We really did not know what we were walking into. I do not know anybody and my father often forgets who is who. He also is not one for hanging about his club listening to gossip, so he would have missed the lady's identity. And then, there was nothing said on the invitation that... that... a certain type of lady would be there."

"No, of course there would not be anything on the invitation. It is my understanding that Doanellen is doing everything in his power to establish Mrs. Featherby in society. He will get nowhere with it, though."

Grace nodded. "Is it true that he's left his wife in the country-side? My aunt said so, but then I thought there must be a good reason for it."

"That is a rather sad case, if what I've heard about it is true.

Lady Doanellen came with a pile of money and as far as I can tell, he married her for it. He played the devoted husband until he had an heir and now he's cast her aside."

"That is wicked."

"Yes, it is. I do not know what Doanellen is about. He's enraged every matron in Town and half of his gentlemen friends too. It is one thing to carry on with a mistress and another thing to expect one's friends to acknowledge the lady."

"It is a usual thing?" Grace asked. "To carry on with… such ladies?"

The idea was a little shocking. She was not entirely naïve, she had heard of such things, but she'd not thought it a usual thing. Her father had certainly never done anything of the sort.

"No, no, not usual. Not among decent men, at any rate."

Grace nodded, rather relieved to hear it. "Your cousin was there."

"Montclave? Yes, I thought that was where he might have gone. He does not keep a house in Town."

"But he is not welcome at your house?"

"He is not."

Grace burned to know why not. Was there something to know about Lord Montclave? Or were they simply oil and water? But, she could not bring herself to ask such a direct and personal question.

"I did mention to him that we had met when you were shipwrecked on the beach. He was very interested in whether or not you swallowed seawater."

"I bet he was."

"I told him I did not know. He also opportuned me about coming to the dinner on Tuesday, but I said only my father could issue invitations. It was quite the fib, I will admit."

"I am glad. My cousin and I do not get on."

Grace could see that, though Lord Dashlend had not given out any clues as to why. She remembered Lord Montclave had said they lived on neighboring estates. Perhaps they both carried forward some old boyhood grudges?

Seeing that she would not discover anything firm, Grace turned the conversation to the other thing that had weighed on her mind.

"Lady Lavender was at the dinner too. I do not know if you know the lady, but she seemed very pleasant."

"Lady Lavender?" Lord Dashlend asked. "What on earth was Wembly thinking?"

"Oh, you are acquainted with the lady?"

"Only recently, it is her first season out. She played the pianoforte at Lady Elspeth's musical evening last night."

"I suppose she was very good."

"Yes, indeed she was. She seemed to have a very natural ear."

"Yes, she seemed the sort of lady who is good at everything," Grace said pensively.

Lord Dashlend laughed. "Yes, I suppose some ladies are. Accomplished, is what I believe they are called."

Accomplished. That short time they'd had a governess, Miss Pynchon, she'd gone on and on about developing accomplishments. She and her sisters had laughed over it, but now she was beginning to think Miss Pynchon had been right all along.

Lady Lavender had accomplishments, one of which had been on display last evening. What accomplishments could Grace Nicolet claim? Certainly nothing to do with the pianoforte.

"What will you do to ensure you do not accept another invitation that might be better declined?" Lord Dashlend asked. "I would look them over if you like."

"That is very kind, Lord Dashlend. My father has determined that my brother-in-law, Mr. Percy Stratton, will be given the task."

"Stratton, yes, he's sensible. He will be sure to steer you in the right direction."

Grace thought that while she could not turn over her social calendar to Lord Dashlend, she should not lose the opportunity to inform him of what events she and her father were to attend in the near future. She listed them out as best as she could remember them. She was gratified that Lord Dashlend seemed to be paying close attention. She was not quite as gratified that he would not attend Lady Luthering's ball on the morrow, as he was committed to dining with one of his father's oldest friends. She was both nervous and looking forward to dancing with Lord Dashlend.

But then, perhaps it was best that she get some practice being at a ball before dancing with him.

"We ought to return to the others, lest Lady Margaret begins to think I step over a gentlemanly line."

Grace nodded and they made their way back. Winsome and Verity were debating some point, while Patience toe tapped over it and interjected the occasional, "Nobody cares, nobody has ever cared, nobody will ever care." Valor was telling Lady Margaret all about Mrs. Wendover.

Lady Margaret patted Valor's hand. "It's a very fine thing to have your own particular friend."

"You could be my friend too," Valor said.

"I'd be delighted. Should we correspond?"

"You mean write letters?" Valor said, looking deeply impressed over the idea. "I should like to get letters in the post."

"Very good," Lady Margaret said. "I'll write the first one and then you write me back. Write whatever is on your mind, poppet."

"Grace," Valor said, "Lady Margaret is my new friend and we are going to write to each other. I'm to get letters."

"That's very kind, Lady Margaret," Grace said. "I do hope though, that you know you are welcome to come to us in person at any time."

"Careful, my dear," Lady Margaret said, "I may well take you up on that."

"As well, we hope you will attend us at dinner on Tuesday?" Grace asked. "Lord Dashlend kindly accepted my father's invitation when we met by the seaside."

"Delighted."

Lord Dashlend had remained standing and Grace very well knew why. The time had elapsed for a call a quarter hour ago.

"Lady Margaret, we'd best take our leave," Lord Dashlend said.

"As you wish," Lady Margaret said, outstretching her hand. Lord Dashlend pulled her to her feet.

All five sisters, and Nelson too, followed them out to the pavement and waved them off. Grace thought it might have been obvious or forward or not exactly right to do so. Perhaps she ought to have stayed in the drawing room and pretended disinterest in the departure. But then, it seemed to be well received.

LADY MARGARET HAD been settled into the carriage and Miles had climbed in after her. Lady Grace and her five sisters, along with the three-legged dog, waved them off.

"Lovely people," Lady Margaret said.

"Yes, I believe so," Miles said.

"I sized them up the minute I walked into the drawing room. Do you know how I did it?"

"You ascertained that they were well-dressed and courteous?" Miles ventured.

"No. Anybody can throw on decent clothes and manners. I knew they were good people because they have a three-legged dog who is obviously delighted with his circumstances."

"Ah, the dog. They found him at an inn. He also seems to be blind in one eye."

"Even better," Lady Margaret said.

"Is it?"

"Of course it is. There are opportunities, from time to time, to glimpse a person's character, or even a whole family's character. Another family might have kicked such a dog out of their way and passed it by, never thinking of it again. Yet another family might have felt bad and paid for its upkeep. Another family might have gone so far as to relegate him to their stables in the countryside. This dog, though, is living the life of a lord in the family's drawing room in Town."

"I hadn't thought… they *were* very sentimental about his case. They could not bear the idea that he was living on scraps. Scraps were mentioned more than once."

"As I said, lovely people. Well! I will be most interested in attending this dinner. I would like to get a look at the duke. Even in my relative isolation I've heard he's a bit of a corker."

"Yes, the duke does lean toward the eccentric," Miles said, thinking Lady Margaret was not so far behind on that quality.

"I'll have to speak to… what is that girl's name again?"

"What girl?"

"My new maid who used to burn the toast."

"Ah, I believe it is Meg."

"Yes, that's it, Meg. I'll have to speak to her about what sort of dress can be dug up and have her polish my jewelry. Gwen can direct her on how it's done. I'll want to look my best. Goodness, I have some smashing dresses stored away. Time to dig them out and don the armor for battle once more. Your dear mother is at home in the country caring for your father and his gout— somebody has got to keep them informed on your progress."

"My progress? No, really I do not think that is at all necessary," Miles said, alarmed that Lady Margaret was going to send letters home describing his activities.

She patted his hand and said, "You let me worry about what is necessary."

For such a little bird of a lady, she was rather free with imposing her will.

For all that, Miles could not definitely say he was uninterested in making progress. He was astute enough to recognize in himself that his level of concern over Lady Grace being exposed to Mrs.

Featherby was higher than it might have been. He'd not been nearly as concerned upon hearing that Lady Lavender had attended the dinner as well. They were very like—two ladies new to the town—and yet he felt he must extend his protection to Lady Grace, where Lady Lavender could fend for herself.

CHAPTER NINE

HAD MRS. RIGHT been alone in her efforts to display offense over Mr. Button's alleged flirtation toward her, it might not have gone over as well as it had. After all, had it only been her acting alone, Mr. Button might have successfully written her off as a flighty and delusional woman.

In most households, the junior staff were all too enthusiastic about seeing a senior servant knocked down a peg. The duke's household was different though, because Mrs. Right had made it so.

The housekeeper in this household was their protector—she was the head of the table who ensured they were not worked too hard, were paid a superior wage, and had more time off than most. If one of them chose to move on to another venture, Mrs. Right wrote a glowing recommendation and got the duke to sign it. She was the healer of cuts and bruises, the sympathetic listener, and the keeper of secrets.

Her housekeeper's closet was often the scene of somebody pouring out a frustration or outlining a hope for the future. The housemaids might propose an easier way to get through their duties, Cook might make the case for a second kitchen maid, the stablemaster might petition for a late evening plate of meats and cheeses for his grooms as they were growing boys who were always ravenous. The average butler delighted in denying requests. Mrs. Right delighted in approving them. Nobody who worked for the duke wished that recipe to be changed one bit.

Mrs. Right was the general of a loyal army both above and below stairs. The army had been issued orders to drive Mr. Button to distraction and she would lead her forces forward.

Just now, an opportunity was presenting itself. She knew the footmen and maids were at table with their tea and just ahead was Mr. Button in the corridor heading toward them.

Mrs. Right picked up her pace, pushed past him and cried, "Mr. Button! I will not tolerate these impertinences!"

She raced ahead and found her loyal staff all well-prepared to playact with her.

Thomas stood and said, "What's he done now, Mrs. Right?"

Mr. Button hurried into the room. "I've done nothing! I do not know why she keeps accusing me of doing something!"

The footman and the maids frowned. Charlie said, "Mr. Button, we've known Mrs. Right ever so many years. She don't make things up."

"But she is now," Mr. Button said. "I was just walking down the corridor doing nothing at all!"

Mrs. Right sniffed and pulled her shawl tight round her shoulders. "For the first time in twenty years living in the duke's household, I feel unsafe."

The maids leapt to their feet and one of the girls moved a chair between them. "Sit with us, Mrs. Right. We'll protect you."

"We'll *all* protect you," Charlie said darkly.

Mr. Button had got very red in the face, as Mrs. Right supposed anybody would who'd been accused of taking liberties with a middle-aged housekeeper.

"I will not stand for this, this, whatever this is," he shouted. "I will take steps!"

He turned on his heel and marched out of the room.

"Let's hope them steps he's taking lead him right out of the house," Cook said.

There was much nodding round the table and a very pleasant tea commenced.

GRACE HAD SO far been to one dinner, and it was a dinner she should not have gone to. This evening was Lady Luthering's ball and must be considered her first real foray into society. Lady Marchfield had arranged to have Felicity's dresses made last year, but such was her aggravation with the duke she had not done it this year.

All was not lost though. Felicity had been so good as to send over all of her first year's wardrobe. The styles were timeless so they looked as new, and they were close in size, enabling Mrs. Right to take in a bit here and there to make the fit.

Grace chose a lovely blue green silk with a delicate organza overlay dotted with embroidered white daisies. Felicity had particularly recommended it as everything that was fresh and young.

Grace paired it with an aquamarine necklace that had belonged to her mother. When Valor had been old enough to participate, the duke had laid out all of his deceased wife's jewelry and allowed his daughters to choose what they would. It had been a rather frenetic exercise, she and Patience even scouring the floor for loose seed pearls in the fracas. It had eventually calmed when Mrs. Right pointed out that not everything could be worn at once and they would greatly increase their choices if they agreed to share.

That was probably for the best, as Valor had been only five and had gone for the gaudiest paste among the jewels, including an enameled parrot pin she wore regularly which was really very awful. Grace's youngest sister would no doubt notice, as she matured, that her taste had not been what it could have been.

In preparation for the ball, Mrs. Right had been very careful with her hair as her sisters had looked on and peppered her with questions. They were, all of them including Grace, disappointed that Lord Dashlend was not to attend.

Their approval of the gentleman had grown since his visit, and even Valor said he must be a fine gentleman to have such a relation as Lady Margaret. Valor had received her first letter from that lady, and it had outlined Lady Margaret's great and long-lasting friendship with a certain Doodle-do, who had been the stuffed rooster companion of her youth. The lady still had that item in a closet somewhere and it was her hope that Doodle-do and Mrs. Wendover might meet someday.

Valor was to spend the evening composing her response to this news.

Mrs. Right had very astutely chosen a dark blue velvet pelisse to complete Grace's dress, and she and her father had been waved off by the rest of the family.

"Did you notice?" the duke asked as the carriage rumbled through the dark streets.

"Notice what, Papa?"

"Mr. Button. Where was he?"

"That is true," Grace said. Mr. Button was so recently arrived that she'd not even noticed he was absent at their departure.

"Perhaps he's already gone," the duke said. "Mrs. Right has a certain spring in her step at the moment."

"I wonder," Grace said. "She's given us no direction so far regarding her plans."

The duke turned to her. "Do you imply that you and your sisters played a part in Mr. Sykes-Wycliff's exit last year?"

"Only that we told him about the servants' hunt. You were meant to chase the servants round the moors and shoot at them."

The duke laughed long and hard. "Nobody has an imagination like Mrs. Right. Servants' hunt, indeed. Though, it might be amusing with slingshots, eh?"

Grace laughed despite herself. That really might be amusing. She suspected the footmen would be all in on the idea.

"Now Gracie, what's it to be? I understand Dashlend made a point to return the borrowed clothes himself and brought along some sort of relation too. Are you to settle your eyes on him or are you to meander through the season pretending you haven't, just as Felicity did?"

"Papa, it is too soon to settle my eyes anywhere. Though, Lord Dashlend certainly has caught my eye."

The duke chuckled. "I see, you feel you do not know him well enough."

"Well, I do not," she said. "But the more pressing thing is… he does not know *me* well enough."

The duke looked at her quizzically. "You think he might be put off because you are clumsy on occasion?"

"He might be," Grace said.

"If he is, then he is not the man I think he is. I suppose we just wait and see. What's say you purposefully fall on the floor when he's nearby and we'll see what he says."

"I will do no such thing and I know you are joking."

"Maybe," the duke said enigmatically.

The carriage rolled to a stop. "Here we are," Grace said. "My first real ball."

"Chin up, you are a duke's daughter. You fear nobody and require nobody's approval."

Grace smiled. Perhaps she did not *require* anybody's approval, but she wished for the approval of one gentleman in particular. He would not be there to approve on this particular occasion, but he would be soon enough.

Lady Luthering greeted them at the door. She was exceedingly gracious, even when the duke noted that he'd heard Lord Luthering had kicked off. Grace was certain a lady hosting a ball would not like to be reminded of a dead husband but she was very civil about it, only noting the sad event was "last March."

They proceeded to the cloak room to deposit their coats and retrieve Grace's dance card.

A dance card. An empty dance card. Would it be filled? Would she acquit herself creditably on the ballroom floor? She felt she had a very good chance of it. Some days she felt steadier than others and today she was solid on her two feet.

"Lady Grace!"

Grace turned to find Lady Lavender behind her. She curtsied. "Lady Lavender."

Lady Lavender in turn curtsied. "Your Grace," she said to the duke.

"Hah! Another victim of Lord Doanellen's dinner," the duke said. "I hope you escaped it as fast as we did."

Lady Lavender nodded. "Almost as fast. When the gentlemen came in from their port, I marched my father right out the doors."

The duke hooked a thumb toward Lady Lavender. "She's got good sense."

"My father has just made his way to the card room, Your Grace. If you care to do the same, Lady Grace and I can chaperone one another. We will be quite safe in Lady Luthering's ballroom."

"What say you, Gracie?"

"I am certain I will be very safe, Papa, go ahead and find a card table."

"And a glass of claret too, I hope," the duke said. He kissed Grace's cheek and strolled off.

Lady Lavender took her arm as they made their way to the ballroom. "I was hoping your father would agree to it as I wished to have a confidential conversation about that dinner."

"I did not know what it would be," Grace said. "I went through the invitations sent to us on my own and while I did not know who was who, he was an earl at a good address."

Lady Lavender nodded. "The same happened to me. My father left it to me as my mother is long gone and he has been renting out his house in Town for years. He's quite lost any idea of the societal landscape. I have since asked a cousin to review all of my engagements."

Grace said, "I am to have my brother-in-law do the same."

"Gracious, we got ourselves into an awkward situation. My father has been much chastened by it. I suppose the duke feels the same."

Grace laughed. "I cannot recall a time my father was chastened over anything."

"Ah, I imagine a duke never does. I suppose we will discover this evening whether it is widely spoken of or not."

"Will we?" Grace asked.

"If it is bandied about, if we are condemned by the matrons of society for attending, we may find ourselves ostracized."

"Ostracized?" Grace asked, horrified over the idea.

"My cousin who is going into her third season explained it all to me. She knows absolutely everybody."

Grace glanced down at her empty card. Would it stay empty? What was she to do—just stand at the edges of the room, doused in shame and humiliation?

"Oh, I am sure gentlemen will put themselves down on our cards," Lady Lavender said, as if reading her thoughts. "But if certain gentlemen do not, we may make a guess as to why. For instance, the Marquess of Stonehelm is here, and so is his mother, the duchess. She is a stern old thing and seems to run him with an iron hand on his shoulder. If she's heard anything, she will give him strict instructions to give us a wide berth."

Grace sighed. "Last year, my aunt, Lady Marchfield, arranged the calendar for my sister. But my father does not get on with her and refused to let her do it again. That's how I ended up with the task. I should have asked somebody for help, though."

Lady Lavender patted her hand. "You were not to know."

Grace would very much like to dislike Lady Lavender, on account of her being so accomplished at everything, but it was no use. The lady was also very accomplished at being kind.

"Lady Grace, Lady Lavender."

It was Lord Montclave. She and Lady Lavender curtsied, though neither of them were enthusiastic to see him. He was a reminder of Lord Doanellen's dinner and to be seen speaking to him might set talk flying.

Seeming to note their discomfort, he said, "I was hoping to

encounter you. I wish to explain that I counseled Doanellen not to send invitations to people such as yourself. He insisted on doing it anyway and then was triumphant when both of your houses accepted. He was less triumphant when both of your fathers took you away upon noting who the hostess was. He will not try it again, I do not think."

"Lord Montclave," Grace said, "Lord Doanellen, through his carelessness and low morals, may have damaged our reputations. I hardly think I care that he has learned his lesson."

The baron had the good grace to blush. "I apologize on his behalf and I can assure you it will not be widely known unless either of you put it about."

"How are we to know that others who were there will not talk about it?" Lady Lavender asked.

"Because they are the sort of people who straddle two sides of the Town," Lord Montclave said. "They like to be accepted everywhere and they also like to attend the sorts of parties Lord Doanellen hosts. They will not speak of it. Had I known you had accepted the invitations, I would have stopped you at the door."

"But you, yourself, enjoy those sorts of parties?" Grace asked.

"I do not. However, my family does not keep a house in Town and Doanellen offered to have me. When I accepted, I had no idea of any of it, including the existence of Mrs. Featherby."

Grace was satisfied with the explanation, and very relieved that it did not seem as if reports of that dinner would be widely spoken of.

"May I?" Lord Montclave said, motioning toward her card.

"Yes, yes, of course," Grace said.

Lord Montclave put himself down for the dance before Lady Luthering's supper. Grace was not certain how she felt about it, but she supposed at least she would dine with someone she had already met.

The lord put himself down for Lady Lavender's first. Then he bowed and strolled away.

"I cannot decide if I like him or dislike him," Lady Lavender said.

Grace nodded, and then proceeded with a shameless fishing expedition. "He is no Lord Dashlend, in my estimation."

"Gracious no," Lady Lavender said. "Lord Dashlend is a deal more sophisticated in his manner, I think."

Grace was not entirely satisfied with that answer. She supposed she was hoping Lady Lavender would wrinkle her nose at the mention of Lord Dashlend. It was a rather stupid hope, of course, as who would not admire that gentleman?

"I understood he attended a musical evening you played at and he noted you were very accomplished."

Lady Lavender laughed. "He is very kind to say so. I believe the truth is I am like most ladies—I applied myself just enough to learn in the middling style."

Grace did not answer, as she had done far less than middling. She'd done next to nothing. Their pianoforte at home had been gathering dust for years, they did not even bother to have it tuned anymore.

This uncomfortable conversation was interrupted by a series of gentlemen approaching and writing their names down. Grace's card was filled, including by a certain marquess with a stern duchess for a mother.

It seemed the secret of Lord Doanellen's dinner was safe.

MILES WAS NOT certain he'd ever sat through a dinner that felt as long as this one did. He'd promised his father to accept the invitation in his stead, as it was from one of the earl's oldest friends in the world.

Viscount Harraby was an elderly gentleman that Miles had known since he was a young boy. Harraby and his father had met while the earl attended Eton, and then Miles himself when it was his turn to go to the school. The viscount was closely connected to the institution as he had an estate nearby. He'd acted as mentor and host to the legions of boys coming through those halls. It was considered an honor to be invited to one of the viscount's Friday evening dinners.

The headmaster looked upon Harraby as a mentor and appropriate example of manhood to his young charges, which he was. However, he was also the person to call upon when one was short of funds, got into a scrape, or required a few bottles of wine for a party.

Miles' father had maintained a regular correspondence with Lord Harraby ever since his boyhood days. The gentleman, and his lady before she passed on, were often guests at the house, especially during the shooting.

The problem was, the old man looked upon Miles as if he were still a fifteen-year-old lad. The other problem was that Lady Margaret had insisted on requesting an invitation, as those two people had long known one another but not set eyes on each other for some years. Miles had been forced to write Harraby with the request and got a speedy reply in the affirmative.

This had prompted Meg, former burner of toast and current lady's maid, to be sent with a footman to Lady Margaret's house with a long list of items to be retrieved from various trunks and closets. A carriageful of who knew what had arrived and been hauled up to the lady's bedchamber.

When the time came to depart for Lord Harraby's house, Miles was apprised of precisely what had been gathered from Lady Margaret's house.

In some sort of bid to be fashionable, Lady Margaret had arrived to the great hall in a puce-colored taffeta concoction that must have long ago, very long ago, been just the thing. It must also have fit better, as the lady had shrunk in her later years and the crinolines puffing it out lent her the appearance of a miniature sailing ship setting off for America. She wore a heavy gilded gold necklace decorated with birds on trees and her fingers sported an array of enameled and jeweled rings. This startling ensemble was topped off by a towering tiara and two molting ostrich feathers waving dangerously atop her head as if they were scanning the savannah for predators. Miles thought Wainwright's eyes might fall out of his head and roll across the marble floor.

Naturally, they could not escape curious onlookers as they got in the carriage. Miles supposed people *would* be curious to see a little bird of a lady swimming in purple taffeta and sporting overwhelming headgear who needed to be picked up and put inside, as she could not manage the step. Nevertheless, they had set off.

Miles had thought it was to be a usual dinner party of at least fourteen, and perhaps far more. But no, it was just himself, Harraby, and Lady Margaret.

Lord Harraby, being of the same generation as Lady Margaret, was bowled over by her dress, noting he'd not seen such elegance in years. It seemed the old gentleman deplored the simpler cuts of today's ladies' dress as the style had "no panache."

The evening was made even more uncomfortable as Lady Margaret had decided to put herself in charge of Miles' future and was quickly luring Harraby into the idea too.

"I see what you say, Lady Margaret," Lord Harraby said. "A young man does well to wed, it settles him, you see."

"I do not require settling, though," Miles said.

Lady Margaret and Lord Harraby exchanged looks and then laughed heartily.

"Leave it to us, Dashlend," Lady Margaret said. "It is time Lord Harraby and I got out and about so we might size up the ladies of the season."

"Very good notion, Lady Margaret," Lord Harraby said with enthusiasm. "I've got a pile of invitations I was not planning to accept, but now, with a purpose in mind, I find I have a bit of a spring in my step. I'll write to the ones I know well and ask that you be included."

"Excellent idea."

"I could even arrange for you to ride in my carriage, if that would suit."

Miles could not imagine how that would work. Harraby did not look as if he had the strength to lift Lady Margaret in and out of carriages, and she had conveniently not bothered to mention that requirement.

"Your carriage? That would suit very well, Lord Harraby. I sold my carriage and all my horses when my stablemaster died of old age."

"Old age," Harraby said thoughtfully, "it is a menace, is it not?"

Lady Margaret nodded. "Just two months ago, one of my aging footmen fell down the stairs and broke his frail old neck. Of course, he'd fallen down them several times, so I suppose his luck was bound to run out."

"If these young ones only knew what old bones feel like… well, no time to think of that now! We'll down a bit of brandy and carry on—we have a job to do!"

Miles whipped his head back and forth between them. It seemed he was not even to be consulted. How had this happened to him? How was he in possession of two old busybodies who were determined to direct his future? His own father was not so importuning.

How had Lady Margaret gone from shabby and deteriorating isolation to out on the town with Lord Harraby? Those two should not be let loose on society, Miles could not imagine what they'd get up to.

"Now Lady Margaret, you did mention one promising candidate already," Lord Harraby said.

"Ah yes, Lady Grace, she is lovely inside and out."

"That does sound promising indeed," Harraby said. "Though, if we are to do a proper job of it, we must not put blinders on! All eligible ladies must be considered and thoroughly examined."

"You have a very good head on your shoulders, Lord Harraby. That is full of sense."

The dessert course had been cleared and there came a bit of

an awkward moment. It would be the time the ladies would retire to the drawing room for tea, but that would have left Lady Margaret on her own.

"Might I suggest, Lady Margaret," Harraby said, "that you stay on at table. If your bones are anything like mine, I imagine they will be gratified by a tipple of port."

"Excellent notion, Lord Harraby."

And so a glass of port was set in front of Lady Margaret. To Harraby's credit, his butler did a terrific job of pretending nothing was amiss.

Miles took a long draught and signaled a footman for a refill. He had somehow acquired two elderly duennas and he was inclined to drown his sorrows in strong drink.

CHAPTER TEN

MONTCLAVE HAD DONE his best to smooth things over with Lady Grace and Lady Lavender. In truth, he could not care less for Lady Lavender's opinion, but Lady Grace was of possible interest to Dashlend, and so of interest to him.

He'd kept a close eye on the lady, and it might serve him that he did so. There was something odd in her dancing. She did not miss steps, but there were times she seemed to almost fall behind the tempo or otherwise look just the slightest bit awkward.

He was not certain how that information would serve him, but he was a firm believer in noticing details and storing them away for future use. He could not read Dashlend's mind, but he did know that the fellow considered himself a Corinthian. Perhaps he would not be enthusiastic over a lady who could not keep a tempo or had no ear for music and rhythm?

As to how to steer Lady Grace away from Dashlend, as he'd mulled over the situation this way and that, his own situation had seeped into the various considerations and seemed to offer a possible solution.

He was, as always, short on funds. Two days before, he'd approached Lady Margaret for a loan, but the old bird had been in a mood and turned him away. All he could manage to leave with was a silver salver he picked up on his way out, counting on her bad eyesight to miss the maneuver. He'd promptly sold it, but it had not come to much.

This afternoon, he'd returned to Lady Margaret's house, hoping to find her in more generous spirits. Most perplexingly, he'd found her departed from the house and a couple of burly watchmen employed to keep an eye on things. Those two fellows either did not know where she went or had been ordered not to say. All they would say was that her lady's maid, who used to be the cook, had come and taken some of her things away.

What lady's maid was this? As far as he knew, the cook was dead and Lady Margaret's maid had been with her for twenty years. Where could Lady Margaret have gone? Why did she relocate herself? It made no sense.

He'd briefly thought of helping himself to some of her things some late night, as the house was empty, but the watchmen posed too much of a risk. He'd checked the newspapers for a notice of funeral, but no, she was still alive somewhere.

He was short of money, a duke's daughter came with money, this particular duke's daughter needed to be lured away from Dashlend. It seemed the answer to a multitude of problems was to court Lady Grace.

And then, if he were successful in eventually becoming the earl's heir, who best to become the next countess than a duke's daughter? It would confer an instant legitimacy.

Of course, there was the current problem of convincing the lady. At the moment, he could only promise a future as a baroness of a middling estate. He could say nothing of his hopes for anything higher. As well, as much as he despised Dashlend, he was not clouded in his judgments. The fellow was suave and seemed to be well-liked by the ladies, including Lady Grace.

His own allurements were not quite as interesting. But he had cleverness and the ability to conceive of and execute an intricate game. That was what he must do—find the right hook for this lady fish and carefully reel her to his banks. He must find a weakness, a flaw, and exploit it to his advantage.

Montclave collected Lady Grace for the dance before supper and led her to the floor. "I presume you have enjoyed the ball so far?" he asked as an opening gambit.

"Indeed, yes," Lady Grace said. "Everyone has been so genial."

The orchestra struck up for the cotillion, as Lady Luthering was in the habit of placing that dance before supper.

They began Le Grand Rond. Montclave said, "And the dancing? Do you enjoy it?"

A flash of worry crossed Lady Grace's expression and Montclave knew he was on to something. He had hit on an insecurity.

He did not know precisely why it was a sore spot. Certainly, the duke would have seen to his daughters having a dancing master and she seemed to know all the steps. And yet, he'd noticed that she sometimes fell behind the tempo. Perhaps she knew it as a fault?

"Oh yes, the dancing," Lady Grace said. "Very enjoyable."

He did not quite believe that. He led Lady Grace through the figure and then an allemande. There it was again. She completed the step but ended with just the slightest wobble. One would not catch it if one were not looking out for it.

He did not know if this particular knowledge was significant enough to use in an effective manner, but he had to work with what he'd got.

"I will admit something shocking, Lady Grace," he said. "I do find dancing overrated. It is simply a pastime, and somehow the skill has been elevated into a measure of a lady's worth. I find it odd."

Lady Grace's expression told him all he needed to know. Her expression was one of relief. Perhaps even gratitude.

"If we are to be rational creatures," he continued, "I would prefer to judge a lady by means more important—her mind and discernment, kindness and graciousness. These are the things that really matter."

Lady Grace did not answer. But she nodded.

Montclave smiled. This was the crack in the armor. Furthermore, he knew it and Dashlend would not. Surely, there was something he could do with that.

"I've often had the debate with my cousin on this idea," he said as they executed a Rigadoon.

"Lord Dashlend?" Lady Grace asked, looking rather aflutter over it.

Montclave nodded. "Indeed. As you are probably aware, all society knows him as a Corinthian of the first stare. He takes pride in it, he is all physicality and respects it in others. Too much so, in my mind. I've said to him—you cannot judge a person's worth with such a yardstick." He pretended at a great sigh and said, "He can be hardheaded, though, and cemented in his opinions."

He was gratified to see the lady's complexion fade to a whiter shade than it had been. This was certainly the ticket—play on the lady's insecurities and the idea that Dashlend would disdain her weakness.

It was not much of a weakness, really. But then, people always viewed their perceived weaknesses as being bigger and more obvious to others than they were.

Montclave had long been a student of the human condition. One thing he knew for certain—people did not like other people who did not like *them*. To be disapproved of set a person's back up and it was very difficult to undo.

For once, perhaps human nature could work in his favor.

GRACE COULD NOT say her first outing to a ball had been wonderful or awful, as it had been both of those things. She'd been reasonably steady on her feet, which had been her foremost worry. Nothing had been said about Lord Doanellen's dinner, which had been her second worry.

She'd met with more than a few gentlemen. None of them

were Lord Dashlend, of course, but genial all the same.

She'd conducted herself well, and it was very gratifying.

And yet, she could not forget what Lord Montclave had said about Lord Dashlend. He claimed the lord judged very severely on physicality. He was a Corinthian of the first stare and compared everything to that. The way she moved in the world was her primary fault! How could she hide it?

Grace could, perhaps, hide it for now. She'd not given anything away yet. But that could not hold forever. So many times in the past, when she'd least expected it, that swimming feeling would come over her. She'd be getting out of the carriage for church and suddenly find herself on the ground. Or even just walking into a room with nothing at all amiss. She'd got rather skilled at dropping without injuring herself.

In any case, her father had already told Lord Dashlend that she was clumsy. Perhaps seeing it was not even necessary.

He was coming to dine this evening. Would he be examining her for signs of clumsiness? Did he like her enough to overlook it?

There was a short rap on the door and Mrs. Right hurried in. "Have you decided on a dress?" she asked.

Grace of course had. There was nothing she'd given as much thought to. She'd been thinking about it ever since Lord Dashlend had accepted her papa's invitation.

She nodded toward the bed where it was laid out.

"Ah, the violet silk with the tulle overlay. Excellent choice, it will do something well for your coloring. Now, tell me what's on your mind," Mrs. Right said. "You've got that worried look on your face that used to tell me, when you were a little girl, that you'd broken something."

Mrs. Right could always see straight into all of their hearts. And really, it was a relief to be asked.

"Last evening, Lord Montclave, who is Lord Dashlend's cousin and lives on a neighboring estate, so he knows Lord Dashlend ever so well, he said…"

Grace drifted off. She did not even like to speak aloud what he'd said.

"What did he say?"

"He said that Lord Dashlend, being the Corinthian that he is, holds physicality as superior to all else. Lord Montclave has argued against that opinion to no avail."

"Has he now?" Mrs. Right said, narrowing her eyes.

"Yes, indeed, that is what he said. And Mrs. Right, you know my particular situation. My particular… flaw. It is precisely what Lord Dashlend will not like." Grace paused to wring her hands, which she'd done quite a lot of all day. "I ought not to like him as he will be so inclined to not like me, and yet I do. I really cannot help it. I met no end of gentlemen last evening and all I could think was, they were not Lord Dashlend."

"Lord Montclave made a point to inform you of this?" Mrs. Right said thoughtfully.

"He did, though I cannot think how the subject came up."

"Here's my advice—do not pay any mind to Lord Montclave. Form your opinions through your own eyes and ears. It's my experience that a gentleman wishing to impress often takes the low road of trying to make other fellows less appealing than they are."

"You think Lord Montclave might have invented what he told me?"

"Might have. We'll see."

"But that would be so underhanded, so base, so ungentlemanly."

Mrs. Right shrugged. "All's fair in love and war, as they say. Before I wed, I had another suitor besides my Charlie. Mr. Winchum was his name and he told me, quite confidentially of course, that my Charlie only had three toes on his right foot. Well, I wasn't put off, mind, as who goes round staring at a person's toes anyway? When the time came, I did have a peek and wouldn't you know—all five were present and accounted for."

"Mr. Winchum must have been terribly embarrassed that you eventually found out his fib."

"Oh yes, whenever I saw him, I waved at him by wiggling all five of my fingers. He got my meaning. Now, we'd best get you dressed and downstairs, as Felicity and Mr. Stratton are to come early."

Mr. Stratton was to look over her calendar to ensure she had not made any mistakes like she'd done with Lord Doanellen's dinner.

Grace hurried into her dress and Mrs. Right did the buttons up the back. She fussed with the tulle until it was laying right and it really did look charming.

Grace was out the door and down the stairs in good time. She found Valor pacing the drawing room with a rather wild look on her face. She had a letter in one hand, and Mrs. Wendover swinging from the other. Nelson seemed to take the whole thing as a game and made little leaps at Mrs. Wendover, between losing his balance and rolling on the carpet.

"Grace, I am stunned," Valor said. "Lady Margaret and I are friends and we correspond, as you may know. I maintain a correspondence now like any grown lady does. She told me to write about anything I liked and so I did and she has just wrote me back. I am shocked to my shoes."

Grace stood frozen where she stood. Was it something about Lord Dashlend? What could it be? What would Lady Margaret write about? What could be shocking and stunning? Was it news of an engagement?

"I have been looking at things all wrong," Valor said, throwing up her hands. The letter flew one way and Mrs. Wendover flew the other way. Mrs. Wendover was not long on the carpet as Nelson grabbed her by the neck and returned her to Valor, wagging his tail and hoping for another throw.

"What?" Grace asked. "What has so affected you?"

"I wrote to her about how I have nightmares about monsters or I wake in the night and think there is a monster in my room or under my bed. Guess what she says?"

Grace allowed herself to breathe again. It was not an engagement. She could not give a toss for what Lady Margaret had to say about monsters. It was nothing to do with Lord Dashlend. "I have no idea. What does Lady Margaret say about it?"

"She says they are like village boys who like to bully but if you laugh at them and tell them to be off, they run away ashamed of themselves. Then, while they are running away, you tell them you are going to talk to the vicar about their behavior and they will not dare to come back. They are terrified of the church—it is their great weakness."

"Yes, indeed, that does make sense," Grace said, biting her lip to stop her laughter.

"Why didn't anybody tell me! How many hours of sleep have I lost? Mrs. Right doesn't know, else she would have said. Wait until I tell her, she will be just as shocked as Mrs. Wendover was."

Fortunately, Grace was not pressed to explain why nobody had told Valor of the unique weaknesses of monsters until this late date. Mr. Button announced Felicity and Mr. Stratton.

"Felicity!" Valor cried, throwing herself at her eldest sister. "You've been gone from us for so long!"

"I know, poppet," Felicity said. "Grace, how do you get on?"

Grace kissed her sister's cheek. "Perhaps I save that description for a confidential conversation," she said. "Mr. Stratton, how do you do?"

Mr. Stratton bowed and said, "Married life suits me, so I do very well. Now, as we are relations, you ought to just call me Stratton."

Grace nodded, though she could not quite imagine doing so. "You are very kind to agree to look through my calendar."

"Not at all." Mr. Stratton paused and peered at Nelson.

"Gracious," Felicity said, "you've got a three-legged dog."

"And blind in one eye," Valor said proudly.

"Of course you do," Mr. Stratton said, laughing. "I suppose we ought to get to your calendar before Dashlend arrives."

"Oh yes, it is just here, along with some invitations I've yet to do anything with."

Grace and Stratton sat across from each other and laid the calendar out on a table. While they reviewed the invitations she had accepted and opened the pile just arrived, Valor gave Felicity a full accounting of her new understanding of monsters. Nelson sat at Felicity's feet, seeming very taken with this new arrival to the house.

It was not long before the rest of the sisters arrived. Valor informed them of the information she had received regarding the nature of monsters. Naturally, Verity nodded sagely and said it was commonly understood. She was less successful in answering why she'd never bothered to mention it if she'd known it all along.

Verity dodged that question by turning the subject to Felicity. Their eldest sister was surrounded and peppered with questions regarding married life. Some of the questions made Mr. Stratton downright blush, though he pretended not to hear.

Was it genial to wake up and find a gentleman had been in the room all night? Did he stare at you while you were sleeping? Had Felicity seen Mr. Stratton's scars from the tiger, as they were under his clothes? Would she have a baby soon? Had Mr. Stratton seen Felicity's hair unpinned and what did he think about it?

Felicity answered with all good humor. It was very genial to wake to somebody in the room, she did not know if he stared as she was asleep, she had seen the scars and they were terribly attractive, she did not know when she would have a baby but not in the next months, and Mr. Stratton had seen her hair unpinned and thought it smashing.

Mr. Stratton, while not always enthusiastic to see the duke, did seem to welcome the interruption of this sisterly discussion on the finer points of marriage.

"Ho there, Stratton," the duke said, "I hope you keep my girl happy?"

"I do my best, Your Grace," Mr. Stratton said.

Felicity kissed her father's cheek and said, "He does very well, Papa."

"He's seen Felicity's hair unpinned and thinks it's smashing," Valor put in for good measure. "Though we don't know if he stares at her in her sleep."

The duke merely raised his brows, rather than answer, as a father cannot be expected to inquire into such matters.

"How goes it with the calendar, Stratton?" the duke asked. "Have we committed ourselves to any more shocking evenings?"

"No, there is nothing to worry over. Some I may have passed on, only because they may be dull, but everything is very respectable. I did wonder though, why you sent your regrets to all the evenings that showcase the musical talents of the ladies new to the season?"

The duke looked over Mr. Stratton's head. The sisters all looked at each other wide-eyed.

Felicity said, "That sort of evening is not really the right showcase for us."

"Oh I see," Mr. Stratton said. "We do not have a pianoforte in the cottage, so I hadn't known."

"We should never get one," Felicity said.

Mr. Stratton took in the idea that none of them could play a note, which had heretofore escaped his notice. Mr. Button announced Lord Dashlend and Lady Margaret.

While it might be usual for the duke to step forward in greeting first, Valor pushed past him. "My friend Lady Margaret," she said, grasping the lady's hands, "you have done me a real service—all this information about monsters is very good to know."

"Ah yes, it is always an advantage to know who or what you deal with," Lady Margaret said.

Grace's eyes traveled between Lord Dashlend and Lady Margaret. Lord Dashlend was looking very well put together. His coat was well-cut and his neckcloth was neatly done. The lord went in for a clean and unfussy style—he did not pretend at being a dandy, and yet his clothes were impeccable.

Lady Margaret, on the other hand, was looking rather surprising. She wore a purple brocade dress with crinolines underneath, and her hair was piled high atop her head and held in place by a bright green silk turban that sported a heavy diamond broach.

"All right now, Valor," the duke said jovially, moving his youngest daughter out of the way. He greeted Lord Dashlend with a joke about the shipwreck and bowed to Lady Margaret.

"Ah, Duke," Lady Margaret said, dispensing with the need to address him as Your Grace, "I've been very interested to make your acquaintance."

"Have you now? I can't think why."

"I've heard you're a bit of a corker," Lady Margaret said.

This set the duke into roars of laughter. "Very good, very good," he said, catching his breath.

Lord Dashlend and Mr. Stratton greeted one another, as they were previously known to each other. Then Lord Dashlend very kindly mentioned all of her sisters' names before bowing and saying, "Lady Grace, you are looking very well."

Grace bobbed a curtsy. She was looking very well, he said.

"Well, Mr. Button," the duke said to the butler, "are we ready to go through, no sense in dilly-dallying about it."

"Yes, Your Grace," Mr. Button said.

The duke put his arm out for Lady Margaret and led her through. As he did so, he said, "He's the butler at the moment. No idea how long he'll be here."

Mr. Button's eyes widened. Then they widened a bit more as Lady Margaret said, "At least he's alive. Mine has been dead for months."

CHAPTER ELEVEN

M ILES HAD TO give the duke credit—while the gentleman held no compunction over joking about Miles shipwrecking his boat, he'd not shown a flicker of surprise over Lady Margaret's appearance.

He certainly must have been surprised. The turban had been a new and alarming addition to her repertoire. It was not so much the idea that she wore a turban. It was that it was an eye-popping shade of green silk while her dress was bright purple brocade that billowed out in all directions as if her maid had put her into every crinoline in London. When he'd first spotted her coming down the stairs, he had the impression of Lunardi's hydrogen balloon being filled for its flight.

In the carriage, he'd even floated the idea of hiring a dressmaker, but Lady Margaret said the older styles suited her, as Lord Harraby had rightly pointed out.

Lady Grace, on the other hand, looked perfection. She wore a violet silk dress with a delicate tulle overlay in the same shade, embellished with silver thread using a restrained hand. Her blond curls were wrestled into order, though some of the bolder of their number had escaped their pins. Her eyes sparkled and her cheeks bloomed. There could not be a prettier lady in all London.

He was placed on Lady Felicity's right, as she would hostess for the duke. Lady Grace was on Miles' other side. Lady Margaret was to the duke's right, with Lady Valor on her other side.

Miles had not thought the younger sisters would be at table, but then he supposed the duke did not constrain himself to any preconceived notions on how things were done. In any other house, the younger girls who were not out would be taking their dinner above stairs with a governess. Nobody not closely associated with the family would likely be aware of their existence until they were older. As far as he knew, the duke did not even employ a governess. Just a rather frightening house-keeper who had no use for a butler.

"Lord Dashlend," Lady Grace said, "you mentioned you were to dine with one of your father's oldest friends last evening. I pray it was enjoyable."

It was a perfectly polite question and Miles intended to an-swer it perfectly politely, though it would not be a truthful answer. "Yes, it was very enjoyable. May I ask how you found Lady Luthering's ball?"

"Oh very nice," Lady Grace said. She paused and then said, "Your cousin was there. Lord Montclave. He took me into supper."

"Did he," Miles said. He found he did not like that idea at all. Montclave was no gentleman for a lady like Lady Grace. Montclave was no gentleman, period.

Lady Grace nodded. "He spoke of you, actually."

"I do not know why he should," Miles said, careful to keep utter disdain from his tone.

"I am not entirely certain why he did either," Lady Grace said.

There was something sad in the way she said it. What had Montclave said about him?

Before he could press for an answer, the sound of the door knocker being soundly rapped was heard in the dining room. Mr. Button directed the footman to continue serving and hurried out to the front hall.

Shortly after, a matron's raised voice was heard by everyone at table.

"Never fear, Mr. Button, I have received your communication, and I have come to sort out this shameful situation."

The sound of the voice seemed to send chills down the spines of the ladies at table. Lady Valor disappeared under it with her rather worn-out stuffed rabbit.

The duke took a long swig of wine and said, "Lady Misery has arrived. We are in for it now!"

For some reason, the duke seemed to think the idea vastly amusing.

"It is Lady Marchfield, my aunt," Lady Grace said softly.

"Why does everyone seem to be so stricken over her arrival?" Miles whispered.

"We told her the wrong day for the dinner," Lady Grace said. "She was told it was to be on the morrow. She is on the verge of discovering the ruse."

To his other side, Lady Felicity, who had obviously overheard, said, "Oh my."

"She can be very cross," Lady Grace said, by way of explanation. "And so, when Verity said the wrong day, none of us corrected her."

Out in the hall, Mr. Button was speaking and Miles could tell he was speaking rapidly, but it was not so loud that he could make out the words.

He could hear Lady Marchfield's response, though.

"Lead me in, Mr. Button!"

"Here we go," the duke said, raising his glass as if there was cause for celebration.

Lady Marchfield stormed into the dining room. She halted, and Miles thought it took her a moment to comprehend what she was seeing. As far as he could gather, having been told the wrong day for the dinner was just now dawning on her.

"Roland," she said in a rather deadly tone, "step out into the hall for a moment."

"What now, Lady Misery? Say your piece, if you will—I need not get up on my feet for it."

"You will not like what I have to say in front of your guests."

"I never do like what you say!" the duke said, laughing at his own joke.

Lady Marchfield, who Miles was only vaguely acquainted with, looked as if her head would explode.

"Very well, you uncouth excuse for a duke," she said.

Miles dropped his fork. That was rather direct.

"Aside from hosting this dinner tonight, when I was told by your daughters that it was to be held on the morrow, I received this missive from Mr. Button."

She waved the letter back and forth threateningly.

"That woman has finally gone too far," Lady Marchfield said.

Who that woman was, Miles had not the first idea. Until he recalled that the duke's housekeeper had been dead set against having a butler in the house.

"Hand it over," the duke said. "Let me see what you've got yourself in a lather over."

Lady Marchfield practically threw it at the duke. He swept it up from the table and scanned it.

Then, inconceivably, the duke read it aloud.

Dear Lady Marchfield,

It is with deep regret and trepidation that I must communicate some very uncomfortable developments. Mrs. Right has taken to accusing me of improprieties. She refers to herself as an innocent maiden and trumps up wild accusations out of nowhere and always in front of the staff. She seems to have them all fairly bewitched, as they believe these outlandish claims.

I am not at all certain that this situation is tenable. I am not certain I can continue on in a household dominated by an aging matron who can convince the staff that I, or anybody, frankly, has designs on her. Personally, I have never had designs on any lady and if I did ever have designs, those designs would not be directed at Mrs. Right!

With all due respect,

Harold Button

The duke laid the letter on the table and heaved with laughter. He turned to the footmen. "Well? Has Mr. Button been making eyes at our Mrs. Right?"

One of the footmen shrugged and said, "That's what it looked like to us, Your Grace."

The other footman was biting his lip, had gone red in the face, and pinched his leg.

The duke's daughters attempted a bit more decorum, but as most of them had napkins firmly pressed over their mouths and shoulders shaking, he could guess they found the situation equally amusing.

"Designs on my housekeeper, Mr. Button?" the duke asked facetiously.

The youngest, Lady Valor, piped up from under the table. "What are designs?"

Lady Marchfield glared toward the area of the table that question had emanated from, seeming to just have comprehended that the empty chair had so recently been occupied by the youngest and that youngest had dived under the table at her approach.

Of all of them, Stratton seemed entirely unsurprised by this unusual scene.

The duke attempted to speak several times, but he could not manage it between gasps of laughter.

"Mr. Button," Lady Marchfield said gravely, "I had hoped that my brother would, for any better phrase for it, grow up. I had hoped he would finally become cognizant of his standing as a duke and the outrageousness of his housekeeper. That clearly is not to be. I cannot in good conscience leave you in this house. You will pack your things—I happen to know of a very good situation that has just come up and I will see that you get it! I will await you in my carriage."

With that, Lady Marchfield turned on her heel and stormed

out.

Mr. Button, who had lingered by the sideboard appearing unsure where the whole thing was going, suddenly puffed his chest out.

"Your Grace," he said, looking down his nose, "I give my resignation, effective this minute. Furthermore, you can tell that old harridan downstairs that neither I, nor anybody else in the world, will ever have designs on her. She can very safely leave her door unlocked for the rest of her days!"

Mr. Button strode from the room, head held high.

The duke finally caught his breath. "Au revoir, Mr. Button!" he called after the departing butler. He beamed round the table. "I suppose the moral of this story is one never knows where entertainment might come from."

Lady Margaret, who had been taking everything in, said, "Those two people seem very high-strung."

The duke nodded. "My sister is strung like a bow and ready to snap at any and all moments. She does not comprehend that I am beholden to nobody, including herself, and I am free to run my household as I see fit. That misconception provides for hours of amusement."

Lady Margaret nodded, as if this was an accepted fact. She pulled up the tablecloth and peered underneath it. "Come child, there is no cause to be hiding under there. The monsters are gone."

Lady Valor emerged. "What are designs?" she asked.

This caused the duke to heave with laughter all over again. Lady Margaret said, "Apparently, Mrs. Right has accused Mr. Button of attempting to court her."

Lady Valor collapsed in giggles. "That is so stupid, though. If she got married she would have to leave us—she would never do it!"

Miles supposed it was just as well that the accusations that had just flown around the dining room had gone over Lady Valor's head.

The footmen took up the service again, looking exceedingly cheerful.

The table returned to some semblance of normality for a half hour, but Miles was beginning to think normality could not hold in the duke's household.

Mr. Button's departure, which he chose to daringly do through the front doors rather than the servants' entrance, was capped off by the three-legged dog growling and biting at his pant leg. The dining room doors had been left open after his storming out of it and now everyone peered out to watch the butler struggle with the canine of the house.

Miles had no idea what was to come next, but Lady Winsome and Lady Patience had begun suggesting that when they were all gathered in the drawing room, they might play a game called Fact or Fib.

Stratton, who had been rather sanguine throughout the recent goings-on, began to look alarmed.

If Stratton was alarmed, Miles supposed he better be too.

He did not know what he'd been expecting from the Duke of Pelham's dinner, but it was rather more lively than he'd imagined.

MONTCLAVE HAD FOUND himself at loose ends this particular night. He was received in some houses, but not every house. The high and mighty took little notice of a country baron and it was probably a further strike against him that he currently resided in Lord Doanellen's house.

He might have wiled away the time drinking Doanellen's brandy, but Mrs. Featherby was fluttering round the house, making things uncomfortable.

With no money in his pocket and no club to go to, he had contemplated walking the streets for a few hours. With any luck, he could return home to find Mrs. Featherby retired for the evening.

As he mulled over which direction to walk, he recalled it was the night of the Duke of Pelham's dinner. Dashlend and Lady Grace would be in the same house together for an extended period of time. As long as he was walking somewhere, why did he not walk to Grosvenor Square and see what he could see?

He might see nothing at all, but then there were times when the servants forgot to pull the curtains at sunset or closed them but left a gap. Especially when the house was sent topsy-turvy over an entertainment to be hosted. If he understood servants at all, it was that they silently resented the extra work of it, and that brand of resentment showed itself in things being not exactly as precise as they should be.

Though, even if the duke's servants were scrupulous and made no small mistakes to express their dissatisfaction, it gave him a direction that did not feel entirely pointless.

Montclave strode through the dark streets and arrived at the square not a quarter hour later. He slipped into the shadows as the duke's door had just been flung open. Lady Marchfield came steaming out of it and got into her carriage.

She did not immediately depart though.

Why was she just sitting there? Had somebody said something to offend her and she'd made a dramatic exit and now waited for the duke to beg her pardon and lead her back into the house? If she planned to go, why did she not go? He wished she'd move on, as the drawing room curtains had been left open. There was nothing to see at the moment, as he supposed they were all still in the dining room, but there would be.

Montclave climbed the fence into the square, where he might be better hidden amongst the foliage. He would like to light a cigar, but that would give him away to the watchmen.

Over a half hour must have passed and Montclave was beginning to think this was how it would be for the rest of the evening. Lady Marchfield sitting in her carriage and himself hiding in bushes.

But then, the duke's door flew open once more. A man who must certainly be the butler was attempting to shake off a dog who'd got hold of his pant leg. The three-legged dog he'd heard about from Lady Grace.

The fellow had a portmanteau in one hand. He finally did shake off the dog and shut the door behind him. Inexplicably, he got into Lady Marchfield's carriage and they set off.

What in the world did he just witness? Was Lady Marchfield having some sort of assignation with a butler?

No, that could not be it. For one, it was Lady Marchfield. Montclave doubted she even tolerated assignations with her own husband. And two, if a butler were to slip away on account of a lady, he would hardly do it in the middle of a dinner and through the front doors.

It was mystifying. It was also interesting. He did not know if there was anything to be done with the information. However, he *did* know he would not have the information if he'd stayed at home to listen to Mrs. Featherby's inane blathering. How long could that lady talk about the charming, enameled pin she'd seen at Rundell & Bridge before Doanellen went and bought it for her? If he had any money himself, he'd buy it for her just to shut her up about it.

Montclave made himself as comfortable as he could. Sooner or later, the duke's guests would enter the drawing room. He did not know what he would see, but he could not have predicted Lady Marchfield making off with the duke's butler, so anything was possible.

An hour later, the drawing room was lit up with candles and the ladies entered it. Inexplicably, one of the ladies was Lady Margaret.

What was she doing there?

LADY FELICITY HAD led the ladies from the dining room. Now Miles, Stratton, and the duke were left to their port.

"We will not stay long, gentlemen," the duke said. "Eh, Stratton? He knows how we do it—a half glass here and then I'll bring the bottle into the drawing room."

Miles attempted to cover his surprise at the idea, though he'd seen the same done at the inn. He supposed Lady Margaret would not mind it; she'd probably help herself.

Stratton only nodded. "You'll be grateful for a drink, Dashlend. I heard mention of Fact or Fib."

"Yes, what is that game, exactly?" Miles asked. "I do not believe I am familiar with it."

The duke laughed surprisingly heartily at that inquiry. "It is a chance for my daughters to quiz you mercilessly, denounce you as a fibber if you do not answer the way they wish you to, and trounce you at it. You cannot win, therefore it's best to just pour a deep glass and let them have their way."

Miles looked to Stratton, who nodded sadly. "They'll ask you questions, then they decide if it is a fact or a fib. Doesn't really matter if they're right—they decide. Then they'll give you a ticket—blue for fib and yellow for fact. Two yellow tickets wins the game, but a blue ticket cancels a yellow ticket."

"Don't even bother attempting to keep track of it, you'll be drowning in blue tickets no matter what you do," the duke said.

"They can ask anything at all?" Miles asked. It sounded as if it could get very personal.

Stratton nodded. "I am fully prepared to be asked if I stare at my wife while she's sleeping. I do not, by the by. Not often, anyway."

The duke chuckled. "We put old Stratton through the mangle last year. I thought he might jump out the nearest window."

"I might have, had one been open."

"Well," the duke said in a genial tone, "if a gentleman has not got enough stalwartness in him, he's got no business in this house."

Miles did not comment, but he thought that must be true. It was only a dinner, and yet he'd seen a matron barge in and name the host "an uncouth excuse for a duke," a letter written by the butler was read at the table, accusing the housekeeper of delusions in matters of the heart, the butler had dramatically exited from the house while shaking off a three-legged dog, and now he had Fact or Fib hanging over his head.

Being lost at sea was not as harrowing.

"What's it to be, Dashlend?" the duke asked. "Are you to make a run at my Grace?"

Miles was momentarily stunned. Make a run? Did he inquire into Miles' intentions? He had not set any intentions yet. Not firmly. Or maybe a little firmly but not written in stone. Not yet.

"Do not answer him, Dashlend," Stratton counseled.

"Hah!" the duke cried. "Stratton begins to know me too well! No matter, we ought to rejoin the ladies. I'll bring the bottle, you two bring your glasses." The duke paused. "Ought I to bring in a glass for Lady Margaret? My instincts tell me she would not be opposed."

"That is very astute, Your Grace. Though, I believe the lady prefers brandy."

"Charlie?" the duke said. "See to it. You'll need to be on your toes now that we've sent Mr. Button packing."

"Yes, Your Grace," Charlie said, seeming delighted.

Miles took a deep breath. He was to go in and face Fact or Fib. Afterward, he was to lead a tipsy elderly lady to his carriage, get her in there, and then make certain she reached her bedchamber without breaking her neck on the stairs on account of wine and brandy. He must bring all his stalwartness to bear.

CHAPTER TWELVE

GRACE HAD BEEN pleased that Lady Margaret had made it a point of taking her aside in the drawing room and making various sorts of comments and asking questions, all of them round the subject of Lord Dashlend.

Her sisters were all in a corner, conspiring together on what sorts of questions they would pepper Lord Dashlend and Mr. Stratton with. Even Felicity was in on it.

Lady Margaret said, "I always wonder, when two people have met under extraordinary circumstances, if fate did not have a hand in it."

Grace had wondered just the same, though the vicar had often railed against praying for things like love and luck—he said God had more pressing matters to attend to.

"I suppose he looked a very interesting picture, emerging from the sea," Lady Margaret said.

"Very dashing," Grace admitted.

"And there you were, a regular Queen Boudica, bravely facing the elements to rescue him."

Grace felt her eyes go a bit wide at that picture. There had not been any particular elements to face and she'd been there with her family. She really could not claim any resemblance to Queen Boudica.

"He told me your eyes were olive-colored, and that it lent a sophistication to your appearance," Lady Margaret said.

"Did he? Did he say that?"

Lady Margaret nodded.

Just then, the drawing room doors opened. The duke had not kept the gentlemen long at their port. As was his usual habit, her papa had brought the bottle in with him.

"Lady Margaret," the duke said, "I've sent for the brandy decanter. I think you will not be opposed?"

"Gracious no," Lady Margaret said. "These old bones do need to be greased up on occasion."

"We ought to get started," Patience said. "Else Valor gets too tired to play."

"I am not tired," Valor said.

"No, but you will be."

Valor sighed, as if she was much put upon. "It is one of the problems of youth—I *do* get sleepy!"

Patience set the piles of blue and yellow tickets on an ottoman and dragged it to the center of the room.

The footman returned and poured a modest amount of brandy into a glass for Lady Margaret. Then he noticed the lady frowning at it and topped it up.

Valor was waving her hand back and forth at the duke.

"All right, all right, Valor is to go first," the duke said.

"Mr. Stratton," Valor said, "do you stare at Felicity when she's sleeping?"

Mr. Stratton seemed not the least bit alarmed to be asked. He nodded, "Only once or twice."

"Fibber!" Verity cried. "We already talked about it and we are sure it is at least three times."

Felicity giggled and handed her husband a blue ticket. "In the hole already, my love."

They moved round the circle to Winsome. "Lord Dashlend, what was the first thing you noticed about our Grace?"

Though Grace had expected the question, or something very like it, it was still painfully embarrassing.

"Oh, well, let us see," Lord Dashlend said. "I suppose it must have been her eyes."

"Liar!" Winsome, Verity, Patience and Serenity cried.

"It was her hair," Winsome said. "Everybody knows it."

"Well of course, that is very good too," Lord Dashlend said.

Grace thought she might die of embarrassment. But then, she also could not help but to be flattered by his noticing her eyes. Lady Margaret had said as much.

How funny it should be her eyes. All her life, she'd thought she'd been somehow cheated out of a blue color. She'd thought blue superior. Now she understood that Lord Dashlend did not find blue superior.

"I'll go, I'll go," Patience said. "Grace, what was the first thing you noticed about Lord Dashlend?"

Grace had been fully expecting the question and had, therefore, composed an answer.

"Well, I would say his bearing. I was certain he was a gentleman, even though he was washed up on the beach with no coat."

The sisters stared at each other, as if attempting to decide whether the answer would be a fact or fib. Serenity said softly, "I thought it would be his hair, he has very good hair."

The other sisters nodded.

"It must be true, though," Verity said. "Grace is very bad at fibbing."

"Fact!" Valor said, handing Grace a yellow ticket.

"Duke," Lady Margaret said, downing her brandy. "I have one—what is it you wish for your daughters?"

"That is all too easy, Lady Margaret," the duke said. "I hope to get every last one of them out of my house with all speed."

The shouts of fibber echoed throughout the room and the duke was promptly in possession of a blue ticket.

"This is how it starts, Dashlend," the duke said. "They get you in the hole and you can never get out."

This earned the duke a second blue ticket, though it was perfectly true.

The game went merrily on until Valor fell to a sulk over not being asked anything. Then the duke asked her if she was overtired. She said she'd never felt more awake in her life and was instantly named a fibber.

Mrs. Right came to collect her and take her to bed. Valor delivered a pretty curtsy to Lord Dashlend and she held Lady Margaret's hand and said, "Goodnight, my friend. I am almost done writing you a letter and I'll send it to you first thing in the morning. Also, Mrs. Wendover sends her deepest regards."

"What a charming young person," Lady Margaret said after she'd gone. "Well now, after that brandy I find I am quite in my cups. Dashlend, be so good as to call the carriage, and then pour me into it."

MONTCLAVE HAD WATCHED as the gentlemen entered the duke's drawing room. In that first moment, he'd thought they did not stay very long over their port. But then, he noticed they all held glasses and the duke had a bottle in his other hand.

He supposed that was one of the advantages of being a duke. One might look over the various rules and procedures of society and discard them at will. He would not mind having that sort of power himself.

What followed was a game of some sort. It involved bits of blue and yellow colored paper and Montclave had no idea what game it was. All he could tell from it was that men got the majority of the blue tickets, while the ladies received mostly yellow tickets. Whatever it was, they seemed to find it very jolly.

It was rather too comfortable a scene. It was only the duke's extended family attending this dinner, but for Dashlend and Lady Margaret. Even Lady Marchfield had attended, which gave some sort of societal stamp of approval. Though, he might never be able to work out why she'd left early with the butler in tow.

When Dashlend and Lady Margaret departed, he'd wondered

if his cousin was somehow keeping the lady inebriated to gain her cooperation in some matter. Dashlend had supported her and then picked her up and put her in the carriage, as she did not seem as if she could do it herself. Perhaps the devil had designs on her house or hoped to be the sole benefactor of her will?

Worse, Lady Grace and a slew of sisters had followed them out to the pavement. Dashlend paid his compliments to them and then said, "Until tomorrow at Almack's."

As far as he could gather, they'd had some conversation about meeting there for the Wednesday ball. It was aggravating in the extreme, as none of those idiot patronesses had ever seen fit to send *him* a voucher, and certainly would not countenance it while he resided in Doanellen's house. He'd already heard both Doanellen and Mrs. Featherby complain about it. Doanellen got one every year, but for this one. Mrs. Featherby claimed the patronesses were jealous.

The patronesses were many things, but jealous of Mrs. Featherby was not on that list.

Montclave watched the carriage set off and then jogged behind it, staying a good distance from it and keeping to the shadows so that he would not be spotted. He was determined to discover where Lady Margaret would be taken.

Then he did discover it. Lady Margaret was just now living in Dashlend's house. Why, though? Was he after Lady Margaret's money himself? Or had Dashlend somehow discovered that he, himself, had pressed Lady Margaret for money? It would be just like Dashlend to spitefully cut off that avenue of funds. That fellow would like it all too well if he were forced to return home for lack of it.

Montclave had slowly walked back to Bolton Street, considering his options. Dashlend was getting too cozy with Lady Grace. Dashlend had somehow moved their elderly cousin, Lady Margaret, into his house and out of reach.

He must get control of the situation. But how to do it?

Montclave was certain he would find no success in wooing

Lady Grace unless she had firmly turned from Dashlend. That had to be accomplished first.

The most effective thing would be to convince Lady Grace that Dashlend preferred some other lady. There was nothing a woman despised more than to understand someone else was preferred. It put a woman's back up like nothing else could.

Should he start a rumor?

No, that was too dangerous. If he sent round the idea that Dashlend was pursuing some lady or other, it would be well to remember that the lady had a father who would not be amused. That father would work very hard to discover the source of such talk.

He was not so stupid as to find himself on an early morning green, facing an outraged father.

The knowledge of Dashlend's supposed preference must be subtly communicated to Lady Grace herself, not gossiped about all over Town.

Then it came to him, as the right idea always did when he kept his thoughts moving forward.

He would send two sets of flowers to Lady Grace. Only, one of those bouquets would appear to be mistakenly delivered. It would seem as if Dashlend had ordered two arrangements and the florist had made a mistake in the addresses to be used.

Both of the bouquets would arrive to the duke's house, both would be from Dashlend. The one with the note for Lady Grace would be something pedestrian that indicated mild friendship. The one addressed to the duke's house but with a note for another lady, Lady Lavender perhaps, would send the message of love.

Montclave paused, smiling into the night air. It would not only point to love, but there must be some hint toward Lady Grace's insecurity. It must point out the other lady's skill on a ballroom floor, perhaps.

Lady Grace would see that Dashlend sent his love to another lady, and it had only been the florist's mistake to wrongly deliver the bouquet. She would feel she had discovered a secret, and it was not a secret that favored her.

There was only one flaw in the plan that he could see. What if Lady Grace were to order the flowers for the other lady forwarded on to their right destination?

That could be managed. She would not send them directly. She would send the flowers back to the florist, as what else could she do? It would be too humiliating to send them on to the lady, explaining what had happened. He could arrange things with the florist. He'd pay extra for the florist to take them back and forward them nowhere. Any florist would be happy with that proposal, as he could resell the flowers.

He must just find a florist who would take him on account.

Montclave whistled the rest of the way to Lord Doanellen's house, satisfied that he was about to shake things up. When they settled, they were bound to settle in his favor.

GRACE HAD THOUGHT she might like to skip an appearance at Almack's altogether. After all, her father was agreeable to forgo it as he did not care for the patronesses' idea of supper. He further thought it was not at all a necessary appearance for a duke's daughter—they needed nobody's approval. As for Grace, herself, she felt she did not require so many elevated matrons' eyes examining her dancing and its grace. Or lack of it.

But then, Lord Dashlend had said he would attend and asked if she would too. Of course she would go. She would jump up and down in her bedchamber to steady herself, and then she would go.

If only the rules were not so strict. If only she could swan in, dance with Lord Dashlend and ignore everybody else.

She had made her curtsy to the patronesses, who had none too subtly inquired why they had not seen her the week before.

Her dear papa explained that Grace had been struck down with a cold and did not wish to displease the ladies by appearing with a red nose.

They all nodded in sympathy and approval, as evidently a red nose would have been ill-received.

As they left the matrons behind, her father whispered, "As deep and thoughtful as rain puddles, that lot."

Then, there he was, waiting by the cloak room. Lord Dashlend was waiting for her. She was certain that was what had brought him there.

He bowed. "Your Grace, Lady Grace."

"Well met, Dashlend," the duke said. "Now, I will give you a hint before you put your name down on my daughter's card—we will on no account stay for that ridiculous excuse for a supper."

"I see," Lord Dashlend said. "Then I'd better take the first, if Lady Grace is agreeable."

"I am most agreeable," Grace said in a rush, and likely far too enthusiastically.

Lord Dashlend smiled. He penciled in his name and handed her a card as her father handed her cloak to a footman. "I took the liberty of retrieving a card."

"Very efficient, Dashlend," the duke said, laughing.

It *was* very efficient, Grace thought. And certainly it must be more evidence of his interest.

"Here we are," her sister Felicity said, approaching them. She was accompanied by Mr. Stratton, who was looking in high spirits.

"My dear wife informed me that we must turn up in force once she was apprised that Lady Grace would attend this evening," Mr. Stratton said. "Well, Dashlend, you survived Fact or Fib, so I suppose you can stand up to anything now."

Lord Dashlend laughed. "A most interesting game," he said.

"Will we see Lady Margaret?" Felicity asked.

This seemed to give Lord Dashlend pause. Then he said, "You would be hard-pressed to miss her, I think. Lord Harraby brings her." At the mention of those two people, Grace saw the lord's eyes widen as he looked past her. Softly, he said, "It is more astonishing than my imagination could conjure."

Grace peeked over her shoulder. There indeed was Lady Margaret. Lord Harraby escorted her forward as she left a line of stunned patronesses in her wake. The lady had seemed to reach very far back into her wardrobe and retrieved a yellow striped damask gown with a short train that was lifted on either side to give the lady the appearance of her hips being four times their usual width.

"Here we go," the duke said, chuckling. "She's gone for panniers."

Lord Harraby looked exceedingly proud to lead Lady Margaret through the throng, making way for her. It was well he did, as the lady did need room to get through.

"Here we all are," Lady Margaret said. "Goodness, it is rather wonderful to have so many friends these days. My social calendar has really filled up."

Grace could not help but be charmed by the lady, regardless of what interesting fashion she chose to wear.

"When I set eyes on Lady Margaret this evening," Lord Harraby said, "I was transported back to my youth."

Lady Margaret fanned herself. "Lord Harraby is most considerate of me. He has hired a giant of a fellow to carry me in and out of his carriage."

"The lady deserves nothing less!" Lord Harraby said.

Grace thought that was a very sensible idea, as she did not see how Lord Harraby would accomplish the operation on his own. Especially not with the oversized dimensions of her dress.

"Lord Dashlend," Lady Margaret said, "I wonder if you would retrieve a card for me."

Lord Dashlend looked taken aback. "Ah, I see, you will dance?"

"Only the first with Lord Harraby," Lady Margaret said. "He was quite insistent, you see. Look, I brought my dance fan."

Lady Margaret unfurled a fan that had perhaps seen better days. It was covered in tiny writing, each fold outlining the dance steps for… dances that had been popular long ago.

"We've poured over it," Lord Harraby said, jerking a thumb toward the fan, "it all came back to us as if it were yesterday."

"I feel quite up to tossing aside my cane and taking to the floor, but perhaps I ought to save my steps," Lady Margaret said.

"I'm saving my steps too," Lord Harraby noted, no doubt the reason why somebody else must retrieve the lady's card. "Your Grace, if you might carry those two chairs over there into the ballroom, we will sit until it is time for us to go forward in the endeavor."

With that, the couple toddled off toward the ballroom.

Her father snorted and motioned to Mr. Stratton. They picked up two chairs that sat against the wall and followed the couple.

Lord Dashlend held out his arms to Grace and Felicity. "Shall we follow this circus?"

Grace laughed. "I feel we ought to ensure we are in Lady Margaret's vicinity, in case she or Lord Harraby require assistance of some sort. I am rather afraid they will not know the steps."

"Indeed, or have the stamina they are hoping for. Lady Margaret is my relation and living in my house, I must be certain she comes out of this unscathed. Let us keep the couple nearby the chairs Lord Harraby very boldly ordered the duke to carry in, lest they require them at some point."

"I do so like interesting people," Felicity said.

Lord Dashlend laughed and they followed their party into the ballroom.

The duke and Mr. Stratton had already situated Lady Margaret and Lord Harraby in their chairs. Lord Harraby looked longingly in Lady Margaret's direction as he seemed to be sitting further away from her than he would like. However, her panniers demanded their own space.

The musicians were already tuning and the ball would soon

begin.

"Lady Grace, Lord Dashlend, Your Grace," Lady Lavender said, approaching them.

"Lady Lavender, well met," Lord Dashlend said. "Do you know Mr. Stratton and Lady Felicity?"

"I've not had the honor," Mr. Stratton said with a bow.

"A pleasure, Mr. Stratton, Lady Felicity."

"Goodness, you are pretty," Felicity said. "I suppose you must be this season's diamond of the first water." She looked mischievously at her husband and Mr. Stratton had the good grace to pink. When his unusual courtship of Felicity had begun, he'd pointed out another lady as the season's diamond of the first water. Felicity had inquired why she was not thus named and Mr. Stratton had very ill-advisedly told her she could be a diamond of the second water—things had gone downhill from there.

Lady Lavender was looking elegant and graceful and all the things Lady Lavender was. She really was a diamond of the first water. Lord Dashlend was penciling in his name on her card, which very ridiculously gave Grace a pang. What else was he to do?

She did not know what he'd put himself down for, but she dearly hoped they would not dine together. Her papa might disdain the patronesses' offerings at table, but it did permit for extended conversation.

Grace had never viewed herself as a lady who would fall victim to jealousy and envy, but whatever she felt just now, it was very like those two things.

The musicians gave the signal that the ball was to begin. Lady Lavender's first partner came to collect her. Lord Harraby pulled Lady Margaret from her chair and she boldly flung away her cane. That item hit Lord Rasherby in the legs, but she did not seem to notice.

Lord Dashlend led Grace to their places.

The Duchess of Devonshire called the dance and the orchestra struck up. What followed was not a moment in time that

Grace would soon forget.

Lady Margaret and Lord Harraby had no acquaintance whatsoever with the steps. This seemed to occur to them rather rapidly. Lady Margaret shrugged, Lord Harraby smiled. Then they proceeded to execute steps that had no relation whatsoever to what had been called, or the tempo being played. Grace presumed they were the steps memorized from a fold on her fan.

That, in itself, might not have posed an unsurmountable problem. That was, had those two people been in the ballroom alone. They were not, however.

Dancers dodged them, stared at them, leapt out of the way of Lady Margaret's panniers, and some even kindly attempted to do something like the steps they were staggering through. Grace's part of the line of dancers had devolved into some sort of unmanageable chaos, the only people seeming not to notice being the elderly couple who caused it.

Lord Dashlend had just grabbed her hand and pulled her out of the way of another surge forward by Lord Harraby. They both began to laugh uncontrollably. It was too ridiculous.

It was not many minutes, though, when it became apparent that Lady Margaret and Lord Harraby began to run out of steam.

As they attempted some sort of allemande, Lord Harraby shouted, "What do you think, my springtime? Have we acquitted ourselves?"

"Yes, indeed," Lady Margaret said, "we have acquitted and now we may quit."

The couple unceremoniously staggered out of the line, sending the other dancers into further disarray. Both of them appeared none too steady on their feet. Lord Dashlend hurried after them and steadied Lady Margaret as Grace's father, who was guffawing at the whole spectacle, pushed forward a chair for Lord Harraby.

The couple sat down, heaving in breaths, as Lady Margaret's panniers spread out like a bird taking flight.

Lord Dashlend returned to her. "My apologies, Lady Grace."

"Whatever for, Lord Dashlend? If you can persevere through

Fact or Fib, I suppose I can do the same through… what this was."

They spent the rest of the dance laughing, though far more organized in their steps than they had been.

The rest of the ball was not half so interesting. Grace was engaged to dance with various gentlemen who were all very genial. They were not as genial as Lord Dashlend, however. She worked to make conversation and watch her steps so she did not falter, but spent more time looking at Lord Dashlend than anything else.

Sometimes he caught her looking and he smiled. Sometimes she caught *him* looking at her and *she* smiled. All in all, it was lovely.

CHAPTER THIRTEEN

MILES HAD NOT expected to see Lady Margaret in the breakfast room. So far, she had taken her morning meal while still abed, which was quite right for a lady of her age and station. Especially after last evening he did not expect her to be up and about so early. After she and Lord Harraby had staggered to their chairs, they sent the duke off to find them refreshments of the fortifying kind.

Aside from the preposterousness of sending the duke on errands as if he were their footman, the patronesses did not supply the sort of refreshments the couple was looking for. Fortunately, or unfortunately, depending on who was viewing it, the duke had come with his flask of brandy in his pocket. He'd retrieved two cups of punch and liberally dosed them.

It certainly raised their spirits, but Lord Harraby's burly hired man had been forced to enter the ballroom and carry Lady Margaret out, as there was not the least chance she would get out to the carriage under her own propulsion.

Miles had then carried her up the stairs and deposited her with her lady's maid.

Despite that adventure, Lady Margaret hurried in and perched on a chair. Wainwright poured her a cup of tea. She said, "As promised, I received a letter from Lady Valor first thing this morning."

Miles nodded, though he was at a loss as to why such a thing would be of interest to him.

"She spends the first part of the letter explaining how she's getting on with driving the monsters out of her room. It did not go as well as she'd hoped on her first run at it, it was not a complete triumph. The monsters did flee when ordered, but they gained a habit of creeping back in later. However, she realized it was because she was not being forceful enough."

"That all sounds very promising," Miles said, for lack of anything better to say.

"Yes, yes, but then we get to the second part of the letter. That part is all about *you*."

Miles set down his coffee. "She's written about me? Why? She does not still think I might be a murderer?"

Lady Margaret shook her head. "I will read it to you."

You are my wisest friend, so I wonder if you have any advice. Lord D seems nice enough for an older gentleman and I am convinced that I was wrong when I thought he might be a murderer. (Mrs. Wendover agrees with me. She says if he is a murderer, then why are we all still alive? I could not argue with that.)

"Older gentleman?" Miles asked.

"Yes, well, she is eight, so anybody over the age of fifteen is Methuselah to her. The good news is, you are no longer suspected of murder—Mrs. Wendover has pleaded your case. Now, let me continue."

Our Grace likes Lord D ever so well. She even likes his nose! Why? Nobody nose/knows. (That was a joke—I'm still laughing about it.)

I've seen this kind of liking before. Guess what happened last time? Felicity left us and now she lives forever with Mr. Stratton. (When she got married, nobody said it was permanent) So that's the problem—I want Grace to be happy, but I don't want her to leave like Felicity did.

What if all my sisters do that? I would be all alone! I would still have Mrs. Right, Mrs. Wendover, and my papa, and Thomas is my friend too. I'm not sure about Nelson, I think Serenity would take him away with her.

"Thomas is one of the footmen," Lady Margaret added for clarity.

It is so hard to have Felicity gone. We have so much fun all together. Verity tells tales and Winsome says they're not true, and Grace falls over something, and Papa says we all have to get out of the house and we laugh at him, and Serenity cries over the weather and Patience tells her it's only a sunset, and Felicity always led us all as she is the oldest—am I expected to give up all my sisters because of gentlemen? I am glad I don't have brothers!

I really feel you will have a good answer about what we should do. Your truest faithful friend, Valor Nicolet.

Lady Margaret laid down the letter. "She also drew a picture of Mrs. Wendover at the bottom. Goodness, there is quite a lot to take in."

Yes, indeed there was. Foremost, Lady Grace liked him ever so well. He supposed he'd known it, as he liked her ever so well too. He'd been instantly struck by her and still had a clear vision of seeing her for the first time on that beach. Ever since, whenever they were in the vicinity of one another, they were iron and lodestone—inexorably drawn to one another.

Still, it was one thing to sense something and another thing to hear that it was clearly known to others and it was written about. And then, he'd hardly expected his nose to be singled out. He'd always thought it not a particularly attractive feature as it did have the slightest curve to it.

"What do you suppose she means by Lady Grace falling over something?" Lady Margaret asked. "Was there some sort of amusing accident? Though, at my age, no accident is amusing. By the by, I do appreciate you getting me up to my room last evening—that could have gone very wrong, we all know what happened to one of my footmen that last time he went headlong down the stairs. He's dead."

Miles tapped his chin, ignoring any reference to last night. Or the tragic fate of her footman. "The duke said something about Lady Grace having two left feet. When we dined at the inn. I did not think much of it at the time."

"Oh dear," Lady Margaret said, "there are those people who come into the world clumsy and never get past it. My sister in Bath, who I do not get on with and who is dead now, was a master at dropping things. If there was a decent china cup in reach, that girl would drop it. She's dead these days, so I suppose the cups are safe."

Miles had not the first idea of how to respond to another of Lady Margaret's macabre reflections. Further, he'd not seen any evidence from Lady Grace of any sort of inordinate clumsiness. Even if he did, would it put him off? He did not think it would. After all, if one were to have a fault, it was about as minor a fault as he could think of.

"Well, I suppose there are worse things," Lady Margaret said. "But I must not get ahead of myself. Lord Harraby is to collect me at two o'clock and we are to make calls. I will keep you apprised of my opinions regarding the young ladies we encounter. Do not worry, Lord Dashlend—she is out there. Is it Lady Grace? Is it another lady? It's too soon to tell."

"There really is no need for that, Lady Margaret," Miles said, alarmed that she and Lord Harraby were to take their ideas to the streets.

"It is no trouble at all," Lady Margaret said, as if she were proposing to do him a favor. She rose. "I'd best go upstairs. Meg says she has a new idea for my hair. What's left of it, anyway. Wainwright, might you send me a tray? And a tray for Gwen too—her feet are swelling up something terrible these days. And a bit of brandy for both of us. Well! At least we are not dead."

With that, Lady Margaret toddled from the room.

He did not have a good feeling about Lady Margaret and Lord Harraby out on the town looking into his business and trying to arrange his future.

Miles decided there was no point in brewing over it as there did not seem to be a way to stop Lady Margaret from nosing into his business. In any case, he had things to do.

Lady Grace had mentioned that the family would be taking a turn round the park that afternoon and he had some business to attend to before he would set off to coincidentally encounter them.

Miles wondered if Lady Grace knew what Lady Valor had written. Perhaps she even encouraged it? He felt exceedingly buoyed by recent events. During Fact or Fib she had mentioned his gentlemanly bearing. Now his nose was singled out as exceptional too.

He jogged up the stairs and entered his bedchamber, which was comprised of a suite of rooms. There was the main room that overlooked the back garden, then another good-sized chamber acting as a dressing room on one side, and a sitting room of sorts with a desk on the other.

Moreau marched out of the dressing room as soon as he heard Miles come in. "She knows nothing! Nothing at all! Who pays the price for this ignorance? Moreau, who else?"

Miles did not have the first idea who had got into Moreau's bad books. It could be anybody at all. As far as Moreau was concerned, all the world was ranged against him.

As he did not speculate on who might be his valet's latest enemy, Moreau continued on. "How is it that a lady's maid can barely sew a stitch, I wonder? Oh, never mind, it is because she is a *kitchen* maid, that is how."

"I presume you refer to Meg," Miles said. "Lady Margaret seems happy with her."

This, apparently, was not the looked-for response.

"Lady Margaret is happy with her? Why not? Every time I set foot into the servants' hall, this Meg individual is right behind me.

Moreau, how do I fix this hem? Moreau, how do I remove this spot? Moreau, how do I use the irons? I do not see why Moreau is not the lady's maid."

"I suspect Lady Margaret would not prefer it. In any case, Meg is new to the position," Miles said. "She is bound to have questions."

"Oh yes, she has questions all day long. She does not harass *you* with these questions. Only Moreau."

Miles did not bother to point out that even a very inexperienced lady's maid would not be so harebrained as to ask the lord of the house how to use the irons.

"As Meg does harass you with questions," Miles said, "perhaps you might drop some hints she might pass on to her mistress. I've been hoping Lady Margaret might…update her style of dress."

Moreau sniffed. "Oh really? You do not find favor with towering turbans and molting feathers and skirts so voluminous they might serve for a curtsy to the queen?"

"Yes, all of that."

"Well, guess what? This Meg person does a lot of talking. When she is not pestering me with questions, she talks about other things. And guess what? Lord Harraby thinks Lady Margaret's style is marvelous. Good luck prying those limp ostrich feathers from her tiny, wrinkled hands!"

Moreau strode off to go and stew in the dressing room. Miles was certain his valet would collapse in apoplexy one day. If that came to pass and he was forced to find a new valet, his primary requirement would be for a fellow a deal more unflappable.

GRACE WAS JUMPING up and down in her bedchamber, as it really did seem to help when she felt a bit dizzy. Valor burst into the room without so much as a knock.

Then she jumped up and down too and said, "What are we doing?"

"Just getting some exercise," Grace said.

"Oh. I don't like it." Valor climbed onto her bed and said, "I am only waiting to hear back from my friend, Lady Margaret."

"Hear back about what?" Grace said, ceasing her jumping.

"About how you can be happy but not leave the house," Valor said, as if this were a much-discussed point between them.

Grace thought she might need more information about the idea. "Valor, do expand on this notion, if you will."

Valor examined the trim on the pelisse that had been laid out on the bed. "Well, you know how it is. You like Lord Dashlend, just like Felicity liked Mr. Stratton and look what happened there."

"First, I have not said I like Lord Dashlend *that* much. It is far too soon for that. Second, Felicity married, which was quite right."

"Felicity does not live here anymore, Grace," Valor said, as if she were explaining a simple matter to a young child. "That's the problem. It started out exactly the same with Felicity pretending she didn't like Mr. Stratton *that* much, and then she did not like him at all, and then she did and she's gone."

"We will all get married eventually," Grace said. "At least, I hope so."

"Why?"

"It is what ladies do," Grace said. "They grow up and marry and leave their houses."

"I though Papa was joking about that."

"Well, he is. At least, the way he poses it."

"I do not like this at all and I've told Lady Margaret my views. I think she will agree with me."

Grace paused. "Valor, what exactly have you told Lady Margaret?"

Valor jumped off the bed. "Sometimes I feel like you are not really listening, Grace. I told her that you liked Lord Dashlend ever so well and how could it be that you stayed in the house anyway. You see? How can you be happy without going anywhere."

"You said all that?" Grace said, rather horrified that Lady Margaret might repeat any of it to Lord Dashlend.

Valor patted Grace's hand. "I *wrote* all that. I'm glad you were really listening this time, well done. I hope that means I won't have to repeat myself. Now, I have to track down Nelson—I think he's taken Mrs. Wendover somewhere."

Valor skipped out of the room. Grace sank down into a chair. They really had better start monitoring Valor's missives—last season she'd scolded Mr. Stratton terribly, including the wish that he was wrapped in chains and drowned in a lake. Now she was informing Lady Margaret about other people's feelings!

GRACE HAD PLANNED that they would get to the park at four o'clock, and very sensibly had the idea that they had to start getting ready at two-thirty. A half hour should have been sufficient, though Grace knew it was not realistic, and she had casually mentioned the time they expected to be there to Lord Dashlend. She would not like to miss him on account of her sisters' failure to leave the house on time.

As it happened, her practicality served her well. Verity could not find her pelisse, Winsome wondered if she was lying about it and then later hid it from her, Grace had her hair done twice by Mrs. Right before she was satisfied with the results, Serenity went back and forth on the idea of whether Nelson should come with them, finally deciding that he should, Patience spent her time going in and out of the house waiting for the carriages to arrive, and, not unexpectedly, Valor lost track of Mrs. Wendover. It took quite some time to locate the stuffed rabbit, as Nelson had become very attached to it and had taken to hiding it in various locations in the house.

As all that activity swirled around him, the duke merely read a book in the drawing room, occasionally laughing over the confusion. He often noted that as the father of seven daughters, he did not ever expect to leave the house in a timely manner. A more foolish person might be crying with frustration by the second time Verity lost track of her pelisse, but the duke would have been surprised if she didn't.

They finally did set off though, and so many were they, as of course Mrs. Right would come too, they went in two carriages.

Grace was in a carriage with the duke, Patience, and Verity. Mrs. Right supervised the other carriage with Valor, Serenity, Winsome, and Nelson.

"So what's it to be, Gracie, are we to coincidentally bump into Dashlend?" the duke asked.

"How should I know, Papa?" Grace said, though she knew her father understood the truth of it.

"Running into a gentleman in the park is a very common thing, Papa," Verity said.

"Is it?" the duke asked, with one brow raised.

Verity shrugged. "I don't know."

"If we are to see him," Patience said, "I do hope it does not take hours to find him. Riding in the carriage is not as interesting as riding round the dales on our ponies, shooting at things."

"Yes, well, probably best we leave off that for a while," the duke said. "That rascally neighbor of ours claims his sheep get upset about all the shooting. I don't know why—none of the creatures have ever been hit." The duke paused. "They haven't been, have they?"

"Certainly not," Patience said. "We would never hurt a sheep. We only shoot in the farmer's direction, and we always go wide. He and his sheep are in no danger whatsoever."

"Regardless, he's got the vicar's ear about it. He keeps telling the fellow that our Mrs. Right went so far as to tack a cotton wolf's head near his gate to frighten his flock. I do not know if she did or she didn't—I only hope she did!"

"She did," Verity said.

Patience snorted. "It took him ages to find it, but the sheep saw it at once."

All through the family chatter, Grace kept her eyes open and looking out the window for Lord Dashlend.

"Montclave," the duke said. "What do you do here?"

"Good afternoon, Your Grace, Lady Grace," Lord Montclave said. "I am just out exercising my horse. How propitious to encounter you."

Grace turned her head to find the baron walking alongside her father's window while Patience and Verity gave him the once over.

"If you say so," the duke said.

Grace pressed her lips together. Baron Montclave would not be accustomed to her father's unique way of being in the world. He would not understand that he was teased.

"Baron Montclave," Grace said, "these are my sisters, Lady Patience and Lady Verity."

The baron bowed from his saddle. "Lady Patience, Lady Verity, charmed."

"You're just a baron, though?" Patience asked. "Do you have any higher prospects?"

The duke roared with laughter. "You see what I put up with, Montclave. That's our Patience, saying what everybody was thinking. Don't ask Verity anything, you'll never get at the truth."

"Papa!" Verity said, as if somehow surprised by this assessment.

"Ah, oh, I see," Lord Montclave said, sounding nonplussed by the duke's comments about his daughters.

Just then, Grace heard the voice she'd been waiting for on her other side. She whipped round and found Lord Dashlend at her window.

"Lady Grace," he said.

He was looking very fine on his large stallion, his bottle green riding coat with polished silver buttons fitting to perfection.

"Lord Dashlend," she said.

The lord then seemed to notice his cousin on the other side of the carriage. "Montclave," he said through the window, "what do you do here?"

"Exercising my horse," Lord Montclave said with a note of irritation. "What do *you* do here?"

"Lady Grace informed me she would be in the park at this hour," Lord Dashlend said, "so I made my way here forthwith."

"He's got you there, eh, Montclave?" the duke said, laughing. "You claim a happenstance and he says there was no luck or coincidence involved for himself!"

"I believe encountering another person in the park is a very common thing," Verity said.

Lord Montclave looked about him at the endless array of carriages and people on horseback. Grace was certain he was thinking that it would indeed be a very common thing, as half of London was there.

"Lord Dashlend," Grace said, "How does Lady Margaret do after her exertions of last evening?"

"Uh, she does very well. Surprisingly."

"Exertions?" the duke said, laughing. "Is that what we're calling that ludicrous display? Well, Montclave, you would have missed it—patronesses are a persnickety bunch. Very careful of who they let in."

Grace could see Lord Montclave redden to have it pointed to that he would not be in receipt of a voucher.

"In fact, Lady Grace," Lord Dashlend said, "Lady Margaret was just asking about you this morning."

Grace could see very well that Lord Dashlend was somehow embarrassed that Lady Margaret was mentioned. She wondered if the lady had communicated anything that Valor had written in her letter. Grace certainly hoped not, as she would be entirely embarrassed herself.

"I wonder, Lady Grace, if you plan on attending Lady Montague's ball on the morrow?"

"Indeed, we have engaged ourselves," Grace said.

"Perhaps I might linger in the foyer," Lord Dashlend said.

"When you arrive, I could escort you to get your dance card."

"That would be very acceptable, Lord Dashlend," Grace said, feeling a little bit idiotic in her answer. Nevertheless, perhaps there was something non-committal and sophisticated about it? Probably not though. She probably just sounded like an idiot.

On the other hand, she could not very well say what she really thought. It would be even more idiotic if she claimed she was wildly approving of the idea, which she was.

From across the carriage, Lord Montclave called. "I will linger in the foyer as well."

The duke roared with laughter. "Well, Gracie, Lady Montague's foyer will be like shark infested waters. How many gentlemen will be circling, waiting for your arrival?"

Grace was pleased to see that Lord Dashlend did not look very approving of the idea of Lord Montclave haunting the foyer too. If she were to be honest, she did not have strong feelings one way or the other. She did not like Lord Montclave, but she did not hold anything positively against him either. In any case, she would dance with more gentlemen than only Lord Dashlend, and so she supposed that Lord Montclave on her card was of no significance either way.

"Wonderful," Patience said. "Everyone will be wandering around the foyer. When does anything actually happen though?"

"We will proceed to the ballroom," Lord Montclave said. "And then in not too long a time the dancing will begin."

"I know that part," Patience said. "What I mean is, when will something exciting happen? Last year, Mr. Stratton was almost killed by a tiger. Felicity says his scars are wonderful, though we haven't seen them."

"They're under his clothes," Verity clarified.

"The point is, it was very exciting. When can we expect something like that?" Patience asked.

Lord Montclave clearly did not know how to answer that question.

"Lady Patience," Lord Dashlend said, "I am sorry to tell you that I have no expectation of any of us running into a tiger or anything like it at Lady Montague's ball. The best we could hope for is the lady's bad-tempered Pomeranian will make a run at an unsuspecting guest's ankles."

Patience looked a bit let down to hear it.

"We've brought Nelson along today," Verity said. "He's in our other carriage. He does not make a run at anybody's ankles, he is a very charming dog and we all love him excessively."

The duke laughed. "Good luck to Nelson trying to make a run at anyone, what with just the three legs and one blind eye."

"That is the very basis of his charm, Papa." Patience said.

"Yes, I suppose so, my girl. Well, I think you two gentlemen have spent long enough following our carriage. I would not like any sort of talk to go around until there is something definite to talk about."

The duke stared determinedly at Lord Dashlend as he said it. Grace wanted to sink through her seat at the bold hint. Lord Dashlend, for his part, only smiled, while Lord Montclave looked very disgruntled.

Nevertheless, the two gentlemen had been dismissed. They both bowed from their saddles and set off in different directions, seeming to have no inclination for a family reunion.

Chapter Fourteen

G RACE WATCHED LORD Dashlend set off from the road and across the grass at a trot, quickly picking up speed to a gallop. He was an expert horseman and a pleasure to watch. As for where Lord Montclave went, she did not know nor did she particularly care.

"It seems that Grace has two suitors, Papa," Patience said.

"I certainly do not," Grace said. "Nothing at all has been said."

Patience ignored this for the fan-waving that it was. "Which do you prefer?" she asked the duke.

"I'll leave it up to Gracie," the duke said. "If my collection of nonsensical daughters cannot reasonably pick out a mate for life, I'd wonder what their governess was doing all these years."

Grace laughed. "Papa, Miss Pynchon was only with us for a few months. Remember? She disappeared one day and just left a note."

Both Patience and Verity doubled over in laughter. Patience said, "It only said 'GOODBYE.'"

"That's right," the duke said. "I forgot she did not last long. Well, I'm sure our Mrs. Right has packed some sense into your heads about such things. Felicity seemed to do all right for herself."

"I favor Lord Dashlend," Patience said. "For one, we met him first and while it was very foolish to become shipwrecked, it was at least interesting. For another, I do not care for Lord Montclave. Why? He doesn't laugh. What are we to do with a fellow who doesn't laugh?"

"It's my understanding," Verity said, "that people can be taught to laugh."

"I don't believe it," Patience said. "And anyway, who has the time to bother with it? It's the sort of thing one learns as a child."

Grace did not participate much in the long debate about Lord Dashlend and Lord Montclave. There was no reason that she should. Her thoughts felt very settled on the matter. Lord Dashlend was superior to Lord Montclave, as Lord Dashlend was superior to all other gentlemen.

In any case, she would see them both at the ball on the morrow. She had high hopes that Lord Dashlend found her in the foyer first.

She planned on jumping in her bedchamber for at least an hour before she set off for the ball to be sure her head would cooperate with her feet. She had acquitted herself well enough at Almack's, but at Lady Montague's ball there would not be the distraction of Lady Margaret and Lord Harraby to cover any little missteps she may have made.

Everything must be perfect.

MONTCLAVE LEFT THE park irritated. He'd been lingering and looking in the park for days and just when he spotted the duke's carriage, Dashlend made an appearance. Apparently, his cousin had been told when to come.

It was clear enough that the duke favored his cousin. It was also clear enough that the duke leaned heavily to the eccentric. He'd thought to approach their carriage on the duke's side, rather than go directly to Lady Grace, thinking that would somehow ingratiate him. It would have, had the duke been a more regular sort of man. But it had not.

He entered Doanellen's house, only to find Mrs. Featherby lounging in the drawing room. He forced himself to be cheerful and speak of the weather, and then hightailed it up the stairs to his bedchamber before she could wax on about something she saw in a shop that Doanellen ought to buy her.

As he paced back and forth, he thought through what must happen next. He briefly considered ideas to keep Dashlend away from Lady Montague's ball, or at least make him late so he would not be lurking in the foyer. The only thing that came to him was loosening his horse's shoes, but that was associated with too much peril if he were caught.

He would have to depend on the flowers scheme doing the job and turning Lady Grace away from Dashlend. Then it would not matter if he were in the foyer or not. The deliveries had been arranged, as he'd finally found a florist on a side street who was happy to believe in the integrity of the credit of a well-dressed baron. This very afternoon, two arrangements would be delivered at the same time—one of yellow daisies, addressed to Lady Grace and speaking of friendship, the other of pink roses addressed to Lady Lavender and speaking of new love.

The note to Lady Grace would say, "To new friendships."

The note allegedly for Lady Lavender would say, "To the most graceful lady at the ball. I allow the flowers to speak for themselves."

Lady Lavender's flowers would seem to be misaddressed, putting Lady Grace into an exceedingly uncomfortable position. Not only would she believe that she'd accidentally peeked into Dashlend's real inclinations, but that Dashlend admired Lady Lavender's grace. A sore spot for a lady who had been named Grace, but was lacking in it. Then, Lady Grace must return the arrangement to the florist. The florist had already been told to expect it and keep the flowers for himself for resale. The shopkeeper did not pretend to understand the thing, but was led to believe it was a typical gambit for a dandy of the *ton*. The fact that the fellow had believed he was a dandy said all too clearly that he did not know the first thing about it.

Really, he did not see how the flowers could fail. If he were a lady and received those two arrangements from a gentleman, he would be irate.

There was a soft knock on the door. "Enter," he said.

One of Doanellen's footmen came in with a letter on a silver salver. "This just arrived, my lord. The messenger said it is from your dowager and must be delivered upon arrival."

Montclave took the letter and dismissed the boy. He tore it open. His mother would not have written if there was not news. What had she found out?

Son—

I write this in haste. It is told to me that Dashlend has written his father. The earl is in such high spirits over it that he has risen from his bed and talks to all in sundry about it. Dashlend wrote him about his near-miss at sea and how it has given him perspective, and how he has come to recognize his duty to the family. Dashlend went so far as to mention a certain Lady Grace Nicolet, daughter of a duke. It seems as if a proposal is in the offing. Do not allow it to occur.

Your ever-hopeful mother.

Montclave laid the letter down. He had not expected things to move quite so fast. Dashlend had, for all intents and purposes, made a declaration to his father. How long would it be before he made a declaration to Lady Grace herself?

His cousin might propose at Lady Montague's ball. After all, what was stopping him?

And if he did, would that not collapse any ideas he may have stirred up in Lady Grace with the flowers' ruse? Would not the truth come out? That Dashlend had not sent either of those posies?

He wracked his mind for an idea of what else he could do, but nothing came to him. He realized he'd have to fall back on his mother's oft communicated counsel—sometimes, one must just go into a situation and look for the opportunities.

Baron Montclave would be eyes wide, looking for an opportunity.

MILES HAD MADE up his mind—if Lady Grace would have him, he would wed. How could it be otherwise? She was the most charming lady alive in both looks and manner. He'd been so struck by her the moment he laid eyes on her. It was not at all sensible or careful, but it was real all the same. Her family was exceedingly odd, but he liked them very well and would be happy to be connected to them. They might go on eccentric, but Lady Margaret was right about them, they were a family of good character. For that matter, he could not very well turn his nose up regarding a little eccentricity when he had Lady Margaret on display.

It was funny that he now viewed the married state so differently than he had in the past. When he'd thought of it before, there was no particular lady associated with it. That had run his thoughts toward boredom and duty. A wedding was just something to be accomplished, like seeing that the wine cellar was in good order, or the tenants were both paying and content, or arranging to have a leaky roof repaired.

As he'd floated on his wrecked boat for two days, it was as if he'd traveled the River Styx, and then been pulled from the underworld into a new age, a new era. And then, if the fates had a hand in his survival, as surely they must have, Lady Grace was waiting for him on that beach.

He had originally, when his thoughts began to travel toward marriage, counseled himself to be cautious. To look around. To see if there was anyone else he preferred.

There was not. How could there be? There would never be, and he would be a consummate fool to let her get away. That idea really spurred him on. How many gentlemen had dithered with their thoughts until it was too late? They finally came to their conclusion to find the lady had accepted another? A lady as perfect as Lady Grace did not drift round long before somebody moved in to secure her.

"Moreau," he said, as his valet fussed with his dressing table, "I will wear my best coat to Lady Montague's ball on the morrow. See that it's in good order."

Moreau slowly laid down a brush. "See that it is in good order?" he said, his tone full of faint outrage. "What does the great Lord Dashlend think Moreau does all day, if it is not to keep his things in good order? Or perfect order, if one is to be accurate?"

"No need to get on your high horse about it."

Moreau laughed. "Moreau is amused that anybody imagines he owns a horse, much less a high horse. No, poor Moreau does not have such luxuries."

"I see. So if you had a horse, you would ride him regularly."

Moreau sniffed. "Perhaps. But we will never know, as Moreau will go in the carriage."

Miles smiled to himself. Moreau made very free with his carriage and delighted in being seen round the town, peering out of it.

"This best coat idea," Moreau said thoughtfully, "is there some reason for it? I do not recall you ever going to great lengths to impress Lady Montague."

"There *is* a lady I wish to impress, though it is not Lady Montague. It is Lady Grace."

"Impress how? How impressed is she to be?" Moreau asked suspiciously.

"Impressed enough to accept me, I hope," Miles said.

"Mon Dieu," Moreau said. "Lord Dashlend comes to the great city of London, full of ladies everywhere, and he goes right to the strangest family in England."

"I do not think it is your place to provide those sorts of opinions," Miles said sternly.

"Of course not, my lord. Poor Moreau, only a valet, cannot have opinions. But there is one opinion that shall not be wrenched from my breast! I will never stay in a house with that duke, because that duke has a valet I would like to smother in his sleep! Have I received any note of thanks for returning his oldest set of clothes looking better than they did when they were foisted upon me? No I have not!"

Miles stared at his valet. The man really was impossible. However, he was in too high spirits to be bothered about it. "You ought to go below stairs and calm yourself with a cup of tea," he said.

Moreau shook his head sadly and did as he was bid. Cook would shortly be hearing all about the oldest set of clothes and the barbaric English failure to send a note of thanks. As the cook was French too, and they delighted in commiserating with one another over the inferior English, they should both be happily occupied for at least an hour over it.

After the door closed, Miles sat on the balcony overlooking the garden, thinking about what he would say to Lady Grace. His whole future would hang on that moment, and he had to get it right.

EVERYONE HAD GATHERED in the drawing room after their ride in the park and a tea tray and rather expansive tray of cakes and biscuits had come in. Cook had gone so far as to make his famous miniature apple cakes with a generous coating of icing. Mrs. Right told them the cook was in a celebratory frame of mind on account of the departure of Mr. Button.

Very shortly after this communication, a letter arrived for the duke from Lady Marchfield. It was almost as if the very mention of Mr. Button had conjured a missive from the ether.

The duke tore it open and scanned its contents.

"Well now, it seems our Mr. Button has been satisfactorily settled in a house full of regular people, which we are not."

"Do we wish to be regular, Papa?" Valor asked, rearranging Mrs. Wendover's pelisse, given to her by Mr. Stratton the season before. As she did so, Nelson watched longingly, no doubt wishing to get hold of the stuffed rabbit and make off with her.

"We are a ducal family, Valor," the duke said. "We do not need or want to become some sort of pedestrian regular people. Your aunt has that stance well in hand, to everyone's boredom and irritation."

Grace thought that was all perfectly true. Though she did, at times, feel sorry for Lady Marchfield. The lady did really believe all the precepts she flung round, as grim and tedious as they always were.

Grace had written her a note the day before, just a pleasant one to smooth things over. Lady Marchfield had answered, claiming it was not Grace's fault that she had a lunatic for a father.

"What happened today in the park?" Serenity asked. "We saw Lord Dashlend and Lord Montclave at your carriage when we hung out the windows, but we could not hear what was said."

"They were both very pleasant," Grace said, availing herself of one of the tiny apple cakes.

"What Gracie means to say," the duke said laughing, "is that she's got two fish on the hook. We await her reeling in the right fish."

"Papa!" Grace said.

"Lady Margaret wrote me back," Valor said, "and she says she does not know of any way to keep Grace home forever. But I had an idea. Grace, if you marry Lord Dashlend, why cannot he come and live with us? We could give him one of the extra rooms. It would be tiresome, but we would put up with it to keep you at home."

"He won't like it," Winsome said. "Remember? Mr. Stratton stays in the same room with Felicity all night. And probably stares at her while she's sleeping."

Valor sighed. "I guess Lord Dashlend could stay in Grace's room. If that's really necessary."

"I wonder if Lord Dashlend has scars, like Mr. Stratton does," Serenity said. "You could tell us, Grace, once you've had a look under his clothes."

"That is quite enough nonsensical talk," Grace said.

It was probably a hopeless scolding, as once her sisters got on to a subject, they would examine it backward and forward.

Fortunately, Charlie took that moment to come into the drawing room, almost disappeared behind two large flower arrangements.

"What have we here?" the duke asked. "The two fish on a hook both having the same idea?"

Grace did not know who had sent the flowers, she only hoped one was from Lord Dashlend. She did not much care who the other arrangement was from.

Charlie set them down and went to look for two suitable vases. Grace and her sisters gathered round them. There was an arrangement of yellow daisies, and an arrangement of pink roses. Naturally, she put her hopes on roses from Lord Dashlend.

"Open the note with the daisies first, Grace," Patience said. "Save the best for last."

"I ought to read the notes first," the duke said, "but I can well guess where the land lies so go ahead. Daisies first."

Grace fumbled with the folded note tucked into the array of daisies.

To new friendship—Dashlend

"New friendship?" Winsome said. "What does that mean? What does he want a friend for?"

Grace had not the first idea. It seemed a rather… limp…

message to send along with flowers. Though, it matched the daisies meaning. She had hoped Lord Dashlend might feel more than friendship.

The duke laughed heartily. "He takes the slow and cautious road, I see. And let me guess, Montclave has sent the roses. That fellow throws his hat in the ring and caution to the wind."

Grace sighed. "I think I do not care for over-caution, Papa."

"Now, don't let it bring you down. Dashlend is a sensible man, and that is not altogether a bad thing. He'll prove to have a care for a wife's wellbeing. Let him work his way up to roses over time. I suspect he's dipping his toe in the water to get an idea of how you view it."

"Oh, I hadn't thought… well, that is different, then," Grace said, much cheered by the idea. She could simply express her enthusiasm for the daisies, thereby hinting he ought to take a step further. A step further with all haste, if she could subtly communicate such a thing.

Yes, of course that must be right. Lord Dashlend was a real man, not some sort of overwrought hero from one of her novels. Surely it was right that he take things step by step. It would have been foolish to do otherwise, and Lord Dashlend was not foolish.

"All right," the duke said, "let us see what ridiculous thing Montclave has written with those roses. Certainly it must be from him. He shoots too high and too fast, but I think that is the sort of fellow he is—a foolhardy Icarus about to melt his wings."

"You do not like him at all, Papa," Valor said, wrestling Mrs. Wendover out of Nelson's mouth.

"Not particularly."

Grace could not care less what Lord Montclave had written, but she supposed she'd better find it out. She unfolded the note tucked into the pink roses.

Lady Lavender—the most graceful lady in London. I allow the flowers to speak for themselves. Dashlend.

Grace dropped the note as if it were on fire. "I do not understand this," she murmured.

"What does he say?" the duke asked. "Has he foolishly professed his undying love?"

Valor laughed. "That *would* be foolish—none of us even like him very much."

"No," Grace said slowly, examining both the note and the address, "the arrangement is addressed to me, but the note itself is addressed to…"

She could hardly bear to say it.

"To who, Grace? Certainly not to one of us, unless he's been so deranged as to send Papa flowers," Patience said.

"It is addressed to Lady Lavender," Grace said, perceiving what must have happened. The florist received two orders, and in his haste sent them both to the same address. "The note says Lord Dashlend views Lady Lavender as the most graceful lady in London. He allows the flowers to speak for themselves."

"Lord Dashlend?" Winsome exclaimed. "Why should Lord Dashlend send flowers here that are supposed to go to somebody else?"

"And why should he send flowers to somebody else?" Winsome asked. "Pink roses, too."

"I could just cry and I do not even know what's happened," Serenity said, dabbing at her eyes.

"It seems there was simply a mix-up," Grace said, trying very hard not to weep with Serenity. "The florist has made a mistake. The daisies were for me… for friendship. The roses were meant to be delivered to Lady Lavender and the florist accidentally sent both arrangements here."

"Let me see that note," the duke said.

Grace handed it over, though she knew very well that her father would not see anything in it that she had not seen herself.

The duke examined it and laid it on a table. "Does not make a lick of sense. I am not blind, I know what I'm looking at when I look at a young gentleman. No reason for Dashlend to go sending roses to Lady Lavender."

"But he has done," Grace said. "Why should he not? Lady Lavender is everything genial and she is pretty, and she is good at nearly everything in the world. She is graceful, which I already know he values. She is a diamond of the first water. Why should I have supposed that Lord Dashlend preferred me over the glorious Lady Lavender?"

"Because he does," the duke said.

"I fear you are mistaken, Papa," Grace said. "Well, goodness, what a day. I think I will just repair to my room and lie down for a while. I am developing a headache. A rest will cure me, I'm sure. We will just return the roses to the florist so they might correct their mistake. Now, nobody is to bother me in my room, as that will not help my headache."

With that, Grace hurried from the drawing room. She could not bear the pitying looks from her sisters, nor her father's unwillingness to believe what was right in front of them.

Everything had been so wonderful and full of promise and then she'd read that note. It was a crushing blow, as if the note had stolen the air from her lungs. In that instant, everything she thought was happening had been ripped from her, leaving her with the awful and sad truth. Lord Dashlend had merely been friendly, or amusing himself.

She should have known! Mrs. Right had warned them all, over and over, about London people. Grace Nicolet could not compare to Lady Lavender, she was not of the same caliber, she was not accomplished. And, to top it off, she had two left feet, which Lord Dashlend had been early informed of.

Perhaps he'd been so friendly because it would not occur to him that she would imagine herself worthy of anything more serious. He'd not had to caution himself, or worry that he led a lady on, because it would be too absurd for her to imagine it.

There was a quick knock on the door and Mrs. Right hurried through it. Though Grace had warned her sisters from following her, of course Mrs. Right would not be put off.

"There, love, what's happened?" she said, coming to the bed

and chafing her hand.

Between fits of weeping, Grace poured out the whole story of the misdirected flowers and her misdirected thoughts about Lord Dashlend.

Mrs. Right's expression grew darker the more she heard of it. Grace could not fail to recall what had happened to Mr. Stratton at the hands of their housekeeper last season, when it looked as if he'd misled Felicity about his intentions.

"Mrs. Right," she said, "you must promise me you are not to meddle in Lord Dashlend's grocery order, or make him an enemy to his wine merchant, or have his laundress donate all his clothes to a charity."

Mrs. Right delicately raised her brows. "Certainly not, dove. Now I suppose you really do have a headache. I will have one of the maids bring up a cold cloth for your brow and a cup of tea with the smallest drop of laudanum. That will allow you to sleep for a few hours and things will look better for you when you wake up."

Grace nodded. She did not really think she would feel better after sleeping, but just now sleeping would be a welcome escape. She'd been exceedingly foolish, perhaps even conceited and entertaining an overblown opinion of her charms. At least she might awaken with more sense than she'd had so far.

CHAPTER FIFTEEN

Mrs. Right was not amused by the day's events. How dare anyone impose on her Grace in such a manner? To pay such marked attention, only to prefer another lady? And then, to be the author of this florist mix-up? Had the man hired the stupidest florist in London?

It was enraging.

Mrs. Right did not know this Lady Lavender who was to receive roses, but she was certain the lady could not hold a candle to Grace Nicolet. She would not stand idly by while her dear Grace had been so cruelly humiliated.

No. Mrs. Agnes Right did not stand by when one of her girls was insulted. These girls were in her charge and she protected them as fiercely as she would her own. She'd not had her own, and so these girls had become her own. Lord Dashlend must pay for this insult. He must pay dearly. She would rip him limb from limb if she could.

As she could not accomplish that feat, Mrs. Right paced her quarters, thinking of what she *could* do. Grace had already elicited a promise that she would not meddle with Lord Dashlend's grocery order or wine order or the clothes he sent out to the laundress.

What did she know about Lord Dashlend's household? She knew he had a high-strung valet; Reynolds had done no end of complaining about Mr. Moreau. She knew Dashlend had just now

Lady Margaret staying in his house, a lady of older years and even older fashion. She knew he seemed to love the boat he'd come near to sinking, as when he'd been at the inn he'd made all sorts of arrangements about it. She knew he was considered a Corinthian.

Certainly, something could be made of one of those things.

She might arrange to have one of his legs broken, thereby ending his days as a Corinthian. But she could not break a man's leg on her own, she'd have to hire somebody. That did give her pause. Everybody knew that a secret was no longer a secret if more than one person knew about it. It was bound to get out that she was at the bottom of it.

Paying to have his boat hauled out to sea and set afire would be fitting and glorious, but it came with precisely the same risk.

Mrs. Right did not know what could be done regarding Lady Margaret, but something might come to mind.

Then, the first thing she *could* do arrived in her head. It might not be the last thing, but it was a place to start. Unlike Reynolds, Mr. Moreau was of an unsteady temperament. He was the type of fellow who might be set off.

Mrs. Right well knew that all gentlemen despised having to find a new valet. A valet was like a lady's maid, privy to everything personal, and it was a hard road to find the right one and get comfortable with the arrangement. Even though Mr. Moreau was a silly sort, it seemed he'd been with Lord Dashlend a good amount of time.

Certainly, she could cause trouble there, and it would not be hard to do. She would simply place an advertisement in the newspapers for a valet to serve Lord Dashlend. She would carefully send out the news to certain quarters that the gentleman in the advertisement was Dashlend, and where he lived. There was nothing in the world that moved faster than gossip through servants' circles. Every other person had a relative hanging about, looking for a situation.

Not only would the letters come flying in from across England, but the more ambitious fellows who were already haunting Town would turn up at the doorstep.

Mr. Moreau would go positively mad. He would at least pack his bags and be off, causing great inconvenience. At best, he might set Lord Dashlend's house afire on his way out. After all, who really knew what an insulted and betrayed Frenchman would get up to?

Yes, it was a good plan and trumped the burlap bags of turnips she'd sent to Mr. Stratton.

Which of course she now regretted as it seemed she'd been mistaken in that.

She was not mistaken in this, though. She would get that advertisement in the newspaper for the morning edition and start spreading the word by dropping the hint to Mr. Cray, the butler next door. He was both chatty and supercilious, and considered himself graciously condescending—he'd tell all and sundry of the opportunity. There were those people who gloried in being the bearer of helpful news and the receiver of grateful thanks that might be the result of it. Mr. Cray was the emperor of the activity.

As well, she would send a copy of the advertisement to Lord Dashlend's house as some kind of confirmation of purchase. With any luck, Lord Dashlend's household would devolve into chaos on the morrow before the breakfast things had been cleared.

That dastardly lord was about to discover the perils of hurting and humiliating a Nicolet girl.

MONTCLAVE MADE HIS way through the late morning streets, irritated at having been collared by Mrs. Featherby before he left the house. That lady was forever sending him on errands that any footman could accomplish. She generally couched these requests with the idea that something must be hand delivered, or looked at carefully, or assessed with a critical eye, and could not be left to a footman. She liked to put herself forward as a woman of lofty standards and discernment for whom only the best would do, which she certainly was not.

This time, it was to be for tea. He must see Mr. Twining for a particular blend, which he'd written down as he never spent any time thinking about tea. He was a coffee man and found tea watery and insipid.

He made his way to the Strand and found the building easily enough as it was clearly marked with the Twining's sign. He let himself into the shop, and immediately found himself face to face with Lady Margaret.

She was, as she always seemed to be, living in another time. Her skirts were far too wide and painfully embellished with all manner of silver braiding and glass baubles. Her bonnet reached for the sky, helped in that endeavor by two waving ostrich feathers. She was a veritable human chandelier.

"Oh it's you," she said, standing next to an elderly gentleman who Montclave believed was named Harraby.

Montclave bowed. "Lady Margaret, how charming to encounter you here. Lord Harraby, is it?"

"Yes, that's my name. Who are you, by the by?"

It irked Montclave no end that he knew people's names far more than anybody knew his.

"Baron Montclave," he answered.

"Ah! The fellow who comes looking for money," Lord Harraby said to Lady Margaret.

The lady nodded. "Do not bother today," she said to Montclave, "I've not brought money, as I have a longstanding account with Mr. Twining. I stay with Lord Dashlend now, and I wished to purchase something as a treat for the staff."

Of course, Montclave was perfectly aware that Lady Margaret was currently housed with his cousin. He pretended he was not aware, though.

"You are with Dashlend?" he said pleasantly. "That must be

genial."

Apparently, he hit the right note with that comment, as Lady Margaret waxed on about the wonders of Dashlend's hospitality. Montclave smiled pleasantly as he was forced to hear about the superiority of that household's fried eggs. All the while she spoke, a middle-aged and neatly dressed gentleman waited patiently for her attention.

Finally, she did give it to him. "My dear Mr. Twining, I wondered if you might fill one of your charming tins with my special blend. The usual amount, if you please."

Mr. Twining nodded and set off on his task. Montclave pulled the note from his pocket that indicated what he was to purchase for Mrs. Featherby.

Lady Margaret glanced at it. "A rather pedestrian choice."

Montclave did not answer, as he assumed it must be. It was for Mrs. Featherby, after all.

"We will not dally here, Lord Montclave. When I have my purchase, we must be off. There is ever so much to do to get Lord Dashlend properly settled."

"We are quite in the midst of it," Lord Harraby said, looking pleased. "It is our raison d'être these days. It's put a real spring in our step."

"To get Dashlend settled?" Montclave asked, in a tone as innocent as he could muster. Why? Why should that be of concern to these two old bats?

"Oh yes, we said, and I think quite rightly, that we must look about us. We must not conclude it is Lady Grace without looking about us," Lady Margaret said.

"Only sensible to my mind," Harraby said.

"Lord Harraby is full of good sense. So, we *have* looked about. It seems it is to be Lady Grace after all. We can see for ourselves that our Lord Dashlend will not be turned from her and we quite approve."

"We are hoping something is said at Lady Montague's ball this evening," Harraby said, "and we plan to be on hand."

"Naturally, I do hope I may be permitted to stay on in Dashlend's house after the wedding. I do enjoy the company and I believe it has done me good," Lady Margaret said.

"Lady Margaret, I again point out that Dashlend's house is not the *only* place you might have company," Harraby said with a ridiculous gleam in his eye.

Good God. What was he suggesting?

Lady Margaret tapped him with her fan. "Be off with that nonsense, Lord Harraby," she said. "I am far too old for those sorts of bold hints."

"Not in my eyes, you are not. You are a spring flower."

Really, this was rather sickening. These two decrepit people were flirting with each other. If anything were to come of it, at least one of them would be dead before the wedding night was through. Maybe both of them.

Of course, there was every hope the lady had left something for him in her will, so perhaps a speedy trip into the ground was not an unwelcome idea.

"Spring flower, indeed. I will not countenance that with an answer, you old devil!" Lady Margaret said, blushing up to her ears.

Mr. Twining returned with a neat package wrapped in printed paper and tied with a silk ribbon. "Your special blend, Lady Margaret."

"You are a dear man, Mr. Twining. The king of teas, to my mind," Lady Margaret said.

Mr. Twining seemed to appreciate the sentiment and delivered an elegant bow.

Montclave said, "So you think Dashlend is to propose at Lady Montague's ball?"

"I have every expectation of it," Lady Margaret said. "I applaud the efforts that I and Lord Harraby made to ensure Lord Dashlend is happily settled. I suppose he is most grateful to us."

"Let us be off, spring flower," Lord Harraby said jocularly. "I must get you home before Dashlend begins to think I've made off with you to Gretna Green."

Montclave did feel the bile rise in his throat over that picture. He bowed. "A pleasure to see you again, Lady Margaret. Lord Harraby, well met."

Lady Margaret nodded vaguely in his direction and they made their way out of the shop. Before the door closed behind her, Lady Margaret looked over her shoulder and said, "I saw you take the silver salver, by the by."

The door closed and he was left alone with Mr. Twining, who looked at him with brows raised.

Montclave shrugged. "Old age," he said. "It does make a person nonsensical. Hopefully Harraby remembers where she lives, as I doubt she can recall addresses anymore."

Mr. Twining did not reply to that idea. Montclave handed over his note. "I'm to get this for Mrs. Featherby, on Lord Doanellen's account."

Mr. Twining, though he did not travel in elevated circles, seemed to be all too aware of Mrs. Featherby and her paramour. He took the note with a look of distaste and went off to fulfill the order.

Montclave stared at the walls full of cabinets, filled with different sorts of tea. It looked like Viscount Petersham's room for collecting snuff boxes, but it was all filled with tedious tea leaves.

What was he to do at Lady Montague's ball? His flowers would have been delivered—had they been a deadly blow to Lady Grace's feelings?

Perhaps she would decline to even attend?

That would be the best outcome he could think of.

But if she did attend, would Dashlend clear things up with her? And then propose?

How could he stop it? He had to ensure it never happened. If they became engaged, he did not see any practical way to undo it. Short of a murder, which he was entirely against as he had no wish to swing for it.

Mr. Twining returned with Mrs. Featherby's order. It was in a plain brown sack. Not exactly the careful wrapping of Lady Margaret's order.

"I send Mrs. Featherby my compliments," Mr. Twining said, in a tone that indicated that he certainly did not, and would prefer her to move on to another tea merchant.

Montclave was not particularly offended. He did not send any compliments to Mrs. Featherby either. In any case, he had far more serious matters to consider than what a tea merchant thought about Lord Doanellen's indecency.

Somehow, he had to stop an engagement that might be in the offing this very night.

MILES HAD BEEN round the town all afternoon, ending with a stop at Rundell & Bridge. Should Lady Grace accept him, he planned to present her with a small gift as a token of his regard.

At least, he'd planned on a small gift. However, when he'd spotted a rather glorious necklace of green garnets branching out around an exquisite emerald, he'd known it was just the thing. It would set off her eyes marvelously, it was delicate and not too heavy or overbearing, and it was suited to her.

Mr. Rundell had placed it in a slim green velvet box that would slip easily into Miles' waistcoat, ready to be pulled out when the time was right.

Now he headed toward Chesterfield Street, intending to relax, eat something, assure himself that his clothes for the evening were in order, and think. He would spend some time alone in the quiet of his study with a strong pot of coffee, contemplating the night that was to come. It was to set the course of his life, and that deserved careful reflection.

He was startled to find Wainwright standing at the top of the street. He was even more startled to see his butler hurtling toward him. He'd never seen his butler run—it was not a graceful operation and might very well be the first time he'd tried it out. As the fellow drew near, Miles could see that he looked near panicked. He briefly glanced down the street toward his house, wondering if it had caught fire or collapsed in a pile of bricks.

"My lord, thank the heavens you have returned. We are in a topsy-turvy just this minute."

"What on earth has gone on?" Miles asked. "Lady Margaret hasn't done something… odd?"

"Well of course she has, but that is the very least of it!"

"You'd better prepare me for whatever it is I am to face before I get there. What has got you looking as if you are ready to expire?"

Wainwright took in a long slow breath to compose himself. "The flowers came. That was the first thing."

Miles smiled. "Allow me to guess—Lord Harraby has sent Lady Margaret red roses? The staff are all fanning themselves over a lady of a certain age daring to have an admirer?"

Wainwright looked at him as if he were mad. "Nobody cares what Lady Margaret gets up to with Lord Harraby. The two of them are as old as the hills—how much could they get up to?"

"Who were the flowers for then?" Miles asked, certain he was to be told some young adventurer was attempting to seduce one of his housemaids. If that were the case, he'd make quick work of ending the attempt. No good could come of it, for the housemaid at least.

"They are for you! Piles and piles of them. Plants, too. The florist had to bring them in a cart."

Miles paused. He did not know why anybody would send him a single flower, much less a cartful of flowers and plants.

Then he did get an idea. "You do not suppose they've been sent up from the estate? Perhaps my father is determined I do something more extensive with the garden?"

Wainwright lowered his voice so he could not be heard by a gentleman passing by. "He would not send what has been sent. It is the *type* of flora that is frightening, my lord. "Marigolds,

Columbine, Lavender, Thistle, Rhododendron, and Basil."

Miles leaned back in his saddle. That was quite the message. He ran through the various meanings. Sorrow, folly, distrust, defiance, danger, and hatred.

He would almost think Montclave must be at the bottom of it, though he could not see how the fellow afforded such an outlay of money. Unless, of course, he managed to slip past the men left to guard Lady Margaret's house and had made off with some of her silver.

But no, Montclave never declared outright war. He was shifty, he did things on the sly, all the while with a smile on his face. He would never challenge directly and give his hand away. Especially with no purpose in mind other than an insult.

"Rhododendron and basil, my lord! Danger and hatred. What can it mean?"

"I do not know. Perhaps they've gone to the wrong address?"

Wainwright shook his head vigorously. "They were addressed to you, my lord."

"No note with them?"

"No, and the fellow who pulled up with the cart would say nothing. He looked frightened witless, though. I do not know who he has dealt with, but he was shaken over it."

This certainly was a mystery, and not one that he could solve without more information.

Wainwright pulled a folded note from his coat pocket. "Then this came on the heels of the flowers, though I do not know if it is in regard to them."

Miles took the paper and broke the seal.

You are a terrible person and I hope bad things happen to you.

He handed the note to Wainwright. "I think it must be connected somehow," he said. "Though I cannot make heads or tails of this."

Wainwright read the one line of the note. "Someone wishes you ill, my lord. You do not suppose, what I mean is, far be it for me to suggest…"

"It is not Montclave," Miles said. "None of this is his style."

Wainwright nodded thoughtfully. "Then there is the other thing, my lord."

"The other thing?" How could there be another thing?

Wainwright's voice dropped to a whisper. "Lady Margaret is just now interviewing a valet in the drawing room."

"What does Lady Margaret want with a valet?" Miles asked. "Has Harraby asked her to manage it for him? Deuced odd if he has—only a gentleman will know what's wanted in a valet."

"No, no, that is not how it's come about, though I hardly know how it *has* come about. My lord, if you wished for a new valet I could perfectly understand why—Moreau is temperamental and tiresome. But perhaps it might have been done in a more… discreet fashion."

"I am well aware that he is temperamental and tiresome, but I am used to him. Why would I want to bring in a new valet?" Miles asked.

"I cannot presume to know, but you did place an advertisement for one. I did get my hopes up, but perhaps you were assisting another gentleman?"

"I placed no advertisement," Miles said, wildly puzzled.

"I cannot understand it," Wainwright said. "A notice with a copy of the advertisement for a valet, franked as fully paid, was hand-delivered a few hours ago. It was not even folded up, a footman read it and then of course shared the news below stairs as fast as his legs could carry him there. It was not a moment before Mr. Moreau had his hands on it. And then, a fellow turned up at the door in response to it."

"He was sent away and told of the mistake, I presume."

Wainwright shuffled his feet on the pavement. "Well, you see, my lord, it was just then that Lady Margaret was let out of a carriage by Lord Harraby. Lady Margaret very kindly purchased her special blend of tea for the staff, by the by—prepared by Mr. Twining himself. She took in what was occurring and insisted on standing in for you through what was sure to be an onerous task. There have been several fellows turned up since, and she's insisted on seeing all of them! I told her it was not the thing, but last I heard her in there she was asking a fellow what his thoughts were on Shrewsbury Cake. Why? He is not a cook."

"Lady Margaret has been interviewing valets that I did not advertise for, and someone has sent me flowers and plants indicating their hatred and distrust, and a note claims I am a terrible person. What is going on here?"

"I do not know, my lord."

Miles had a sudden thought that really gave him pause. "What has Moreau been doing through all this?"

His valet was not likely to manage such a surprise with any sort of stalwartness.

Beads of sweat sprung up on Wainwright's brow. "That is another thing—nobody knows. I would have thought he'd be downstairs, throwing those prospective valets out the door and kicking up like a bad-tempered toddler. But no, he has disappeared up the stairs, locked himself in your chambers, and we only hear the occasional thump."

"Good God, I'd best get in there before he hangs himself or sets my house on fire."

"My thoughts exactly, my lord. A quiet Moreau must be a dangerous Moreau. It is too strange to be otherwise—he is never quiet!"

Miles spurred his horse. This situation was unaccountable. He'd been off on pleasant errands and returned to a house in an uproar. Who was behind this?

CHAPTER SIXTEEN

GRACE HAD SPENT the rest of the prior day working very hard to keep her head up. She had attempted to sleep for an hour or so, but it had not happened, and so she had risen and rejoined the family.

She thought that was surely what she must do. She must not moon around and worry everyone just because all her hopes and dreams were crushed. She was a duke's daughter; she could not allow any feelings of despair to inconvenience anybody.

She was also determined to keep any lightheadedness or dizziness under wraps. It was always the case that a circumstance that was upsetting put her off her feet a bit.

As might be expected, her sisters went to great lengths to cheer her. Valor explained that she'd had a long consultation with Mrs. Wendover, occasionally joined by Nelson, and concluded Lord Dashlend was a terrible person and something bad should happen to him. She declared he would be ashamed to discover her opinion.

Grace had scolded her and ordered that she was not to write any letters about it. Valor had refused to meet her eye and then pretended she heard Mrs. Right calling for her. She ran from the room and so Grace was afraid she already had written down her sentiments.

Patience and Serenity, who so rarely joined together as the twins they were, brought her some of the last miniature apple cakes, which Patience had been hiding in her room.

Winsome attempted to convince Grace that she'd been suspicious of Lord Dashlend from the first, which might have been true, as Winsome was suspicious of everybody.

Verity explained that florists making mistakes was a very usual circumstance. At least, she had heard it said.

Mrs. Right sat by Grace, patted her hand, and hoped that Lord Dashlend would pay dearly for his perfidy.

Even Felicity arrived, and Grace had no doubt she'd been sent for. Felicity needed no explanation of what had happened and came fully prepared to support her sister. She was mightily perplexed, as she had been certain a match was in the offing.

Grace's father, of all of them, seemed more grim than was his usual mien. All he would say was that he'd sent Dashlend a message. A clear message of his contempt.

Of all that she was told, that might be the most worrying. However, the duke could not be pressed into revealing what he'd done. All he would say was that a gentleman so foolish as to not assure himself that the flowers he sent were going to the right address ought to be called to task over it.

There had been some question over whether she would attend Lady Montague's ball. Valor suggested they could stay cozy together and play Fact or Fib. Serenity wept over the idea of Grace dancing as if all was well when it was not—how could she bear it? Patience was of two minds—she presumed Grace did not wish to go and so should stay at home. On the other hand, if she did go she might stumble upon an opportunity to hit Lord Dashlend over the head, which would be gratifying to everybody. When Winsome was apprised of the hitting over the head idea, she began leaning toward Grace going after all. Verity, ever willing to provide a counterpoint, mentioned that Lord Dashlend might hit Grace back, as it was established that he was a terrible person, and then where would they be?

Her father's opinion weighed the heaviest with Grace. He said she ought to go and hold her head high. There were times, he said, when one must just face a thing down.

Grace decided she'd rather not go, but she must go. It was awful enough that she had been informed of the real case of things with Lord Dashlend. He'd no doubt been told by the florist of the mistake that had been made. It would be a thousand times worse if she were to let on that she had been at all affected by it.

Was she to stay at home and allow Lord Dashlend to imagine she was in a puddle of tears over it?

No, she would not do *that*. She had lost enough, she would not throw her pride into the fire too.

As she was to go, she selected the dress she admired the most to give her courage. It had never been worn, as Felicity had not thought it suited her—it was a frothy confection of pale blue silk with a netting overlay in the same shade. The netting was embellished with hundreds of the tiniest crystals that would shimmer in the candlelight.

She would do her best to go to the ball and be cheerful. She would look about her more than she had done so far. She'd shot her arrow too high and now she must lower her bow and aim for the more realistic prospects of the single gentlemen in Town.

Perhaps her own marriage would not be the sort of love match that Felicity had found, but then not all were. Certainly, she could be happy, or at least content, with a genial gentleman who was not as high a flyer as Lord Dashlend.

Grace sighed as she wiled away the afternoon pretending to read a book. She would be realistic and practical, though it would not be as thrilling as her recent experience of being unrealistic and impractical.

MILES ENTERED HIS house with trepidation after being apprised of the note, the awful flowers, and the valets turning up for interviews.

The front hall was a jungle of unwanted vegetation. His first order of business was to direct it to be removed.

Then he'd gone to the drawing room and informed the hopeful fellow being looked over by Lady Margaret that there had been an unfortunate mix-up. He directed the footmen to bar the entrance to anybody else turning up.

Lady Margaret had been surprised that her services were not needed, but happily jumped to the next thing of interest. She would attend Lady Montague's ball, escorted by Lord Harraby. Amidst broad hints that she was expecting to be apprised of welcome news this night, Miles left her with a tea tray.

He jogged up the stairs to his bedchamber and found the door locked.

Miles banged on it. "Open up the door, Moreau."

From the other side, Moreau answered back. "Ah, he still gives Moreau orders though Moreau is to be replaced. Moreau is to be thrown to the road like a stray dog. Moreau—the greatest valet living! The infamy! Perhaps Lord Dashlend might employ the duke's ridiculous valet and have always access to his oldest set of clothes."

Miles was not so certain Moreau was the greatest valet living, but he was competent enough. As for why he would suppose Miles to be interested in the duke's valet's oldest set of clothes, that must remain a mystery. "There has been some sort of mistake. I did not advertise for a valet."

"Moreau saw it with his own eyes!"

"And yet, I did not. I do not know who did, but certainly it was meant to cause me an inconvenience."

This prompted rather hysterical laughter from Moreau. "Now Moreau sees it all! His fate, whatever it is meant to be, is only an inconvenience to the great Lord Dashlend. Moreau is a fly, a speck of dust, a nothing!"

Miles sighed. "Moreau, open this door at once or I will break it down and then I really *will* dismiss you. I do not have time for your histrionics—I have an important ball to attend this evening."

Moreau did not answer, but Miles heard his pacing back and forth. What was he doing in there?

Finally, the door cracked open and Moreau peered his head out. "Moreau wonders, if this really is all a mistake, what a lord might think of…certain actions that were taken."

"What have you done?"

The door opened wider and Moreau shrugged. Moreau's shrugs never indicated good news. Miles pushed his way in.

What assaulted his eyes when he did so was astonishing. Every item of clothing he owned was strewn about the room. Coats were inside out, shirts were crumpled, boots smeared with shaving powder, hats smashed in, gloves in the soot of the hearth, there was even a pair of breeches hanging from the gilded frame of a portrait on the wall. The room looked as if it had been attacked by a wild animal.

"Moreau has been made upset by recent events," his valet said, looking round as if he were seeing it for the first time.

"*I* have been made upset by *these* recent events," Miles said, his eyes scanning the room.

"Oh this?" Moreau said, following his gaze. "This is nothing. A bit of disorder. Due to upset. Moreau feels more calm now."

"How wonderful for Moreau," Miles said drily. "Get this room back in order and I had better have a perfect set of clothes for this evening. I do not care what lengths you have to go to accomplish it."

Miles turned on his heel. He would go to the quiet of his library and contemplate this bizarre homecoming. Somebody, aside from his valet, was enraged with him. The only person he was certain wished him ill was Montclave, but none of this was the sort of thing Montclave would get up to.

What was he missing? Who had he offended?

As he reached the door, he heard Moreau mutter, "What is one expected to do when one hears one is being replaced? Moreau acted quite reasonable."

Miles bit his tongue, lest he point out that Moreau and reasonable were not very well acquainted.

"CHIN UP, GRACIE," the duke said as the carriage rattled along the darkened streets.

Grace smiled at her father in his seat across the carriage. "Papa, I am quite chin up. I have thought deeply regarding this situation and I have begun to understand that I was only being unrealistic. I was shooting too high. Now, I will proceed with good sense tucked in my reticule and I am certain I shall make a match with some acceptable gentleman."

"What on earth are you going on about? You are a Nicolet— there is no 'too high' for *us* to shoot for. No, that is not where we are. Dashlend has proved himself too low and you must turn your aim higher."

Her father really was a darling, though she was not quite convinced of his view on things. Who could be higher than Lord Dashlend?

"Now, what is our plan?" the duke asked. "Dashlend swore he'd be haunting the front hall for our arrival. If he sticks to it, how do we treat him? I'm inclined to throw a vase of flowers at his head and let Lady Montague say what she likes about it. I know your sisters would be all for it and Mrs. Right would happily do it herself, but I'll allow you to set the tone."

Grace fussed with the netting on her skirt. "The tone, Papa, is neutral. I am entirely unaffected. Did I see that roses were misdelivered when they should have gone to Lady Lavender? Oh yes, now that you mention it, Lord Dashlend, I believe one of the footmen handled it. Goodness, I hadn't thought of it until you asked."

The duke nodded approvingly. "Yes, yes, that will do very well. I might have thought of the attitude myself if I weren't so busy imagining cracking a vase over his head. If he thinks he has affected you, indifference will sting that puffed up rogue all the more. Here we are. Let us go in and show these nobodies how it's done."

And so they did proceed in. Lady Montague was an imposing woman, the sort who'd been long in society, knew everybody, and was so established that she did not worry over anybody's opinion. She'd seemed well acquainted with the duke and jokingly told him he'd find no tigers inside.

Of course, they all knew what she meant. Lady Albright had not hosted her annual rout this year, on account of her tiger getting loose last year and putting the duke, Mr. Stratton, and Felicity in grave danger.

"Deuced odd, that woman," the duke said, in a summation of Lady Albright.

Lady Montague had nodded in sympathy.

They proceeded into the great hall. Though only a day ago Grace would have dearly wished that Lord Dashlend would be found waiting for her, now she just as dearly hoped he would be nowhere to be seen.

Aside from masking her grave disappointment, it was all so awkward. He would know his flowers had been misdelivered. What would he say about it?

She had told her father she planned a neutral attitude and she was determined to stick to it. However, it would be very hard.

But there he was and approaching fast.

As he always seemed to be, he was positively dashing. Dashing Dashlend—how that was not his nickname she did not know. His clothes were perfection, his features divine, and his very perfect Roman nose. None of that was for her though. It was all for Lady Lavender.

She felt the familiar rush of lightheadedness, though she had jumped around her bedchamber for nearly an hour before getting dressed. She took in a breath and held her head very still to steady herself.

"Your Grace. Lady Grace," he said, with an elegant bow.

"Dashlend," the duke said flatly.

"If I might have the honor of showing you to the cloak-room?"

The duke shrugged. "Any footman could do it, I suppose."

Not surprisingly, Lord Dashlend seemed a bit thrown on the back foot from that comment. He recovered himself and said, "Excellent, just this way."

The duke squeezed Grace's hand as Lord Dashlend led them forward. Her father took her cloak and Lord Dashlend secured her card. Before handing it over, he said, "Might I put my name down?"

Grace had been expecting it. After all, as the daisies had spelled out, she was a new friend.

She nodded. "Of course, Lord Dashlend."

Though she pretended at disinterest, she did steal a glance at where he put himself down.

She assumed he'd go for somewhere in the middle, but he did not. He put himself down for the last. He would take her into supper.

Why? Did Lady Lavender not attend this evening? Surely that must be the case. As he could not spend extended time with the lady who'd been sent roses, he contented himself with a new friend.

Or even more likely, he wished some time to apologize for the flowers being misdelivered.

It was not very fair that he do it, though. It would put a burden on Grace to carry on with her appearance of neutrality and disinterest. As well, she was meant to be looking further afield, and it would have been sensible for her to dine with a gentleman as yet unknown to her.

He handed her card to her, and just then another familiar voice was heard.

She turned to find Lord Montclave.

"Your Grace, Lady Grace," Lord Montclave said, "I see my cousin has beat me to the punch." He glanced at her card. "May I,

Lady Grace?"

Grace nodded. Lord Montclave wrote himself down for the first. For some reason, he spent just a bit too long a time staring at her card. There was not much to see, as he was only the second gentleman on it. Then, he seemed to collect himself. He smiled and handed it back.

They stood there awkwardly for a moment as her father stared off into the distance. He gave off the impression that he found the company of these two gentlemen just the smallest bit tedious.

Fortunately, Lady Margaret and Lord Harraby appeared to break the uncomfortable silence.

Amidst the greetings, Grace looked with wonder at Lady Margaret's attire. Each time Grace saw the lady, her skirts seemed just the littlest bit wider. This evening, she wore a silver satin gown embellished with strings of seed pearls draped in rows. There was so much fabric to the skirt that it fell into wide folds. The ostrich feathers in her hair were as they had been from the first—a bit thinning but very tall.

"Lady Margaret," the duke said, "you take me back to a simpler time."

Lord Harraby said, "That is just what I think, Your Grace. Remember how it was, when we were all young and full of bounce?"

"Now," Lady Margaret said to Lord Harraby and the duke, "do not attempt to convince me, either of you, that you have lost your bounce."

"If I have not," Lord Harraby said gallantly, "the charge of it must be laid at Lady Margaret's door. Our current interests have been invigorating."

Lady Margaret laughed. "Oh yes, our current interests. There is nothing so good as to see two worthy young people happily settled."

Grace was not at all certain what they referred to. Was Lady Margaret a staunch supporter of a match between Lord Dashlend and Lady Lavender? Why did Lord Montclave appear so stricken over it?

Lord Dashlend appeared rather stricken himself, but then she could well guess the cause. The gentleman had not yet had time to apologize for the misdirected flowers. He would not like anything close to the subject mentioned.

"Well now," the duke said, "I will escort my daughter into the ballroom."

It was said very abruptly, and Grace understood her father had reason to pull her away. She curtsied and took his arm.

Once they were away, the duke said, "I do not like what I just heard. Lady Margaret seems to hint that Montclave means to declare himself."

Grace wrinkled her brow. That had not been her guess at all.

"If she were talking about Dashlend and Lady Lavender," the duke went on, "I do not believe she would have said it in our hearing. We've no connection to that business."

That might well be true. She had not thought of it that way.

"Grace, under no circumstance accept that fellow."

"I have no intention of it, Papa," Grace said, finding the idea faintly repugnant.

The duke nodded. "Excellent. I only warn you off as you would not be the first lady to rashly accept someone after receiving a disappointment, and then lived to regret it. The moment can be satisfying, but the years are long."

"You are always full of good sense, Papa."

"Am I? Well, let us see if you can convince my sister of that fact. She sails toward us like a sloop on the downwind."

Indeed, Lady Marchfield was headed right for them. Grace had not seen her since Mr. Button had been removed from the house. They had exchanged several letters and Grace remained on good terms with the lady. Her father, however, remained on the same terms with his sister as always, which were never good.

"It is the talk everywhere, Roland. I heard it from my lady's maid, who heard it from several servants of different houses. I hope you are satisfied with yourself."

Grace had not the first idea what she referred to. The duke said, "I *am* generally satisfied with myself, as I do not factor your opinion into the equation. What this latest bee in your bonnet is, I do not know or care."

"You most certainly do know. It is said that cartfuls of hateful flowers and plants were delivered to Lord Dashlend—Columbine, Marigolds, Thistle, Rhododendron, and I do not know what else. All hateful. Do you deny it?"

"I deny there were cartfuls," the duke said. "There was one cart, but then people do exaggerate. Very eccentric of them, I always think."

Grace's eyes widened just a bit. From her father's prior hints, she knew he'd done something. She'd presumed it had come to nothing since he'd not said anything further about it.

"And then, going so far as to meddle with the staff! Why should you make the poor valet believe he was being dismissed?"

The duke laughed. "*That*, I know nothing about. It sounds like the sort of thing Mrs. Right might manage, though."

"That ridiculous housekeeper!" Lady Marchfield said. "I suppose she sent the threatening note too? She accuses Lord Dashlend of being a terrible person and wishes he comes to a bad end? How dare that woman send such a note to a person above her station?"

"Oh, Aunt, that might have been Valor," Grace said, entirely convinced that it had been. She'd told Valor not to write a letter and her sister had an instant look of guilt and run from the room. As well, Valor had wished Mr. Stratton to come to a bad end too. It seemed to be becoming a habit.

"Valor?" Lady Marchfield said, looking aghast. "Roland, you go so far as to allow your youngest daughter to fire off letters wherever and to whomever she pleases?"

"How should I know what she gets up to?" the duke said.

"That is the point. You ought to know. So far, nobody seems to know you are at the bottom of all this, though I guessed it quick enough. I do not understand what you have been about. Lord Dashlend is a respectable man and has seemed to express an interest in Grace. Why on earth would you ruin it for her?"

Of course, her aunt could not know there was nothing to ruin.

The duke's visage darkened. "Look here, Lady Misery, I have told you time and again to stop your attempts to meddle with me and mine. Be off now and take that sour face with you."

Lady Marchfield, seeming to understand she would get nowhere with her brother, let out a disgusted sigh. "Have a care, Grace, that your lunatic father does not steer you to disaster."

She turned on her heel and marched off.

The duke quietly laughed. "Valor sent him one of her condemning notes. Unsigned, it sounds like. I should have known Mrs. Right would get up to something original—that valet of Dashlend's has the constitution of a newborn chick."

"I do hope, though," Grace said, "none of this is connected to us, Papa. It does not particularly support my attitude of neutrality and indifference."

"No," the duke said thoughtfully, "I suppose it does not. Not to worry, Lady Misery won't put it about. She won't like it to reflect on the family, as that reflects on her."

"I believe you are right about that."

"Pay no mind to her, Gracie. She does not know what has gone on."

Grace nodded. There was the real truth of it—Lady Marchfield did not know where things stood. If she did, she would not wonder that her family had rallied round and exacted revenge. She would still disapprove, but she would not wonder.

Though Grace did not wish Lord Dashlend to know where the troubles that had beset him had originated, she could not help but to be touched that her father, Mrs. Right, and Valor had each taken steps to avenge her feelings.

No matter what happened, they would all support one another.

CHAPTER SEVENTEEN

MILES COULD NOT work out what he'd just witnessed. The duke had led Lady Grace away and he was left with Lady Margaret, Lord Harraby, and Montclave.

It had been such an odd encounter. The duke looked almost unhappy to see him. Lady Grace was… he did not really know. She had smiled on occasion, but it had seemed somehow forced.

He did say he would wait for them in the great hall. Why did they seem the slightest bit annoyed that he had?

Perhaps it was all in his imagination. There was something very fraught about knowing one was hours from proposing. Perhaps it had affected him in some way.

Perhaps they had only left so abruptly to get away from Montclave.

Lady Margaret bounced up and down on her toes, her ostrich feathers waving back and forth. "Is this to be it, Dashlend? Is this to be the momentous evening?"

Miles' eyes widened. Really, there was no amount of indiscretion Lady Margaret would not dare.

"Now, do not worry that we talk out of turn, Dashlend," Lord Harraby said. "Montclave here knows all about it."

"Does he?" Miles asked. He did not like that idea at all. Why should they have spoken to Montclave about anything, much less his personal business?

"We encountered Lord Montclave at Mr. Twining's establishment," Lady Margaret said. "I was determined to purchase some tea for your household staff. They have all been so kind."

Miles was well aware of the tea purchase. That did not explain how or why Lady Margaret would have revealed any of his personal aims. She must encounter people everywhere, all the time, is that what she was in the habit of doing?

"Lady Margaret was so good as to inform me that you intend on proposing to Lady Grace," Montclave said drily. "They are fingers crossed that tonight is to be the momentous occasion."

"Lady Margaret," Miles said, "I have communicated no such ideas."

"Ha, but that is just it!" Lord Harraby said. "We have been busy observing."

"And deducing," Lady Margaret said, nodding vigorously.

"You are most welcome in my house, Lady Margaret," Miles said gravely, "but I must ask you to steer clear of predicting anything I may or may not do. Now, I will go into the ballroom. There are other ladies who wait for me to put myself down for a set. Other ladies, who I may or may not be interested in."

Miles turned and strode off. Of course, not before hearing Lady Margaret say, "Poor lad, he's got a case of the lovestruck nerves."

"No doubt," Lord Harraby answered.

Miles did not quite hear what Lord Harraby said next, but it might have been some mention of his own lovestruck nerves. Miles had high hopes the lord was planning on taking Lady Margaret off his hands sometime in the near future.

He could not say if he had himself fallen victim to lovestruck nerves. He did not think so, in any event. What he was sure of though, was that this entire day was like a dream. Dreams so rarely made sense and were one odd scene strung to the next. That was exactly what this day had been like.

Nevertheless, he maintained high hopes that the very end of this day would conclude in his favor.

He patted the pocket that held the necklace he'd purchased

for Lady Grace. His visit to Rundell and Bridge had been the last usual thing he'd experienced.

There was nothing to do but steady on. He knew his purpose and was determined to accomplish it.

MONTCLAVE WAS NOT at all fooled by Dashlend's protestations that he might be interested in other ladies aside from Lady Grace. In fact, his reaction rather told the tale. Dashlend had been made uncomfortable that Lady Margaret had guessed his plans.

The lord doth protest too much.

It was all well and good to be certain of which way the wind blew. But what was he going to do about it? How would he keep them apart to prevent it from happening? Even if he could devise something to stop it this night, what about the morrow and the morrow and the morrow?

What was a permanent solution?

Might he compromise Lady Grace in some way?

No, he did not see how he could do it without landing in the bad books of her duke. Or worse, landing on a dueling green.

He'd already done what he could to reduce Lady Grace's estimation of Dashlend by sending those flowers addressed to Lady Lavender. It seemed to have worked, too. Lady Grace's manner had changed toward Dashlend and the duke seemed even more changed.

Would it hold though? If Dashlend proposed, would not the whole ruse come out? Lady Grace would remain forever mystified over who was the author of the scheme, though Dashlend would probably guess at it. The end result was all that mattered though—Dashlend would deny he sent them, and Lady Grace would probably believe him.

What would his mother advise? What would the dowager do?

Montclave did not know, except to know one thing—she

would take drastic measures to stop an engagement. The dowager never allowed herself to be defeated. The only setback of any consequence she'd ever experienced was when Dashlend was born. Her ideas of her son becoming the next earl had been sunk. And yet, she refused, even at this late date, to consider herself entirely defeated in that plan.

It was just that now, all her hopes were pinned on what he himself would do next.

The orchestra was tuning. He searched the ballroom for Lady Grace and she was not hard to find. She was the prettiest lady attending and had drawn to her side a bevy of admirers like bees to a hive.

He made his way over.

As he led Lady Grace away from the callow youths who'd encircled her, he could not help but to notice that the duke did not appear very approving of him. He did not make too much of it, as the duke did not seem particularly approving of Dashlend either.

The ball would begin with a cotillion, which would afford some little time for talking. He must make the most of it.

As they completed the circle and moved to the allemande, he said, "Lady Margaret is in high spirits this evening, though I imagine her hopes will be dashed—it does not seem as if Lady Lavender attends."

He watched her expression closely. There was no doubt the statement had affected her. Mightily, though she worked to hide it.

"Goodness, I did not know Lady Margaret was so fond of Lady Lavender that her hopes would be dashed by the lady's absence."

"It is not for herself that she hopes for," Montclave said. Then he stuttered just the smallest bit and attempted to appear embarrassed to have said something he ought not have said. "I am sorry, I speak out of turn. I was under the impression that Dashlend's own hopes were widely known. Lady Margaret has taken a great interest in his happiness."

"Yes, of course, she would do," Lady Grace said, her complexion a deal more pale than it had been.

"I suppose they will make quite the dashing couple," Montclave pressed on. "Anybody who has seen them dance together must own it. They are both exceedingly graceful—two swans on a lake, as it were."

Montclave suppressed a smile. It was a nice touch to prey on Lady Grace's own insecurities. She doubted her own grace on the ballroom floor. Really, he thought his mother would be proud of that ingenious stroke.

Something in Lady Grace's manner changed, as if she gathered all her fortitude together. "Yes, of course they will appear very well suited," she said resolutely.

"Ah well, I think the rest of us mere mortals must just struggle on as best we can," he said.

Lady Grace nodded and Montclave was convinced that *she* was convinced of Dashlend's inclination toward Lady Lavender.

The question was, how long would it hold?

GRACE FELT AS if she'd been wounded, and as much as she tried to cover and treat the wound so it might begin to heal, the bandage was ripped away again and again.

Not even just ripped away—ripped away and then scalding water and piles of salt poured over it. She'd worked very hard to maintain an appearance of equanimity all through her dance with Lord Montclave.

She supposed this was how it would be from now on. Everybody would express their admiration for the dashing couple—Lord Dashlend and Lady Lavender.

If there was anything at all bright about the evening, it was that Lady Lavender did not attend. She would at least not be forced to view the couple. Not yet, in any case.

She must hope that when she *was* forced to see them together, she had gained more peace than she was in receipt of at just this moment.

Grace had moved through the sets in almost a dreamlike state. It was very hard to make herself amusing and she was afraid she was not a very genial partner.

How could she be? Every minute that passed brought closer the real test of the evening. She would dance the last set with Lord Dashlend and then he would lead her into supper. She was counting on her father to note her discomfort in the dining room, and certainly she would be so, and take her home abruptly.

It was one of the lovely things about her Papa—he would not give a toss for what anybody, including Lord Dashlend, would think about it. He would happily leave Lord Dashlend to sit alone, entertaining himself, if he sensed the slightest whiff of unhappiness in his daughter.

Just now, Lord Kendrick, a baron from Hertfordshire, was working hard to make conversation.

"It is my first season," the lord said. "My father does not really approve of outlaying so much money for a London season, but my mother pointed out that if he didn't loosen the purse strings for it, I'd end up wedding Miss Granger. She is from our neighborhood, you see."

"Indeed," Grace said mechanically. "Are you partial to Miss Granger?"

The baron laughed. "Nobody is partial to Miss Granger, particularly not myself or my father. She is very purse-lipped and does not approve of…well, anything fun, really. It was only my mother's gambit to frighten my father that he might end with a daughter-in-law frowning from every corner. I reckon Miss Granger weds the vicar and they should go on purse-lipped and happy forevermore."

Grace was rather startled that the lord should insult the lady so thoroughly.

"No, I have my sights set higher than Miss Granger," the baron said. "Do you know Lady Lavender Westcott?"

Grace suppressed a disgusted sigh and nodded. "I have made her acquaintance," she said.

"Now there is a fine lady. She's the sort who would show Miss Granger what is what." In a wistful tone, he said, "I thought she would be here this evening. I wonder where she is."

Grace hardly knew how to answer. In the first moment, she was entirely aggravated to hear of Lady Lavender's charms again. It seemed everyone was bowled over by her. In the second moment, though, she understood that poor Lord Kendrick was on the verge of being as heartbroken as she was herself.

It must be so. The baron from Hertfordshire would not prevail against Lord Dashlend for the hand of Lady Lavender. He was too youthful, too unseasoned, too…not Lord Dashlend.

Grace felt a wave of dizziness wash over her and she leaned just a little bit on Lord Kendrick's arm. He did not seem to notice, as he was engaged in listing out all of Lady Lavender's charms.

She hardly listened. For one, she was already quite conversant regarding the lady's charms. For another, she was thinking about how unsteady she felt just now.

Grace was determined that she did not show it. She would dance with Lord Dashlend soon enough and would not embarrass herself with a stumble. That would be entirely too much to bear.

Between the sets she must steal away somewhere and jump up and down in private. It was the only thing that helped steady her.

That was what she would do. Then, she would get through the set with Lord Dashlend and her father would take her home and she would bandage up her wounds again. They would heal eventually; she must just give it time. She would regain her spirits.

In time.

MONTCLAVE FELT THE minutes moving too fast. He'd escorted one lady after the next through the sets, none of them very interesting and one of them he vowed to never dance with again.

That one he was still dancing with.

Lady Agatha, an earl's daughter, apparently thought the world of herself and was determined to hear that any gentleman coming into her sphere thought the very same. She fished for compliments like she stood on the banks of the River Tay looking to land a fat trout.

"My mother said, Agatha, that color does something well for your eyes," Lady Agatha said. "But I said, Mama, I am certain it does not."

And there it was, the long pause awaiting the compliment. He was not at all inclined to take the bait.

"Well, sometimes eyes are not a lady's best feature," he said. "No shame in that, I always think."

He said it in a genial tone, as if he did not intend it as a slap. Though, he very much did, and well-earned too. Lady Agatha's eyes were a dull brown, on the small side, and set too close together. If he were her, he would not bring any attention to them.

The lady turned several shades of pink and fell to silence.

It was well she did. He needed time to think!

When he could, he watched Lady Grace. She did not seem as if she were enjoying herself very much. However, it would be only another half hour before Dashlend collected her. Only a half hour before Dashlend would have the opportunity of clearing up any misapprehensions about the flowers.

He had to do something. What? What? What?

The set blessedly came to a conclusion. He bowed and said, "Lady Agatha, charmed," as if he had not the first idea that he'd insulted her.

The lady hurried off, no doubt to locate her mama and inquire if her eyes were or were not her best feature.

As there would be a quarter hour between sets, Montclave had hoped to engage Lady Grace in conversation. It felt as if he were only putting off the inevitable, but he must do what he could. An idea might spring upon him, even at the last minute.

As Lady Grace curtsied and broke away from Lord Kendrick, she inexplicably set out toward the great hall. Where was she going?

Could it be that she was going home? Perhaps she felt ill? Would the fates smile upon him in such a manner?

He hurried through the ballroom, silently praying as he did so. He must know—was she leaving?

He passed through the ballroom doors into the hall and saw a wisp of the hem of her gown disappear as she entered a room. The door closed behind her.

Where was she going? The library? Music room? Where? And most importantly, why?

Was Dashlend in there? Had they arranged to meet?

Montclave strode down the corridor. He noted an old brass key hanging by the door she'd just slipped through—the type used when the house was closed up. Many a Londoner locked every door when they departed for the countryside, the idea being that a housebreaker would discover he did not have access to the entire house, just the room he broke into. For the skeleton staff staying behind it was felt an added security measure.

He could lock her in there, and then Dashlend might decide he'd been stood up and leave in a huff. That was, if he was not in there with her. It would not do him any good at all to lock them in together. They would be discovered and a wedding would become a necessity to maintain the lady's honor.

If Dashlend was in there, he could say that Lady Margaret needed him urgently and did not look well. What he would do after that, he did not know.

He must just take one step at a time.

Montclave slowly pressed the door open enough to see inside.

What he saw, he was not even certain he saw, so little sense did it make.

The room was lit up with candles. Lady Grace was near the windows, jumping up and down. She was alone, and just jumping.

In that moment, she perceived that she was not alone. He pulled back, but she could see the door had been opened.

With one eye he peered in from the dim corridor.

"Oh!" she cried. She stumbled into a brass candelabra with eight bright burning candles ranged across it. The candelabra tipped over and the lit candles fell to the floor.

One of the flames caught the netting of her dress. As she beat it out, another was busy setting the curtains alight. Lady Grace pounded at it but it did little good. The flame began its rise up the material.

Montclave felt his mind in a muddle. Without thinking, he shut the door, turned the key in the lock, and threw the key down the dark corridor.

He hurried back into the ballroom, hardly understanding what he'd done.

Should he go back?

He passed through the ballroom doors and the acrid smell of smoke seemed to follow him there. What had he done?

A footman in the hall yelled, "Fire!"

CHAPTER EIGHTEEN

G RACE HAD BEEN jumping up and down to attempt to settle her dizziness when she'd heard the creak of the door.

She could not see the face clearly, but she knew it was a man. Had she been foolish to steal off alone and put herself in a compromising position?

Such was her surprise and confusion, she stumbled and knocked over a candelabra.

The candles seemed to fly everywhere!

She beat at the netting of her dress, as that was the most urgent of the flames. As she did so, her mind raced—what was she to tell everyone? Her dress was burnt beyond repair, was she to say she'd been jumping up and down alone because she was dizzy and knocked over candles? It was too absurd.

As all of that was racing through her mind, the curtains caught fire.

Grace was momentarily frozen. Was she in the midst of burning down a lady's house?

She needed help. She could not rectify this on her own, the flames had grown too high.

Grace raced to the door to fling it open and call for assistance.

And found it locked.

At first, she was convinced she was mistaken. She was not turning the latch correctly.

It did finally dawn on her that she was locked in. The smoke was filling the room. Grace raced to the set of windows away from the flames and threw the sash open. She gasped the cool night air into her lungs. But so did the fire take in the night air. It seemed to feed on the air rushing into the room.

She put her head out the window and looked down. Should she jump?

She might not survive the fall and if she did, might be seriously maimed. Grace shouted for help as loud as she could. Had anyone heard her? Was anybody coming?

WHEN MILES HEARD the shout of fire, his first thought was to get Lady Grace to safety. These old piles of stone were filled to the brim with wood that could go up in a flash.

Where was she?

He searched the room and began to think she might have gone to the lady's retiring room when the duke approached.

"Have you seen my daughter?" he asked.

"No, Your Grace, she is not in the ballroom."

"I do not like this," the duke said gravely. "If she could, she would find me. Come with me, we'd better assist in fighting back whatever has been set afire—probably a chimney that was not cleaned as it should have been."

They pushed their way through the throng, most of whom were leaving the premises. The male staff of the house, along with some of Lady Montague's guests were handing sand buckets in a line. Further down the corridor, two burly men Miles took to be coachmen were throwing their weight against a door.

Then he heard it. The faint cry for help. It was unmistakable. It was Lady Grace.

"Your Grace," he said, catching at the duke's arm, "this way."

He practically dragged the duke forward. As he did so, Lady Grace's cries became clearer. Somehow, she was locked behind a door, and that room was where the smoke was coming from.

"Out of the way," Miles shouted. He threw himself at the door. It did not budge an inch. He did not know what he'd been expecting, the two men who were trying to get it open were veritable giants and had not seen success.

He turned to the men. "It feels like a deadbolt. Try working on the hinges. Your Grace, let us see if we can get in another way."

The duke nodded. Miles raced to the next door in the corridor, throwing it open in hopes of finding a connecting door.

There was none.

He ran to the window and raised the sash, leaning far out to see how close the next window was.

Lady Grace had her head out, breathing the air there as the smoke would have overcome her in the room. He could see it drifting out over her head.

He looked down. The drop was too far to try a jump. He would somehow have to get her on the ledge. It was a foot wide, which was wider than most. It could be done. It must be done.

She stared at him wide-eyed, as if she'd lost the faculty of speech.

Miles climbed out and inched toward her. "Lady Grace, you'll have to climb out." Seeing the look of terror in her eyes, he said, "It's not far to go. I'll steady you."

"I cannot," she whispered. "I am dizzy."

"That's just the smoke. Your head will clear when you are away from it."

"No," she said softly.

No? What choice did she have?

Miles realized she was in a state of panic. He would somehow need to jar her out of it. "Lady Grace, do as I say this instant! Climb out and I will help you over."

She stared at him for a moment. Just then, he could hear the crackling of the fire. They did not have much time.

She nodded, picking up her skirts, and slowly climbed out.

She stood up and then wobbled. Miles grasped at her to stop her from falling, but her balance was giving way.

He threw himself in front of her as they plummeted into the rose bushes below.

The fall seemed to take a very long time, though it could not have been more than a second or two. They crashed into the greenery, the branches and thorns prying their way into every bit of uncovered skin. The final landing was far worse than any fall off a horse he'd ever taken. It felt as if he'd hit a stone pavement rather than earth.

Miles had the wind knocked out of him. He forced air into his lungs, though the pain was immense.

"All right?" he choked out as Lady Grace lay on top of him.

"I think so," she said in a small voice. "I was locked in."

"Who? The fire?"

"Oh, I started it. Accidently."

"Are you alive?" the duke shouted from above.

"Papa," Lady Grace answered.

From his prone position looking up at the sky, Miles saw the duke leaning out. "They finally got the door opened," the duke said helpfully. "The fire was on its way to burning itself out. Stone walls, you know."

The duke's head disappeared.

"We should have waited," Lady Grace said, quite unnecessarily.

She rolled off him, causing further pain to his chest. "You are hurt," she said, again quite unnecessarily.

"Yes."

She took a sharp breath in. In a voice no louder than a whisper on the wind she said, "If you are paralyzed, Lady Lavender will never forgive me."

Lady Lavender? He wiggled his toes to make sure he was not, indeed, paralyzed. He was not, though something was wrong. Speaking had been a monumental effort. Breathing was no less a challenge.

"Papa!" Lady Grace said, fighting her way out of the rose bushes. "Lord Dashlend is hurt!"

"Can't say I'm surprised. I don't know why you two thought to jump. Can you walk, Dashlend?"

Though he would like to say yes, he knew very well that he could not. "No," he said, pushing the word out of his lungs.

"Right," the duke said. "I'll arrange things. Gracie, stay here and keep him awake. On no account allow him to close his eyes."

"Yes, Papa," she said softly.

Lady Grace crawled back to his location in the bushes. She stared down at him with wide eyes. Those very pretty olive-colored eyes. He did not suppose he had ever been this close to her before.

"Not paralyzed," he said with effort.

She did not look at all convinced. "If you were, then I suppose any self-respecting lady would take it on very bravely. You are not to think she would not."

What did she mean? Was she saying she'd wed him even if he was to be in a chair all his life?

It was very cheering if that was what she meant. Also, her perfume was intoxicating.

"It would be challenging, of course," Lady Grace said. "But a lady should not be put off by a challenge. I imagine she would be ready to meet it head on." She sighed long and deep. "This was all my fault. If only I did not get dizzy."

Miles would like to propose to her then and there. He could not though. He could hardly get out the simplest words and he found he must put all his attention into getting air into and out of his lungs.

"Is he still awake?"

The duke had returned. How the gentleman was to get him out of his current predicament he had not the first idea.

"Yes, Papa, though I believe he is in very terrible pain." In a lower voice she said, "He might be paralyzed."

"Do not jump to the worst just yet. Take the flask, throw

some brandy into him. I've commandeered Lady Montague's coachmen and grooms. They're hammering together a litter of sorts and they'll bring round a cart. We'll take him home—I've already sent for my physician."

He saw Lady Grace nod. So that was the plan—somehow, two burly coachmen were to get him out of the bushes and into a cart. He did not, of course, know how painful an operation that would be. He was not an idiot though. It was going to hurt.

Lady Grace crawled back to his side. She held the flask and he drank down as much brandy as he could. The warm liquid did deliver its own particular comfort, though he imagined that would fly out the window once he was moved.

GRACE HARDLY KNEW how she'd created such a mess. And dragged Lord Dashlend into it too. He would suffer for her actions more than she ever would. She'd landed on top of him; he'd broken her fall.

Now, he seemed to be working hard even to take a breath. There was every chance he'd never walk again. She'd ruined his life! She'd ruined Lady Lavender's life too.

She'd tried to be encouraging, to hint that Lady Lavender would not turn from him when she discovered that her dashing gentleman was to be bound to a chair. She was not certain if it were true, though.

Had it been herself, she would have remained resolute in the face of such uncertainty. She would have bravely faced the prospect of failing to have children, of being wed to a man who might at any moment succumb to winter fever or a wasting disease. There were a whole host of things that a person immobilized in a chair might perish from, as she knew very well from Mrs. Lendower. That lady had been struck down three winters in a row, until she finally succumbed. She'd been a lovely lady, but there was something about being immobile that wore a person down.

If she were Lady Lavender, she would value whatever time together they had.

Would the actual Lady Lavender do the same?

All the bitterness that had been in her heart regarding Lady Lavender and Lord Dashlend melted away and disappeared, as if it had never been there at all.

Grace heard a commotion coming. She peered over the rose bushes to see two very large men carrying boards that had been hastily nailed together to form a litter. Behind them followed a collection of footmen and grooms.

She poured the last of the brandy down Lord Dashlend's throat. He drank it eagerly, as if he knew being moved would bring its own sort of torture.

"This is Wellburn, Lady Montague's stablemaster," the duke said. "He's been to war and knows how these things are done. We will follow his lead. Wellburn? Send everybody going in the right direction."

Grace stood and got herself out of the way, as Wellburn did very confidently begin getting everybody going. The first part of the operation entailed cutting down the rose bushes surrounding Lord Dashlend. One of the footmen piped up that Lady Montague was certain to have a fit over it, but Wellburn said, "I think if you were to ask the lady which to save, her roses or one of her guests, she would say goodbye to her roses."

Once the bushes were cut away, six men brought the litter forward. Wellburn directed three on one side to slowly lift Lord Dashlend to his side, all moving as one. Then the litter was slid underneath him and he was laid gently down.

The men carefully lifted the litter and carried it to the waiting cart. The cart had been lined with hay to soften the jostling that would occur during the journey.

Grace did not know how painful an operation it had been, as Lord Dashlend did not utter a sound. His complexion in the moonlight was a deal more pale than she'd ever seen it, so she suspected he'd worked hard not to shout out.

He was gently slid into the cart and Wellburn gave the driver firm instructions to go slow and steady. He and his men would follow on horseback, as when they arrived to the house, the litter would need to be carried up the stairs.

Grace climbed into the back of the cart, alongside the litter. She was certain it was not the thing, but she would not be turned from it. Her father had only raised a brow, but did not cross her on it.

She was determined to stay by Lord Dashlend's side for as long as was necessary.

MONTCLAVE STAYED HIDDEN in the dark garden, listening closely to what was said. A burly coachman was directing everybody on what they were to do to extract Dashlend from the rose bushes.

He needed to know if any mention of him was made. Had Lady Grace seen him clearly? Did she know he'd locked her in a burning room?

He hardly knew why he did it. Some kind of desperation had come over him and it had seemed the only answer.

His mother had often said that life was not like chess, one could not anticipate what the next moves might be after making a move of one's own. People were wildly unpredictable, while chess was not.

Montclave had never entirely understood her meaning until this night. He could never have foreseen that Lady Grace and Dashlend would end up falling from a window.

Dashlend seemed to get the worst of it. It was not at all clear how damaged he'd been from the fall, only clear that he could not rise and walk.

Perhaps he would not regain the use of his legs? If that were the case, he might die at any time. He might just waste away. He would not have children.

If he were to die, Montclave would become the heir. If he did not die, but remained childless, then someday one of his own sons would inherit.

As long as nobody discovered he'd had anything to do with it.

How long would he have to wait to be certain he was in the clear? Would Lady Grace tell her father that she'd seen him at the door? Would some servant step forward and claim he'd been seen throwing the key down the corridor or rushing away from the scene? Had someone noted him hurrying back into the ballroom as a footman yelled fire?

If he even got a whiff of something brewing, of some suspicion falling on him, he would pack his things and go… somewhere. He would not be locked up or swing for it.

And yet, he must hope nobody would suspect him. After all, he'd not set the room on fire. Lady Grace had done that herself.

He'd only locked the door. Which he might claim was an accident?

Perhaps he might claim he locked it to contain the fire, unaware there was anybody inside?

Though, he would then have to account for why he did not tell anybody there was a fire. Or why he threw the key down the corridor.

He must pray he would not come to anybody's notice.

Dashlend was just now loaded into the back of a farmer's cart and Lady Grace had climbed in too. He was being taken to the duke's house. That was not ideal. On the off chance that he was not paralyzed, the close proximity of the couple would likely end in an engagement.

Especially since it appeared Dashlend had broken the lady's fall. How heroic he would appear in the eyes of a young lady.

But then, might not Dashlend lose consciousness at some point? If that were to happen, he could step in as a member of the family and have him removed. If he could get Lady Margaret out of the way, then whatever care or lack of care given to the patient would be up to him.

It was something to hope for, anyway.

For now, he would return home and drink a vast amount of brandy to settle his nerves. He hoped Mrs. Featherby was not haunting Doanellen's drawing room, as he fully intended to locate the brandy decanter and take it to his bedchamber.

MRS. RIGHT HAD spent an enjoyable evening in with her girls. She'd told them all the story of driving Lord Dashlend's valet mad and they speculated he must have quit on the spot and now the lord was left to tie his own knot.

Valor recited the letter she'd sent to Lord Dashlend and everyone was satisfied that she'd wished he would come to a bad end.

Nelson, who was turning out to be a very good sort of dog despite missing a leg and being blind in one eye, had curled up next to Valor on the sofa. He cleverly angled himself to view the door, as he was always on the watch for food coming through it.

As the last tea tray came in before they would retire and Nelson staggered to his three legs in anticipation, they all speculated on how Grace was making out at Lady Montague's ball. Winsome hoped Grace had given Lord Dashlend no end of perishing looks. Verity was adamant that tripping another lady, who may or may not be Lady Lavender, was a very accepted thing. Patience claimed Grace would be better off pretending she did not know Lord Dashlend was even alive, of so little consequence was he. Serenity posited that Grace might stand just to the right of a chandelier, allowing the warm light to present her as an unattainable Venus, so Lord Dashlend might see what he'd lost. Valor was of two minds—Grace might hit him over the head with a wine glass or she might set his coat on fire.

Even Nelson was in agreement as to Lord Dashlend. Whenever the lord's name was mentioned, he gave a little snarl. Mrs. Right knew very well that the dog did not hold any sort of personal grudge against the gentleman, but Winsome had been rewarding him with a bit of biscuit every time he did it.

All in all, it was a very cheery evening.

Therefore, the very last thing they'd been expecting was for Grace to come home on the back of a farmer's cart, with Lord Dashlend in a litter beside her.

For the first few minutes, Mrs. Right did fear that Grace had taken some of her sisters' advice and clobbered the fellow. While it would be satisfying in the extreme, it was the sort of thing that might cause her girl some trouble.

As the men who'd accompanied the cart took the litter above stairs to a spare bedchamber, the duke explained what had happened. Or as much of what happened as he knew.

This explanation did put a damper on all their ideas of destroying Lord Dashlend. It was hard to reconcile that he saved Grace from a fire and was also a scoundrel who ought to die a painful death.

As the duke led the physician above stairs, Mrs. Right poured Grace a large glass of sherry and her sisters gathered round her.

"So you went by yourself to the room so you could jump around in private?" Winsome asked.

"She does it all the time in her own room," Valor said. "I've tried it, it's not very interesting."

"I do not know what anybody else does to settle their dizziness," Grace said, "I only know that it helps me."

"What dizziness?" Serenity asked.

"Dizziness can be a common thing. I've read," Verity said.

"I don't get dizzy," Valor said. "Not unless I close my eyes and spin around."

"I never got dizzy at your age," Grace said. "It comes on later."

"Does it?" Valor shouted, seeming alarmed by this news.

"When, though?" Patience asked. "I'm never dizzy. Serenity is never dizzy. Winsome?"

Winsome shook her head.

Grace turned to her. "Mrs. Right?"

She slowly shook her head. It really did set her to wondering. She had of course known that her Grace was… not all that graceful. She'd not known anything about regularly feeling dizzy. What was causing it?

Just then, the duke entered the room.

"Papa," Grace said, rising from her chair. "He is paralyzed. Just say it. We must pull him through it. It will be a heavy blow for someone like Lord Dashlend."

"He is not paralyzed," the duke said. "According to Phillips, he's got several broken ribs, a badly sprained ankle, and a bang to the head. He'll recover, but he's got to go on quiet for now, so we'll keep him here for the time being."

"Not paralyzed?" Grace said. Mrs. Right got the idea that she'd firmly decided the lord was paralyzed and the idea that he was not was hard to take in.

"He's staying here?" Winsome asked. "He's the enemy, Papa. At least, he was."

Patience nodded. "Papa, are we to be civil to him? We hate him, but now he's saved Grace, so we don't know what to do with him."

"What about that Lady Lavender?" Valor asked. "Are we supposed to let her in to see him? Are we supposed to talk to her and give her tea?"

"I could just cry thinking about it," Serenity said, wiping a tear from her cheek.

"Now settle down," the duke said. "He's done our Gracie wrong, I do not deny it. But on the other hand, he saved her from a fire at great inconvenience to himself. That must count for something, I think."

Mrs. Right nodded gravely, as if she were in full agreement with the duke.

That she was not in agreement need not trouble him. She would set about doing what it was in her purview to do regarding Lord Dashlend's comfort. He would hurry along his recovery once he experienced the meals he could enjoy in the Duke of Pelham's household—salty porridge was suddenly on the menu. She would use the scratchiest sheets she could find for his bedding. In fact, she might get hold of some nettles and snip off little pieces on the bedding. She was certain there was more she could think of if she put her mind to it. If that lord had some idea of being waited on hand and foot and coddled, he had another thing coming.

The faster Lord Dashlend was out of this house, the faster her Grace could regain her spirits.

Mrs. Right rose. "Now then, off to bed with all of you. It is late and do not follow Grace into her room—she will need her rest after this night's adventure."

Grace nodded gratefully and the poor girl really did look worn out. The rest of her girls nodded, though not very enthusiastically. Mrs. Right was certain they'd have been willing to stay up all night discussing the fire at the ball and the gentleman just now relocated into their household.

She knew what was best, though. Particularly for Valor, who was so tired she'd got that look on her face as if she might hysterically laugh or hysterically cry, or both at once.

As for herself, she would see Valor settled and then have her usual glass of brandy with the duke. She suspected there were more details he had not shared with his youngest daughters.

CHAPTER NINETEEN

G RACE DID NOT know how she managed to fall asleep, nor sleep so soundly. Though, she suspected the rather large glass of sherry Mrs. Right had urged her to drink, along with her nerves being exhausted, had certainly helped.

Everything that had happened replayed in her mind over and over again. Particularly, the ride in the cart. Clearly the jostling of the moving conveyance caused Lord Dashlend pain. She'd hardly known what to do about it. He would wince and she would grasp his hand. Then she would realize the impropriety of it and let it go. Then it would happen all over again.

His hand was large and firm and warm. She'd not wished to give it up, but she must. His was not her hand to hold and she could see very well the looks she received from the coachmen and grooms who followed on horseback.

This morning, she and her sisters had spent breakfast glancing up at the ceiling. Their father was up there with Lord Dashlend and the physician.

It was so odd to know that Lord Dashlend was in the house. What was he thinking?

She supposed she could guess at what he was thinking. His injuries were to be laid at her door, it had been all her fault. She'd gone off alone to jump around and then managed to start a fire through her clumsiness.

Grace could not imagine who locked her in there, but she had begun to think that perhaps the person had only noted the flames and not herself and sought to contain it. She did not see how anybody could have missed her, as it had been she knocking over the candelabra, or why the door must be locked and not just closed. But what other explanation could there be?

They had all gone to the drawing room after breakfast and continued on with glancing at the ceiling. They did it so often that Nelson began looking there too.

There had been a prior plan of going to the park but that had been called off. They would stay where they were, just looking at the ceiling.

Thomas opened the drawing room doors and said, "Lady Margaret Hawley, Lady Valor's particular friend."

Valor clapped and said, "Well done, Thomas." To Grace she said, "I told Thomas to always introduce Lady Margaret as my particular friend. Because she is my particular friend. We have a correspondence. Between two ladies."

Lady Margaret came through, her skirts wider than ever. Her signature ostrich feathers had seen an improvement though—the ones she wore today seemed new and not molting like the ones she'd previously displayed.

"What a night. Lady Grace, you are unhurt?"

"I am very well, thank you, Lady Margaret. Thomas? A tea tray, if you will."

As Thomas hurried off, Lady Margaret hurried forward.

"Sit next to me and Nelson, Lady Margaret," Valor said.

"Of course, my little friend," the lady said, taking her seat.

"See?" Valor said. "We are particular friends."

"I understand Dashlend is here?" Lady Margaret asked, nodding at Valor to confirm the idea.

Grace said that he was, and they all glanced at the ceiling again. Nelson, hearing Lord Dashlend's name, gave a little snarl.

Lady Margaret glanced down at the dog in alarm, but then Nelson wagged his tail. "What is my dear relation's condition? Has he regained consciousness? Will he recover?"

"We have been told he never lost consciousness," Grace said. "He was fully conscious when last I saw him. The physician says he will recover, though it might take time. He's broken some ribs and has a badly sprained ankle."

"And he got a knock on the head," Valor added.

"My goodness, the stories that do go round. The *ton* has poor Lord Dashlend lying at death's door, quite unconscious. A relief that it's only talk, yes, it really is," Lady Margaret said. "I came straight over to warn you of something."

"Warn us?" Grace said.

Thomas came in with the tea tray and Lady Margaret fell to silence. Valor patted her hand. "You don't have to be quiet because Thomas might hear," she said. "I tell him everything anyway."

"Oh I see, well then," Lady Margaret said, "I had a very unusual encounter this morning. Lord Montclave came to see me. Of course, I initially thought he'd try to get some money out of me and good luck to that. But no. First, he practically interrogated me about last night, as if I should know what happened. Then he told me that people are saying Dashlend had not regained consciousness."

Nelson growled again. Winsome said, "Never mind Nelson, we taught him to do that."

Lady Margaret's eyes widened just a bit, but she continued on. "Then, Lord Montclave made a speech about him being the senior most family member on the scene and he would need to take charge of his cousin's recovery. Then, if you can believe it, he said *he* must move into the house and *I* must move out!"

"Goodness," Grace said, rather taken aback by Lord Montclave's heavy-handedness. "What did you say to it?"

"I told him he would have to pry me out of Lord Dashlend's house cold and dead, that's what I told him. Among other things."

Valor clapped. "I knew it. I knew my friend would give that fellow the what for. Mrs. Wendover knew it all along too."

Lady Margaret patted Valor's hand. "I am most gratified in your faith in me. And of course, Mrs. Wendover's approbation. Now, aside from the outrage of attempting to throw me out of a house he does not own, I feel there is something underhanded in Lord Montclave's ideas. He will be the earl's heir if Dashlend does not produce one, and I just feel…"

Lady Margaret had trailed off.

"You do not mean he would attempt any sort of violence?" Grace asked.

"Perhaps not violence," Lady Margaret said, "perhaps more like neglect. After all, why does he need me gone from the house? Is it because he wishes to move Lord Dashlend there and enact some plan in secret?" Lady Margaret wrung her hands. "Oh, I do not know. I just have a very bad feeling about it."

Grace poured a cup of tea for Lady Margaret and handed it to her. "My father says Lord Dashlend is to stay here for the moment. I will tell him of your concerns—he does not care for Lord Montclave as it is. In any case, reports of the lord's unconsciousness are not correct, Lord Dashlend can himself determine what ought to be done about his cousin."

Lady Margaret looked much relieved to hear it.

"Now you can set your mind at ease, Lady Margaret," Serenity said.

"Indeed I can. I knew I did right to come here straight away." The lady sipped her tea and then set it down. "Well! I suppose I'd best visit our patient and see how he gets on."

"Visit him?" Grace asked.

"None of us have seen him since he was carried in," Winsome said.

"It's scary that he's up there," Valor said. "Last night, I couldn't fall asleep because he was just down the hall, breathing or whatever he's doing in that room."

Valor shivered, as if to make her point more directly.

"We haven't seen him on account of he's in a bed," Patience said. "Only our Felicity has ever seen a gentleman in a bed."

Valor whispered, "Mr. Stratton sleeps in the same room with Felicity," in a tone that suggested it was hard to believe.

"We think Mr. Stratton stares at Felicity while she's sleeping," Serenity said for added clarity.

"That's rather uncomfortable, I imagine," Lady Margaret said.

Valor shrugged. "Felicity seems to like it, though we don't know why. But Lady Margaret, will you really go into his room?"

"Why should I not? I am an old lady and a relation. I suppose I can charge into any sickroom I like. Thomas, is it? Lead me there."

With that, she rose and sailed majestically from the room. Her skirts were so wide she appeared a ship leaving a wake as she departed a harbor.

Goodness. She was going to see Lord Dashlend.

As the doors to the drawing room were closed, they all stared at the ceiling once more.

MILES HAD BEEN entirely disoriented when he'd woken up. It was very strange to find one was not in one's own house. Even stranger to find a fellow staring down at him.

Then, of course, how he got to be where he was came back to him and who the fellow was, the duke's physician, came back too.

Phillips peered down at him. "You had a restful night, that is good. How is the breathing?"

Miles found it had got easier to take in breaths. The combination of having his ribs wrapped as well as remembering to take in breaths that were not too deep made it more manageable.

"Better, I think."

"Excellent. Well, there is not much to be done now. The sprain will heal itself in time and so will your ribs. Though, you might feel some after effects in cold and damp weather. All you can do is bide your time and not do anything stupid, like trying to rush the healing process." The physician sighed and said, "I cannot count how many times I have issued that warning and how many times it has been ignored."

"How long will I be confined to bed, though?" Miles asked, thinking he should go mad if he were left lingering for days on end. Lady Grace was just below stairs, was he to lie round here all day?

"For today at least with that foot propped up. I will return on the morrow with a chair the footmen can use to transport you downstairs. Which will be perfectly fine as long as you quietly sit, leg elevated, wherever you are taken. Do not do anything foolish. No sitting at a dinner table for now."

It was not ideal, but at least he would not be trapped in this room forever. In any case, he might propose from a chair, might he not? It would not be a typical proposal, but it could be done. After all, Lady Grace had hinted that she'd even accept him if he were paralyzed.

And then, there was the handholding in the cart. Certainly, that had stepped across some lines and indicated her preference for him. She'd done it several times.

Just then, the door swung open and Lady Margaret came through it. Miles pulled the blankets over his bare legs. What was she doing here?

"There you are, my boy," she said. "You gave us a scare, I don't mind telling you."

"I'm perfectly fine, Lady Margaret," he said.

She turned to the physician. "True?"

"Perfectly fine is an exaggeration," the physician said. "He will be though. I will take my leave and return on the morrow unless the duke calls me back beforehand."

He bowed to Lady Margaret and made his exit.

She hurried to his side. Grasping his hand, she said, "I think Lord Montclave is looking for a way to kill you."

That was about the last thing he imagined he'd hear from Lady Margaret. "What?" he said.

She then proceeded to tell him of Montclave's visit to the house that morning.

"He was most forceful. *I* must leave and *he* was moving in," Lady Margaret said.

"He'll do no such thing."

"Naturally, I informed him of how fond you were of my company. You could hardly bear to be parted with me, particularly in your hour of need. I vowed I would stay by your side always. He would have to drag me out cold and dead."

Miles thought the idea that he could not bear to be parted from the lady was painting it on a little thick. As for her staying by his side always, that sounded more like a threat than anything else. However, this was not the time to straighten out any of Lady Margaret's wild ideas.

"Get me some writing things. I will direct Wainwright to hire some guards so that Montclave does not attempt to push you out or insert himself in."

Lady Margaret hopped up and began to rifle through a desk, pulling out what was required.

What was Montclave up to? Miles would never put himself in that villain's hands—why would Montclave imagine he would?

Lady Margaret had set the writing things on what had been his breakfast tray. And a pretty awful breakfast it had been. Why had there been salt in the porridge? Why had there been only porridge? Did the duke not go in for eggs or bacon or sausages?

"Lord Montclave thinks you remain unconscious," Lady Margaret said. "That's the gossip going round."

Ah. So that was why Montclave imagined he could get control of him.

He carefully raised his arm, careful not to jostle his ribs, and wrote out directions for Wainwright. He also wrote a note for Moreau, telling him to bring some clothes and his shaving things. He did not know how long he'd be here, but he did know he would be allowed some amount of time downstairs on the morrow. He'd prefer to appear pulled together. He had some very particular things to say.

Then another thing occurred to him. "Lady Margaret, I do not wish to insult the duke's hospitality, but would you taste that porridge," he asked, pointing at the bowl she had removed from the tray. "I am certain it has salt in it."

Lady Margaret took herself to the bowl and tasted it. She nodded. "Well, well, well."

"Well, well, well? What does that mean?"

"It means, my dear boy, that the housekeeper in this establishment is not fond of you. Salting porridge is not something a cook or housemaid would dare. Only the housekeeper. I would say a butler might try it, but they don't have one."

"Mrs. Right? I do not see how she can have anything against me. I've not insulted the lady in any way."

Lady Margaret shrugged. "Nevertheless, here we have salt in your porridge. Do I suspect that was all that was on your tray? That is another piece of evidence. Where are the eggs? The bacon? The kidneys? The sausages? The rolls? The coffee?"

"Yes, I did notice those things missing."

"Never mind it. I will take care of it without putting the duke's back up."

"What? What would you do? Do not insult Mrs. Right—I suspect that would make whatever this is even worse."

Lady Margaret patted his arm. "Leave it to me. This is not the first time I've dealt with a recalcitrant housekeeper."

Before he could press her for specifics, she took herself out of the room.

He satisfied himself by wiling away the morning thinking of the handholding in the cart that had gone on the night before.

MONTCLAVE PACED HIS bedchamber, swigging brandy. This morning had been a disaster. The night before, he'd not slept at all. He'd tried, but every time he closed his eyes he saw the curtains aflame and himself locking the door and throwing the key. There was no amount of brandy that would wipe it away. He had to stop thinking about it!

Did he look guilty? Could people tell by looking at him?

Every knock on the front doors seemed to jolt his heart and speed it up to a pounding. Were they coming to get him, to lock him up?

Finally, he'd forced himself to dress and go downstairs. Mrs. Featherby had been in the drawing room. She did not look at him strangely, as if she knew his secret. In fact, she seemed rather bored to see him.

She nattered on about this and that. And then she said it—the shred of hope he could hold on to. She said Dashlend was unconscious.

Dashlend had taken a turn for the worse! Perhaps he was dead already? These things could go downhill quickly.

No, if he were dead that news would be a brushfire all over Town. But unconscious, that was better than conscious. Might he not do something with that?

He began to formulate a plan. He must just get hold of Dashlend while he was unconscious and make sure he stayed that way.

Montclave had splashed cold water on his face, taken a fortifying swig of brandy, and set off for Dashlend's house. He would get Lady Margaret out and Dashlend in. Somehow he would rid the house of that idiot valet Moreau. Then he would see what could be done.

It had not worked. He really did not see how it had not worked. That butler of Dashlend's was his usual grim visage but would not have defied him. Lady Margaret had defied him. He told her, as the senior most family member on the scene, that he would take over Dashlend's care and she must leave. He explained to her that she was too chattering a female to be in a sickroom and would only cause harm.

If she would have acted as any old lady might be expected to upon being insulted, she would have tearfully packed her things and been gone. But no, she had the audacity to stand there staring at him and then announce she wouldn't go until she was dead.

He'd briefly wondered if he ought to kill her to hasten things along, but then he decided the brandy was affecting his thoughts.

Montclave had left and had walked the streets for hours. Now he was closeted in his room. He felt he needed to do something but he could not think of what. Or rather, he could think of things but was not certain he had the nerve.

The thing that kept surfacing was a poison of some sort. If he were to poison Dashlend while he was laid low, it would seem as if he'd simply taken a turn for the worse.

If not poison, then something. He must at least get Dashlend moved to his own house so he had some measure of control over the situation. He'd think of something to get blasted Lady Margaret out of the way. And then, then, what? Would he be forced to put a pillow over Dashlend's face?

Montclave recoiled from the idea. He did not want to do something so… close.

Maybe he could order a fire for the patient, then close the flue, shut the door and blame the servants when Dashlend died from the smoke?

If he could only see into everybody's thoughts he would know if anybody suspected him. If he knew if anybody suspected him, he would know how far he could dare. He could not stand the wondering.

All these ideas swirled round his muddled mind as he made his way through Doanellen's brandy.

MRS. RIGHT, EVER aware of the doings of her household, had

watched Lady Margaret come down the stairs. Then, instead of heading toward the drawing room, the lady slipped through the door leading to the stairs and the kitchens below.

What was she doing?

Mrs. Right did not know, but she was determined to find out. She waited long enough for Lady Margaret to get down the stairs and then followed her. In the corridor that led to the kitchens, she paused.

Lady Margaret was talking to Cook. "My good man," she said, "I have been to see Lord Dashlend and his physician. I thought to come to you to give you a hint before that irascible doctor raises the roof. While I, myself, applaud your care in sending Lord Dashlend a hearty porridge for breakfast I cannot say the same for that charlatan of a doctor. It seems he is stubbornly convinced that the lord requires meats of all sorts, ample potatoes, rolls, butter, coffee, wine, and no salt added to it whatsoever. The salt is only to be in a salt cellar and Lord Dashlend has been given strict instructions on its use. A lot of nonsense, I'm sure, but what are we to do?"

"Oh I see," Cook said. "Mrs. Right did think my porridge would be just the thing."

"As do I. Mrs. Right is full of good sense. However, we must keep that physician happy or he will cause all sorts of trouble."

"Damn doctors," Cook said.

"Precisely."

Mrs. Right suppressed a defeated sigh. Lady Margaret was a deal more clever than she seemed. The physician ordered it— what a bit of nonsense that was. It was clear enough the lady was on to the salt in the porridge gambit and would be falcon eyes on the rest of Lord Dashlend's food.

Mrs. Right was rarely crossed in one of her schemes and she found it very inconvenient. Nevertheless, she might need to pull back on this one. She was quite sure that Lady Margaret would have guessed the housekeeper was behind it. Who else would have both the opportunity and nerve to do it? While the duke was generally so approving of any little thing she did for the family, his ire against Lord Dashlend had seemed to soften on account of the lord rescuing his daughter from a fire.

Perhaps she could still locate some nettles and quietly add them to his bedding.

CHAPTER TWENTY

G RACE AND HER sisters had spent the entire day before in the drawing room, glancing up at the ceiling. Unlike that day, which had been filled with the silence of a sickroom, today they heard things. Lord Dashlend's valet had come and apparently he was either a heavy walker, or in the habit of moving furniture.

Her father had informed them that a special chair was to be brought in by the physician today to allow Lord Dashlend some amount of time downstairs. She supposed the valet was preparing Lord Dashlend to be presentable.

What would he say when he arrived in his chair? He must be so aggravated with her.

She had hoped she might mitigate his ire. She had forced herself to write to Lady Lavender, informing the lady that Lord Dashlend was currently recovering in the duke's house and, most importantly, he was not paralyzed. She explained that the lord was to be brought to the drawing room this very afternoon and they would all be pleased to see Lady Lavender at that time.

Grace had presumed the lady would be delighted, but she had received a note back that did not indicate delight at all.

She unfolded it and read it again.

Dear Lady Grace—

It was very kind to alert me to Lord Dashlend's current location and condition. Though, I find I must inquire as to why? I am certain Lord Dashlend requires being surrounded by his closest friends and relations during this difficult time, and so will respectfully decline your offer of a visit. I do look forward to seeing you at future society events.

Lavender Westcott

It was really very outrageous. Was the lady so lacking in fortitude that she would not countenance a gentleman who suffered from broken ribs and a sprained ankle? Grace, herself, would be prepared to face it if the lord was paralyzed—what were broken ribs to that?

Worse, what was she to say to Lord Dashlend about it? He was already injured physically, must she injure his heart too? Might it not cause a setback of some sort?

"I'm glad she's not coming," Winsome said, noting Grace had read the letter once more. "I do not see how we would have managed to be civil."

"Nelson would not have liked her," Valor said. "That's what Mrs. Wendover says."

"Do not worry too much, Grace," Serenity said. "I went and spoke to Cook about the tea tray and he is to make his special miniature apple cakes. You see? Lord Dashlend will be distracted by them and not notice that Lady Lavender has thrown him over."

Grace was not at all sure that apple cakes would distract a gentleman from the loss of the lady he preferred. She was not at all sure about anything anymore, including her own sense. She'd taken great care in selecting what she would wear and had fussed with her hair for a half hour—what did she mean by it?

Just then, the duke came into the drawing room. "Here they all are, awaiting the descent of our patient. Well, I suppose we must be gracious, what with saving Grace from the fire."

"Of course we will be gracious, Papa," Grace said. "We will bring all of our dignity to bear."

The duke laughed. "We're to be dignified now, are we? I hadn't known."

"I hadn't known either, Papa," Valor said. "Is it a lot of work?"

"It is, rather," the duke said, laughing.

They heard the distant knock on the front doors. The room fell to silence. It would be the physician arriving with the chair. Lord Dashlend would be before them in a matter of minutes.

Thomas opened the drawing room doors. "Lady Marchfield, Your Grace. I'm sorry! I assumed it was the doctor... and then it was too late."

"Do not feel bad, Thomas," Valor said. "Charlie hasn't managed to keep out our aunt either and he has more experience."

The lady in question pushed past Thomas. "I heard most of that. I would bother to remind you, Roland, that you are raising these girls with little manners, but it would accomplish little."

"And yet, you managed to say it all the same," the duke said.

"I have come to inquire what you are doing regarding the care of Lord Dashlend. If it is your usual slapdash sort of operation, I have come to manage things. You certainly cannot leave it to that housekeeper of yours."

"As usual, madam, you poke your nose where it is not wanted," the duke said.

Valor laughed hysterically and said, "Papa says you are a polecat going into the wrong henhouse. Or something like that. It was very funny."

Lady Marchfield ignored these various insults. "I will not leave this house until I am assured of his care."

"Aunt," Grace said, "Papa's physician has been here and cared for Lord Dashlend. He is even returning with a special chair so the lord might come to the drawing room for a limited amount of time."

"A chair... but I was led to believe... so he has regained consciousness?"

"He was never unconscious," Grace said. "We do not know where that gossip came from."

Thomas opened the door again. Grace had hoped it was a tea

tray, as that might distract Lady Marchfield. However, it was not.

"Lady Margaret and Lord Harraby," Thomas said, rather white-faced. "She let herself in," he whispered.

"She is my particular friend, Thomas," Valor said. "I would give her a key if I had one."

Lady Margaret waddled into the room in her oversized skirts with Lord Harraby trailing behind her.

"We've come to see the patient," Lady Margaret said. "He told me yesterday that he would be coming down."

"Where Lady Margaret leads, I dutifully follow," Lord Harraby said.

Lady Margaret playfully tapped Lord Harraby's arm with her fan. Then she took that moment to train her eyes on Lady Marchfield. "Lady Marchfield, is it? We encountered one another briefly at the duke's dinner. Before you made off with the butler. This is Lord Harraby."

Lady Marchfield gave Lady Margaret a cold stare. "Lord Harraby and I are acquainted."

"Oh yes, indeed, long time now," Lord Harraby said, not looking particularly enthused over knowing Lady Marchfield for a long time.

Grace would be happy to see any of these people, but she really did not see why they all needed to be here just at this minute. She was hoping for some moment in private with Lord Dashlend, so she might apologize.

Then, yet another person appeared at the door. It was Mr. Moreau, Lord Dashlend's valet.

"Your Grace," Mr. Moreau said, "Lord Dashlend requests your presence above stairs, if you will."

"He hasn't gone south, has he?" the duke asked.

Mr. Moreau appeared mystified by the question. "No, Your Grace, he is still upstairs."

"Right," the duke said. "I'd better go and see for myself."

"Yes, Your Grace," Mr. Moreau said. "That is what he asked."

"Are you French?" Valor asked.

Mr. Moreau bowed. "Oui, Mademoiselle."

"That's why he doesn't understand you, Papa. Speak loudly and slowly," Valor advised.

The duke chucked her chin and headed out of the room. Mr. Moreau hurried after him, no doubt relieved he'd accomplished the task he'd been given and not entirely certain how he'd done so.

What was happening up there? Why did Lord Dashlend require the duke? Had something gone wrong? Or perhaps he had regained his strength and wished to express his feelings over being pulled off the side of a house by the duke's clumsy daughter? Perhaps he wished to send for Lady Lavender, and then have to be told she would not come.

There was something rather fraught in not knowing which way the wind was blowing. She had wondered sometimes, during Felicity's season, why her sister so often appeared nervous. Now she understood. It felt as if her blood contained bubbles that were pinging round her body. She grasped the arm of her chair to steady herself.

MILES WATCHED THE door crash open and Moreau run through it. "I have brought him, my lord."

The duke was on his heels and they were both out of breath. Did they run up the stairs?

"Yes, he has brought me," the duke said, "or rather, raced me up the stairs. I could not get ahead of him."

Moreau nodded, as if beating the duke up the stairs had been part of Miles' directions to him.

"Your Grace," Miles said, "thank you for attending me, and for your hospitality and the services of your physician as well. Moreau, step out and close the door behind you."

Moreau appeared shocked to his shoes to be sent out. He

sniffed, he huffed, he rolled his eyes, he swatted at invisible dust on his coat. Finally, he went.

After the door closed, the duke said, "He's a rather hysterical fellow."

This prompted a very loud stomp from the corridor. Miles only nodded so as not to cause another outburst from his irascible valet.

"Your Grace, considering my current condition, it is probably not the ideal time to broach the subject of nuptials—"

The duke held up a hand. "Listen here, Dashlend, you're free to do what you want with your life, but I will not have my Grace faced with congratulating you and Lady Lavender in her own house. No, I will not have that."

"Lady Lavender? What does she have to do with it?"

The duke snorted. "Don't tell me, you have a *third* lady on the hook? How many bouquets do you send out a week, anyway?"

Miles was well aware that the duke was eccentric, but now he began to fear the man was downright mad. What was this gibberish about Lady Lavender and bouquets of flowers?

"Your Grace, my intentions have not strayed away from Lady Grace since the moment I met her on the beach. My feelings have grown day by day since that fateful encounter. Now, as to flowers, I admit I have been remiss in not sending any. It was really very stupid of me, but I am not in the habit of courting. However, I have not sent any flowers to Lady Lavender or any other lady either. I do not understand how you came to labor under that misapprehension."

"Misapprehension? I see, so the florist was not forthcoming in admitting their mistake and you don't know the whole of it. Well, let me tell you, Dashlend, your secret is out—two bouquets of flowers arrived here, daisies for Grace and roses for Lady Lavender. We promptly sent back the roses so they could be delivered to their correct destination."

"I sent no daisies or roses to anybody," Miles said.

"Who else would have sent them and signed your name to them? Come now, as a gentleman, have the good grace to acknowledge being caught out."

As soon as the question as to who might have signed was posed, the answer presented itself. "The only person I can think of who would have reason to stir trouble between Lady Grace and myself is Lord Montclave. If I die early, he becomes the heir to the earldom, and if I do not produce an issue, his son will eventually inherit. He's done some other things recently that make me think he is actively attempting to prevent me from continuing the line through a wedding and the ensuing children."

The duke narrowed his eyes and stared at him, seeming to consider this idea.

"Hmm. Montclave. I never liked that fellow. I am usually a good judge of character. I was all for you until the flowers arrived. Then I was forced to send you some flowers of my own."

"That was you?" Miles asked.

"Yes," the duke said laughing. "A whole cartful. Things like that soothe me when I find me and mine have been put out."

That mystery was now solved. He supposed he should have guessed that only the duke would go in for such a wild gambit, even if Miles had not known the cause. He presumed the duke had not just constrained himself to flowers either.

"And the note?"

"What note?" the duke asked.

"The one that said I was a terrible person and the author hoped terrible things happened to me."

The duke laughed heartily, though Miles could not see the humor in it. "Valor," he said. "She's seemed to have got very free with her missives."

"What about the advertisement in the newspaper for a new valet?" he asked.

They heard a thump on the door, as clearly the current valet was pressed against it and listening hard.

"Me? No? That'll be the sort of thing Mrs. Right gets up to.

She's very devoted to my girls, you understand."

"Exceedingly so, it seems," Miles said softly. This flower business had caused what he'd sensed at the ball. Lady Grace and the duke had seemed a bit put off by him. They thought he was in love with Lady Lavender. They thought he must have been stringing Lady Grace along for his own amusement.

As if he would harm a hair on her head!

"Your Grace, I assure you that I did not send those flowers. I asked that you attend me so that I might ask for your permission to propose to your daughter."

Just then, there was the sound of a struggle outside the door. It crashed open and the physician stumbled into the room.

"Lord Dashlend! Call off your ridiculous valet!"

The ridiculous valet himself staggered in, his clothes very much askew. "I was only trying to hold him back to give you time, Lord Dashlend."

"By assaulting the doctor?" Miles asked.

Moreau shrugged.

"I think we're done here," the duke said to Miles.

"Your Grace, I beg you to reconsider," Miles said. He would kill Montclave if that rogue had ruined his chances by sending bouquets of flowers.

"Reconsider?" the duke asked, laughing. "I'd rather thought you'd want to get on with the thing."

"Get on with it? Yes, I *would* like to get on with it," Miles said, very much relieved that he'd misunderstood.

"I do not know what I missed," the doctor said, "and I will not inquire. Lord Dashlend, I'll give you a going over to ensure you are fit and, assuming that is the case, you may be carried down the stairs in the chair I've brought with me. It is in the corridor, and it would be in here already if I did not have to fight your valet to get in myself."

Moreau shrugged as if he did not know how it happened.

"I'll send Charlie and Thomas up—they're both strapping lads and should get you down without dropping you," the duke said.

Miles nodded his thanks, though he had not considered the idea of anybody dropping him down the stairs.

After the duke departed, Miles said, "Perhaps it would be more practical to just hop down the stairs on my good foot?"

The physician frowned. "No," he said flatly. He then proceeded to examine the ankle on his bad foot and seemed satisfied that it was still sprained.

There did not seem to be any room for a debate on it, so Miles decided not to argue.

The footmen came bounding into the room, seeming filled with enthusiasm to carry a gentleman in a chair down the stairs. The most senior, Charlie, bowed and said, "My lord, we have been directed by the duke to get you into that chair in the corridor and carry you down the stairs in all haste."

"But without dropping you," the junior footman said. Miles recalled his name was Thomas, as Lady Valor was often in the habit of congratulating him when he accomplished one of his duties successfully.

"As Thomas said, without dropping you," Charlie confirmed.

"It has wheels," Thomas said, "so when we get you down without dropping you, it's a walk in the park to wheel you into the drawing room."

Miles decided to ignore the many assurances about not dropping him and just hope for the best. Moreau hurried over to him and made last minute adjustments to his neckcloth.

The physician had him stand, which he did on one foot, and then felt around his bandaged ribs, poking here and there to assure himself that they still hurt. Which they did.

He was helped to the chair and there began his alarming trip down the stairs.

Despite assurances that he would not be dropped, the two footmen had not seemed to have devised any particular strategy to avoid it. They argued back and forth as the chair tipped to one side then the other on its perilous journey. It seemed the wheels kept catching on the rises and throwing them off balance.

Miles held on to the armrests as the two young men blamed one another for the tipping. Somehow, they managed to get him down to the great hall.

They set him down as Charlie said, "There we go, my lord. Right as rain."

Miles glanced up to the top of the stairs as the physician frowned from the landing and Moreau's knuckles were white as he clutched the balustrade. Neither of them seemed to think the operation went right as rain. However, it was accomplished.

Just then there was a sharp rap on the door. Charlie and Thomas looked at each other. "You answer it, Thomas," Charlie said. "As the senior footman, it must be myself that wheels the lord forward."

Thomas, as junior footmen were wont to do, communicated his sullenness over it by way of facial expressions. Then he jogged round the corner to the foyer. Charlie got behind him to push him to the drawing room. As those doors were currently closed, the footman paused, seeming to realize he'd need Thomas to open them.

From the foyer, Miles heard a distinct and unwelcome voice. Montclave.

"I repeat, I am Lord Dashlend's most senior relation in Town. I insist on seeing him and taking over his care."

In a moment, Montclave was in the hall, having pushed poor Thomas to the side.

The baron stopped in his tracks. "You. You were said to be comatose."

"Well, I am not," Miles asked. He really wondered what Montclave's plan had been. He arrived thinking he would find Miles unconscious and demanded to take over his care? What then? A pillow over his face when nobody was looking?

"I see, yes, there you are, awake, very good news. Further good news—I have arrived. As family. Now, I insist you be moved to your own house, where you will be more comfortable. I will take care of everything. No detail will be too small!"

"You will do no such thing," Miles said. "My staff has been informed that you are not to set foot in the house, nor is Lady Margaret to be thrown out of it. Furthermore, I am certain you sent certain arrangements of flowers to this address."

"What? Flowers?" Montclave said, pointing at himself and then looking over his shoulder as if Miles was accusing somebody else. "Never. What flowers? I do not know what you say."

The drawing room doors opened and Miles saw a crowd of people in there. What was Lady Marchfield doing there? And Lady Margaret and Lord Harraby, too.

Ah, but there was Lady Grace, looking positively lovely. It enraged him that Montclave would have caused her any distress. He had sent his signals of interest clearly enough and she had reciprocated. For her to think it was all just a game… he wanted to strangle his cousin.

The duke strode out and stared at Montclave. "What do you do here?" he asked.

"Your Grace, I was concerned for my relation. I can see, just from speaking to him for a few moments, that he is not steady in his mind. His thoughts are confused. These things are all too common after a fall. I must take him home and hire specialized care."

The duke laughed. "Oh I see, take him home and have this specialized care take him right into a grave I imagine. Do not look so shocked, we know all, Montclave. Thought you might become the next earl, did you?"

Though Miles and his father had long known it to be the case, it had never been said aloud. Not to Montclave anyway. The fellow went positively white. At a shrill and ear-piercing pitch, he screamed, "It was not me! You cannot prove it was me!"

Montclave turned and ran from the house. Lady Grace came into the hall. "Papa, what do you accuse Lord Montclave of?"

"The flowers, my dear. Dashlend did not send those two sets of posies, Montclave did. Trying to stir up some trouble."

"The flowers? Really?" Lady Grace whispered.

"Yes, now you see how it is, Gracie. Charlie, wheel Dashlend to the drawing room. The rest of you but for Grace, out you go. Take yourselves to the dining room and we'll send in a tea tray and set up a sideboard. Out, out, out—you too, Lady Margaret, out with you."

Lady Margaret did look affronted at being ordered out, but Lord Harraby said some soothing words in her ear that seemed to mollify her. Lady Marchfield sniffed as she passed by her brother. Lady Grace's sisters filed out, all looking at Miles suspiciously. Lady Valor whispered to their three-legged dog and he growled at Miles, while wagging his tail at the same time.

Charlie got behind him and wheeled him into the drawing room. Lady Grace had sunk into a sofa and Miles motioned to be taken closer to her.

Then he craned his neck and said to the footman, "Close the doors on your way out."

CHAPTER TWENTY-ONE

GRACE HAD SUNK onto a sofa as everyone in the drawing room but for herself and Lord Dashlend had been ordered out of it by the duke.

What had just happened? Was it true? Lord Montclave had sent the daisies and roses?

If that were true, then perhaps Lord Dashlend was not set on Lady Lavender after all.

The thought made her feel swoony. She gripped the side of the sofa. She might feel swoony, but she would not swoon. Not until she understood the case of things.

Charlie wheeled the lord to her side and then jogged to the doors and closed them behind him.

"Lord Dashlend," she said, determined to go straight to her apology, "I deeply, deeply apologize for pulling you from the side of a house and causing… your current condition. I was dizzy, you see, which I'm afraid is a regular occurrence."

"It is nothing, I assure you," Lord Dashlend said.

"Nothing? You have broken your ribs, sprained your ankle, and are in a wheeled chair!"

"Yes, well, all of that will heal in not too long a time."

Grace twisted her hands together. It would almost be better if he just said what he really felt about it, instead of being so gentlemanly. "I am sure you are angry over it and it is very good of you to pretend you are not but I do not deserve the courtesy. I set that fire myself, because I am clumsy, particularly when I am startled."

"How did you manage to lock yourself in, though?" Lord Dashlend asked. "That was quite the trick."

"Oh, I did not. Someone opened the door and startled me, then they closed it again and I could not get out."

Lord Dashlend had a pensive look and she wondered if he believed her.

"Never mind that mystery for the moment," he said. "Lady Grace, there is no other lady I would rather fall off the side of a building with and it was my honor to break your fall. From the first moment I saw you on the beach I have been drawn to you, and every day that has passed only increases my surety that you are the lady for me. I find myself entirely besotted. Assuming you'd have me. To wed."

Grace was certain she had turned the color of an aubergine, but who cared for that?

"*Have* you?" she cried. "Of course I'll have you. When I thought you were all in for Lady Lavender, well, I wanted to tear her hair. Or yours. Or my own."

"Do not tear a single hair from your head," Lord Dashlend said, hoisting himself from his chair and hopping over to her.

He landed on the sofa with a thud. Grace thought this was the moment. He would kiss her. She stared at him. Then she decided to hurry him up and she kissed him.

That seemed to break apart any constraint that was between them.

Hair pins flying, arms and legs entwined, clothes wrinkled beyond repair, they came together as if they had been always built to be so. There was the occasional wince on account of his broken ribs, but he would not be put off. Grace had not the least inclination to put him off and just reminded herself not to clutch at him too hard.

Before the season, the idea of a gentleman she would wed was a foggy one, all blurry outlines and a faceless head. But now, here he was, exactly how he was meant to be.

"I would have married you even if you were paralyzed," Grace said softly.

Dashlend said, "Thankfully, it's not come to that," as he kissed her neck.

"Oh dear, I wrote Lady Lavender a letter regarding your condition. I thought I would be forced to tell you the terrible truth that she would not come to your side."

Dashlend laughed into her hair. "She must have been startled to receive such a message, as I have not expressed the least interest in her, nor she me. Now, let us not speak of Lady Lavender more."

Grace found herself very agreeable to that request, as being in Dashlend's arms was turning out to be a revelation. Both Felicity and Mrs. Right had told her that such things were very natural when the time was right and she could see that it was so.

They remained engrossed with one another for she knew not how long. Finally, Dashlend kissed her lips once more, which surely were flushed and maybe a bit bruised.

"You have positively mauled me, Dashlend," she whispered.

"Yes, I have, very careless of me."

"You must promise it is to be a lifelong habit."

"Easily promised." He winced as he reached inside his coat. He pulled out a dented velvet box. "I brought this with me to Lady Montague's ball as a token of my affection. It has seemed to survive the fall."

Grace took it in her hands and opened it. "It is positively lovely," she said. It truly was. The garnets and the magnificent emerald in the middle of the piece sparkled in the afternoon light that streamed through the windows.

Lord Dashlend took it and carefully placed it round her neck and did the clasp. Then he kissed that now adorned neck for good measure.

There was a short rap on the door and Lady Marchfield barreled through it. Behind her, the duke shouted, "Keep your nose out of it, you old polecat."

"Grace Nicolet!" Lady Marchfield said, upon seeing Grace's current condition.

"It is all right, Aunt," Grace said. "Look at this lovely necklace. We are to be married."

"I should think so," Lady Marchfield said. "The sooner the better, as far as I can see."

Once Lady Marchfield had stormed into the room, it was not a moment before her sisters followed.

Grace and Lord Dashlend disentangled from each other.

Winsome stopped in her tracks and cried, "What have you done to Grace?"

Patience punched Lord Dashlend in the ribs, which doubled him over.

"It's all right," Grace said, patting Dashlend's hand to try to distract him from his aching ribs. "We are to be married."

"This is what married people do?" Valor asked incredulously. "They fight on a sofa? What's the point of it?"

The duke moved her out of the way. "Well done, Dashlend. Have your solicitor set up a meeting. Now, perhaps both of you pull yourself together. New necklace, is it?"

Grace nodded as Lady Margaret sailed forward with loyal Lord Harraby by her side. "I do not like to claim credit for the match, but where credit is so obviously due…"

"Lady Margaret means to say," Lord Harraby said, "that we are both gratified that our hopes have come to fruition."

Grace did her best to straighten out her clothes and fix her hair amidst the congratulations. It had happened. It seemed impossible that it had happened, but it had. Dashlend had proposed and then mauled her on the sofa, and it was glorious.

"Your Grace," Thomas said from the doorway, "Lady Felicity and Mr. Stratton."

★

MONTCLAVE HAD LEFT the duke's house as fast as his legs could carry him. They knew! They knew everything!

What would they do? Should he run? Where? He had no connections outside of England. Should he stay and attempt to brazen it out?

But what chance would he have against the word of a duke? Even an eccentric duke. What evidence did they have? Was it that Lady Grace had seen him at the door?

Should he kill the florist before the fellow was interrogated? That might be the thread that unraveled the whole thing.

No. He was not a murderer yet. He had tried to be, but he was not. Could they hang him for simply locking a door?

Even if he were not hanged, if word got out, he would be disgraced.

Montclave felt as if his head would explode. He entered Doanellen's house and ignored Mrs. Featherby lounging round the drawing room. He jogged up the stairs and closed the door behind him. It felt as if the dogs were on his heels.

He fumbled with his cases until he found what he was looking for. A bottle of laudanum. He drank down a large swig, washed it down with brandy, and got in bed. He pulled the covers over his head.

He would stay there until somebody dragged him out.

GRACE SMILED DOWN the dining table. The afternoon had been merry indeed. Felicity and Stratton had joined them in the drawing room and now everybody who'd been present for the news of the proposal had stayed on for dinner. Even Lady Marchfield, who was having a time of it deciding if she were pleased over the engagement or aggravated that there was no butler in the house.

Earlier, Grace and Dashlend had used the ridiculous excuse of a sought-after book in the library to slip off for a half hour, or was it longer? The library had the advantage of a loveseat located in an alcove and Grace laid in his arms, careful not to press on his ribs, as they spoke of their future.

Dashlend was keen to wed as soon as possible, but then the practicalities of his condition did give them pause. It was decided that they would at least wait until he could walk, and then they might take a wedding trip wherever they liked.

Wherever they liked was a question that took some thought. Then, it came to Grace like a bolt of lightning from the heavens. There was only one place they should go.

"We ought to return to Hull to see how your boat gets on. If it is fully repaired, perhaps we could go sailing somewhere."

Dashlend had peered down at her. "That sounds like the sort of thing a very considerate fiancée would suggest to her boat-mad fiancé. I insist we go somewhere you would enjoy."

Grace sat up a little. "I think I would enjoy it, though. This will sound strange, but I am always less clumsy when I am on something that is moving. Also, you might as well know now—I sometimes jump up and down to make myself steadier."

"Do you really?" Dashlend asked.

"Indeed, it is my terrible secret."

"Jump away, my love. And if you really want to try sailing, I suggest we hug the coast and stay at inns overnight."

"That sounds lovely."

Now, at dinner, they had flouted the physician's insistence that Dashlend not sit at table, though they did make some adjustments. His sprained ankle was carefully placed on a stool underneath the table to keep it elevated.

"Well now," the duke said, "another daughter unloaded and five more to go—my dream is within reach!"

Lady Marchfield frowned, though Grace could not think why. It was not as if she'd never heard the duke express that particular wish—he'd said it dozens of times.

Valor giggled. "He always says that, but I'm not going anywhere for a long time. Maybe never!"

The duke ignored this threat. "Where will you be off to?" he asked Grace. "Felicity and Stratton went to Scotland for their wedding trip."

"And survived it too," Felicity said, laughing.

Mr. Stratton nodded. "A tip, Dashlend—wherever you go, do not allow your wife to sit on a dock in full sun with nothing to drink for six hours and expect everything to be rosy."

"A minor outburst," Felicity said.

Mr. Stratton laughed. "Tell that to the boat captain—the man was shaken to his core."

"Papa," Grace said, "Dashlend will need to be healed before we set off. By then it will be full summer and we intend to take out *The Marquessa*."

Valor leveled her gaze at Lord Dashlend. "Didn't you almost drown the last time?"

Dashlend nodded. "Yes, that was unfortunate, but we will stay close to the coast this time round."

Some of the guests round the table were dubious of the sense of this plan, some were admiring, all had a comment to make.

Grace did not much care. She was to wed Dashlend, and wherever he went she would follow—north, south, east, west, land, or sea.

After dinner, it was roundly agreed that they would gather in the drawing room for Fact or Fib. Lady Marchfield did not stay for it. For one thing, she did not care for the game. For another, she was incensed that Mrs. Right had been called in to participate. Her aunt did kiss Grace on the cheek, though, and said, "You'll be settled admirably, Grace, though how I do not know."

After her aunt departed, the questions in Fact or Fib came rapid fire to Lord Dashlend. Why had he been fighting with Grace on the sofa? Why did he pull so many of her hairpins out? Would he be sleeping in Grace's room? Was he planning to watch Grace while she was sleeping, like Mr. Stratton does?

It was a credit to Lord Dashlend that he answered all these

questions in high good humor and was not the least perturbed to be named a fibber on multiple occasions.

Perhaps it was even more to his credit that he'd only smiled when Mrs. Right leaned over to him and said, "Sorry about placing an advertisement for a new valet."

He'd said, "I doubt anybody is sorrier about my valet than I am."

"And the salty porridge yesterday," Mrs. Right added.

"I believe Lady Margaret took that in hand?"

Mrs. Right had stolen a glance at that lady. "She is craftier than she looks."

"As are you, Mrs. Right."

Their beloved housekeeper had seemed well-pleased to hear it.

AFTER SEVERAL MONTHS of recovering, all of which were spent in the duke's house, the wedding finally took place. They spent their first night together at Dashlend's own house, which was quite empty. Lord Harraby had prevailed and quietly wed Lady Margaret and they were out terrorizing the town as a married couple. Now that they'd found one another, they spent far less time talking about death, which was a relief to everybody. As Lady Margaret had taken to wearing the panniers of old, Lord Harraby had also ransacked his attics. He now regularly appeared in a powdered wig and impossibly ornate frock coats. The couple looked as if they were always on their way to a masque. They did not give a toss for any raised brows over it.

As for the newly-married younger couple, there was not too terribly much to discover on their wedding night. Having been in close proximity for months, they had perhaps taken things further than the usual engaged couple. Not as far as they could possibly go, but not much short of it.

Grace thought that was well. There was an ease between them and whatever nerves there had been had long fled. It had been a long, slow, and lovely introduction to the relations between a man and a woman. As well, it was rather a relief to not always be listening for footsteps and knocks on the door. Valor, in particular, always seemed to be looking for her and concerned with her mussed appearance.

The next morning, they'd set off for Hull and retrieved *The Marquessa*. She had been entirely restored and she was perfect.

It was late August when they'd set sail to calm seas and a gentle breeze, making their way south along the coast. They occasionally anchored in shallow water to take a bracing dip in the sea or to make good use of the small cabin on the boat. There were occasions where they spent the night in the cabin, but more often they rowed to shore on a dinghy and made their way to the nearest inn.

Grace found her sea legs quickly, as she was always more comfortable on something that moved, whether it be boat or carriage. Dashlend joked that she was born to be a sailor and he taught her about the wind, the riggings, how to set a course, and how to tack when they did not have the wind at their backs.

Eventually, August turned to September and September wore on and the weather began to turn. They took the boat back to Hull and prepared to remove themselves to Dashlend's estate, which did not come without complications.

Dashlend was all but certain that Montclave had locked Grace into the burning room to stop a wedding and an ensuing heir. He did not share the suspicion with his new bride, but she was already leery enough of his cousin after discovering it had been him who had sent the flowers.

He'd written a long letter to his father, outlining what needed to be done. As he could not prove anything, he must just protect himself and his bride in case Montclave had the audacity to try something else. The gatehouse would not permit his cousin entry and extra men would be hired to keep an eye on other ways onto the estate—particularly the wood that bordered his cousin's land.

Dashlend had only been thinking of what *he* must do to keep Montclave away from his wife. He'd failed to take into consideration that terror might have delivered its own retribution in subduing his cousin's ambitions.

After the duke had told Montclave, "We know all," that gentleman had spent every waking moment wondering when someone would come to get him. His imagination spun out every possible disastrous eventuality. In his mind, he saw himself hung or locked up forever.

He hid in his room in Doanellen's house, always listening for footsteps and knocks on the door.

There were times he considered putting a bullet in his head to make the thoughts go away.

The only two measures that seemed to help at all were brandy and laudanum, and he leaned on them heavily.

So heavily, that he deteriorated. He lost weight, his eyes were at once bloodshot and half closed, his words were incoherent.

Lord Doanellen hardly knew what to do with him and eventually wrote the dowager that somebody must come to collect him, as Montclave was in no shape to make such a journey himself.

The dowager did so. She'd sent her strapping son to Town and got back a haggard shell of a man. He would never say what had happened, but the dowager's disapprobation of him drove him ever further into a sea of brandy and laudanum. One night, he dived too deep in that sea, and never came to the surface. Montclave was dead.

Though neither Dashlend nor Grace wished for Montclave's death, both were not over sorry for it. Especially Dashlend, who understood just how much danger his cousin brought.

As it was, they settled happily at the estate and Dashlend's mother and father took to Grace at once, even though they'd heard some alarming things about her father. They liked her so well that they pretended they did not even notice when she occasionally fell on the floor or tripped and broke something.

Quiet instructions were given to the staff to keep ottomans in their same places and not move them around, and candles were always to be set far away from table edges.

When Grace fell with child, her clumsiness only increased. Dashlend made every effort to always be by her side in case she was on the verge of falling over. In the later stages, his adorable wife was tipping over more than she wasn't.

On the night she gave birth to a son, she received more than the gift of a child.

The midwife directed her on when to push and she'd been at it for hours. Near the end of things, entirely exhausted, the midwife told her to push with all the strength she had left. Grace had done so, and she'd felt a strange pop in her left ear. Then there was an odd feeling of wetness there.

Both the midwife and the young girl apprenticing with her stared at her ear.

"Well, that is a first for me," the midwife said.

Grace did not know what had happened, but she did know that everything in the room had got louder. The midwife's voice, the crackle of the fire, it was all so much louder.

"What is it?" the apprentice whispered.

The midwife reached toward Grace's ear. She took something and rubbed it with a cloth. "Ah, I see. Now, Lady Dashlend, might I inquire as to why you've gone and put a seed pearl in your ear?"

"A what?" Certainly she had not.

Why on earth would it be there? How long had it been there?

And then she remembered how it had got there. Years ago, when her father had laid out all of her departed mother's jewelry, there had been such a scramble for pieces. She and Patience had dived for some loose seed pearls that had rolled onto the carpet. In her haste to have it, she supposed—

Another great pain took over. The midwife said, "Push hard now, my lady, this will be the last or very near to it." She glanced at her apprentice and said, "Girl, get warm water and flush every bit of wax from our lady's ear. It's not something she'll want the lord to see."

And so Grace did push very hard and was certain even more wax came from her ear. But then, her son arrived too.

After the birth, it was of course noticed that Grace was not near as clumsy as she had been. That was a relief to all as they had worried about her accidentally dropping the baby. It was presumed that the pregnancy had somehow cured her through the mysterious goings-on of a woman's body when she carries a child.

Which, she supposed it had. Grace never elaborated on the mystery, as she could not bear to paint the picture of what had really happened for her dear husband. The midwife had assured her that there were some things a man could not take on with any sort of equanimity. The details of a birth were one of those things. A seed pearl and a river of wax erupting from his lady's ear must certainly be another.

Blessedly, jumping up and down to steady herself had come to an end. Grace became much bolder in the world without having to always worry about tipping over. Over time, she and Dashlend went on wild rides together and her dancing improved significantly. They became a dashing couple, though Grace had not imagined it as a possibility.

She did not entirely forget what had happened, though. She kept a close eye on all her children and regularly checked them over to be certain they'd not decided to store something in an unfortunate location. She had spent years slightly off kilter and believing everyone felt the same—she would not care for any of her children having the experience.

It was rather surprising how often she found something in an ear or a nose.

Through the first winter of her first child's existence, Grace had watched over him like a falcon. The first year was always dangerous for a baby and she took on all of Mrs. Right's good sense in the matter. She still remembered the care the dear lady had taken of poor motherless Valor. No strangers were allowed to visit the baby. No staff who cared for the baby were to go to the village for the first few months, and they were paid very generously for the inconvenience. The nursery must always be kept to a warm temperature. If it were warm outside, the windows must be opened. If not, there must be a fire, but the air must not be allowed to become too dry—a pot of water must simmer on the hearth.

Mr. Moreau made himself far more helpful than anybody would have expected. He guarded the nursery stairs at all hours and scolded the nursemaids when he thought they were falling short. He harassed the laundress that she must only use very hot water to wash the baby's things and darkly warned her that he would know if she hadn't. He ordered soft lawn and fine knit wools from the shops and then carefully examined them to judge if they were worthy of the earl's grandson. Only then, with his approval, could they go to the seamstress. Once the new-sewn clothes were returned, they were aired out for a full week to get rid of any ill-humors they may have picked up.

Through everybody's care, the jolly little baby came through his first year with only a sniffle to two and one hair-raising chest cold. After that, Grace felt herself relax.

Two years had passed and in the coming season, it would be Patience to take her turn in society. Serenity might have done too, as they were twins, but she claimed she would wait another year. Patience would make her too nervous with all her hurrying and toe-tapping. Grace did not know if that were true or not, but she was determined to be on the scene to assist her sister.

If Lady Patience *were* to toe-tap, then it was to be hoped she would match with an equally hurried fellow who could keep up with her preferred and rather frenzied pace.

The Earl of Stanford could be just the man, if he were not of such a calm and measured temperament. He understands that few things outside of a housefire require immediate action. Well-laid plans and prudence are his guiding lights. Furthermore, he considers marriage the most momentous step he will take in life, and it merits careful and thoughtful reflection. His choice of a wife is not to be rushed, regardless of any lovely lady drumming her fingers over it.

Patience is lightning and the earl is molasses. One of them needs to hurry up or the other one needs to slow down, else they drive each other mad.

The End

About the Author

By the time I was eleven, my Irish Nana and I had formed a book club of sorts. On a timetable only known to herself, Nana would grab her blackthorn walking stick and steam down to the local Woolworth's. There, she would buy the latest Barbara Cartland romance, hurry home to read it accompanied by viciously strong wine, (Wild Irish Rose, if you're wondering) and then pass the book on to me. Though I was not particularly interested in real boys yet, I was *very* interested in the gentlemen in those stories—daring, bold, and often enraging and unaccountable. After my Barbara Cartland phase, I went on to Georgette Heyer, Jane Austen and so many other gifted authors blessed with the ability to bring the Georgian and Regency eras to life.

I would like nothing more than to time travel back to the Regency (and time travel back to my twenties as long as we're going somewhere) to take my chances at a ball. Who would take the first? Who would escort me into supper? What sort of meaningful looks would be exchanged? I would hope, having made the trip, to encounter a gentleman who would give me a very hard time. He ought to be vexatious in the extreme, and *worth* every vexation, to make the journey worthwhile.

I most likely won't be able to work out the time travel gambit, so I will content myself with writing stories of adventure and romance in my beloved time period. There are lives to be created, marvelous gowns to wear, jewels to don, instant attractions that inevitably come with a difficulty, and hearts to break before putting them back together again. In traditional Regency fashion, my stories are clean—the action happens in a drawing room, rather than a bedroom.

As I muse over what will happen next to my H and h, and

wish I were there with them, I will occasionally remind myself that it's also nice to have a microwave, Netflix, cheese popcorn, and steaming hot showers.

Come see me on Facebook! @KateArcherAuthor